FROM THE AUTHOR OF *AN AUDIENCE FOR EINSTEIN*

# A FRIEND LIKE FILBY

## MARK WAKELY

Printed in the United States of America

ISBN: 978-1-953910-89-9 (paperback)
ISBN: 978-1-953910-90-5 (ebook)

**Canoe Tree
Press**

4697 Main Street
Manchester Center, VT 05255

Canoe Tree Press is a division of DartFrog Books.

CHAPTER ONE
# SO IT BEGINS

It's early. *Real* early. Dave and I are the first ones to arrive. It's as quiet as a morgue, with most of the hallway lights still off. With no one else around, I was surprised the doors were open since the place is usually locked down like the prison it vaguely resembles.

Dave picked me up right at dawn. Since he has a car and I don't, I reluctantly agreed to roll out of bed way ahead of my regular schedule. Real early was still better than a terrifying, barely-in-control school bus ride later on, like the ones I had to take when a ride from Dave wasn't possible. He said he had "something to do," and now I know what it is. Dave's standing on a classroom chair, yelling into a security camera. Never mind that it doesn't record sound; I guess his expression and unfriendly gestures are enough to get his message across. The chair seat is flexing and groaning under his weight, and I'm standing by apprehensive, waiting for the seat to splinter and for Dave to come tumbling down like Humpty Dumpty, cradle and all and whatnot.

He's still angry about some decision the school administration announced yesterday regarding student organization budgets or benefits or something. Not that Dave really cared about any of that—he just loves any opportunity to act offended at anything the administration does. I guess putting it all on tape for some unsuspecting security guard or secretary to see was his way of making his displeasure known.

The second week of our senior year and already Dave is in rare form. He's screeching now in full rant, his face just inches away from the camera lens. It was a beautiful performance, gloriously obscene, a marvel of four-letter words strung together like a true maestro.

When he was finished, he gave the camera a lewd gesture with both hands.

Spent and out of breath, he climbed down from the chair and dragged it back where it belonged.

Dave calls our school "The Big Brown Box," where we're "processed" and "churned out like obedient zombies." I guess it's Dave's calling to be a rabble-rouser, but I'm not sure you can make a living at it. If you could, though, Dave would make a very good one.

"So. How was the rant?" Dave asked, still out of breath but beaming with pride.

I thought a moment, comparing it to his past performances.

"Oh, I don't know. I'd give it a solid B, maybe a B-plus."

Dave seemed pleased with the grade. "Thanks. It wasn't a personal best, but it was pretty good, wasn't it?"

"Sure, Dave. Sure."

I patted the big guy on the back, and then we headed off to the cafeteria to sit at our favorite table and wait for them to open so we could get our usual morning cup of joe.

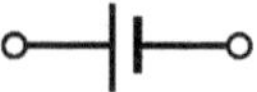

Our Big Brown Box was one of those sprawling eyesores of a building—ominous, pompous, and dreary, not unlike a few of our teachers. Built in what seemed like record time, it towered over the neighborhood.

Metal detectors by the main doors were installed our sophomore year, as were the surveillance cameras and doors that locked electronically when classes began. The joke was they were either trying to keep the bad guys out or the inmates in. Even the drug-sniffing dog they brought in unannounced on occasion seemed afraid of the place and always bolted out the door when its job was done.

"Hear that, people?" Dave said loudly one morning, when all those electronic locks kicked in with their usual *thunk* that reverberated down the halls. "Homeland Security cares about you."

Even though our senior year had just begun, oddly enough I was already getting a bit nostalgic, and was thinking lately about my freshman year. Freshman year was essentially boot camp that never ended. Yeah, we were the scum, the newbies, the dorks and freaks and nerds and geeks that nobody loved or wanted. There were notable exceptions, of course—the few girls with supermodel looks already and an even smaller number of jocks with overactive thyroids who towered over the rest of us and made first team without even breaking a sweat. (Actually, Dave was one of those.) But like I said, they were the exceptions. The rest of us had to bow and scrap to the upperclassmen, even those who had little status otherwise. It got old fast to find all your stuff in the trash if you left it unattended for even a minute, or have someone cut in line in front of you just because you're new.

At least no one ever beat me up cliché-style for my lunch money, although rumors that could actually happen resurface with every freshman class like some kind of cruel urban legend that just won't die. It's one of those stupid things you would think no one would ever believe, but it was always amusing to see the freshman lined up in the cafe with their money clutched tight in their fists while glancing nervously around for any sign of some lurking, hungry bully looking for a free lunch.

It would have been amusing, that is, if I hadn't done that myself when I was a freshman. More out of pity than anything else, I leave the freshman alone. They've got enough problems.

Sadder yet are the handful of recent graduates who just can't let this place go. You see them the first couple of weeks of every new school year hanging around the hallways with their wistful little puppy dog expressions as if hoping they could fit back in somehow.

"Man, when I graduate, I'm putting this place in my rearview mirror and that's it," Dave said when we saw one being gently escorted out because classes were about to begin.

"Agreed," Onion said. "High school's not going to be the high point of *my* life."

But enough about all that.

My name is George Wells. At home there's my dad and my younger brother Kenny. My mom died when I was ten. We live in a ranch house in an older part of town, far from The Big Brown Box, which is why I depend on Dave to get there. I've got my driver's license but never had any great desire to own a car, although on rare occasion Dad will let me drive his buzzy, bouncy econobox he bought for the fuel economy. And that's good enough for me.

Before you write me off as too ordinary, I will admit to one obsession that's a bit unusual. Actually, it's one that drives both Dave and Onion nuts. They're among the few who know about it since it is a bit . . . well . . . strange, and the last thing you want to be known as in high school is strange. You get the whole shunned and scorned deal if that happens, so I mostly keep it to myself. I'm sure Dave and Onion wish I had a normal obsession like jogging or singing or something else totally mundane.

At any rate, here it is. Not long after my mom died, just by chance I saw the classic 1960 version of *The Time Machine* with Rod Taylor and Yvette Mimieux. It was almost as if my whole life I had been destined to see that movie, as if that movie had been made expressly for me, and ever since I've been fascinated with the idea of time travel. That isn't what drives Dave and Onion crazy, though. The problem is that I kept quoting from The Movie—that's all we call it now, just "The Movie"—since I have the whole thing memorized. I think I've watched The Movie at least thirty times through and have yet to grow tired of a single minute. If you haven't seen it yet, you must; if you haven't seen it in a while, see it again—it's an absolute masterpiece, easily one of the best movies ever made.

*The Time Machine* is based on the book by Herbert George Wells—no relation, sad to say. It's the story of the far future, where the human race has been divided into two groups: the peaceful though uneducated Eloi on the surface, and the brainy but monstrous Morlocks who live underground and prey on the Eloi above.

Spoiler alert here: George, the time traveler, helps the Eloi win their freedom from the Morlocks and then rejoins them at the end to restore human civilization.

Shortly after I saw The Movie for the first time, I began collecting wind-up clocks that chimed—mantel clocks, cuckoo clocks, you name it. The time traveler's parlor was full of chiming clocks and I thought that looked beyond cool. After years of garage sales and gifts—"Well, at least you're easy to buy for," Dave once told me—I now had dozens lined up in our living room on the mantel, tables, and walls. Basically, they're everywhere you look, just as I had planned. My favorite is probably the miniature grandfather clock I found in a secondhand store; that's center stage on the mantel. It has a few dings and is missing a decorative piece on the front, so it's probably not worth much, but it has a nice loud chime. Unfortunately, my dad said no way was he going to listen to them all going off every hour on the hour, so I had to silence them. While none of the clocks are priceless heirlooms or anything like that, it's pretty impressive to hear them all ticking, and whenever I was home alone I would un-silence them and try to synchronize them to all chime together. There was usually one or two that sounded a bit early and a couple that sounded a bit late, but still it was just like The Movie, as if the chimes were announcing that hidden somewhere in the house was a time machine of my own, just waiting for me hop on board and explore the far past and future.

My dad thinks my obsession with time travel has something to do with my mom's death and my desire to go back and try to save her—or at least see her again. But that's not it at all. Sure, it would be great to see her again as she was, with her long brown hair and always-glad-to-see-you smile, but I know it would just be a visit, a moment in time that wouldn't change the here and now. Besides, it would be sad to have to leave her behind again, knowing she was to die much too young, although with a time machine I could always pop in to see her again anytime I wanted.

There are lots of people I would like to meet throughout history, and while my mom and grandparents are at the top of the list, they aren't the only ones. I like the idea of owning a time machine for three reasons, really. First, it would be great to witness some of the big moments in history and meet famous people I could talk to, like Ben Franklin, Mark Twain, Edison, and Einstein. You know, the really super important people like that. Second, it would be fascinating to see what's going to happen to mankind in the future near and far. And third and most important, because I want to find a friend like Filby, the time traveler's faithful friend who never abandoned him. That was my ultimate quest. Filby was the best friend anyone could ever have, the nearly perfect friend. Filby and George had a friendship that transcended death and time itself, as you would know if you ever saw The Movie. Filby was forever loyal, Filby was forever caring, Filby would have done anything for George, the intrepid time traveler.

Somehow, somewhere, I was sure to find my own Filby. The only real question in my mind was when.

# CHAPTER TWO

# ONION AND DAVE

Her name is Nancy, but everybody knows her as Onion. Dave gave her that name early in our sophomore year, before the three of us had become best buds. Nancy always wore layers of clothes no matter what the weather. The look was definitely unique, almost to the point of being a classroom distraction.

So one day Dave says to a bunch of us in the cafe, "She's like an onion. If you peeled off all her clothes, layer by layer, soon there would be nothing left."

The name stuck.

Now, you would think a girl would hate a name like Onion, what with the bad smell and bad breath connotations. But the day after Dave's comment went viral, Nancy showed up wearing something like half a dozen blouses—no two alike—two hats, two pairs of pants, and a skirt, willing to go along with the joke. She made of point of coming by our table at lunchtime to show us.

"You look like a pumpkin," Dave said.

"Why, thank you," she said. "Aren't I glamorous?" And she spun about like a rock star, her arms raised as high as all those clothes would let her. "Besides," she said, more seriously, "if you can't laugh at yourself, who can you laugh at?"

Dave stared hard at her. "You mean you don't care what the sheeple say about you?"

I could tell he was testing her the same way he tested me on the bus the day we first met.

She didn't hesitate to answer. "Why should I? I live my life the way I want to, not the way the sheeple do."

It was then that both Dave and I realized she was more than just okay. She was a kindred spirit. We cleared a space for her at our table and she's joined us ever since.

In time, Onion became like the sister I never had and Dave the older brother I never had, even though Dave was older than me by only a few months.

Dave used to joke that Onion's mom and my dad should get married so Onion can be my stepsister, but I could never imagine it. My dad and Onion's mom are two completely different people. While they say that opposites attract, there still has to be some basis for two people to get together in the first place. My dad only spoke when there was something to say; Onion's mom—like Onion—was always talking. My dad never showed any outward signs of worrying about anything, while Mrs. Gordon couldn't wait to tell you what was troubling her. Thanks to his stint in the Navy, my dad liked things orderly and shipshape—"A place for everything and everything in its place" as he said a thousand times—while Onion's house overflowed with their strewn belongings, on the tables, the chairs, everywhere.

"Not too much more than this," Dave once whispered during a visit as we stepped over a pile of Onion's clothes, "and they'll officially be hoarders."

"Maybe that's why Onion wears so many of them," I whispered back. "Just to get them off the floor."

When Dave persisted that my dad and her mom should meet "just to see what happens," Onion finally shut him down.

"Please. Let's not turn this into *The Parent Trap* or anything hokey like that, okay? Just stop already. *Stop.* That's an order."

Dave never brought it up again, which should tell you who's in charge.

And if you ever have any doubt about that, you should see Onion in gym class. She doesn't just want to win—oh no, she wants to crush and thoroughly humiliate her opponents, and usually does. With every goal or point Onion scores, she cackles in delight like it's the most fun she's ever had. Needless to say, nobody wants to play against her, and when players are picked to form teams, she's always picked first. Onion didn't win any friends in gym, but at the same time I think it makes all the girls show her plenty of respect both in and out of it.

"What can I tell you?" she said once at our cafeteria table when I brought up her total lack of mercy. "I'm a tough broad." She grinned.

Dave and I just grinned stiffly at her in return like a couple of idiots. Neither of us would have ever dared call her that, even though it was absolutely true.

Every now and then, Dave would engage me in discussing The Movie since he had a vague interest in time travel from a philosophical point of view. Mostly, though, he just made fun of the plot.

At our usual table in the cafe one day, we were discussing the scene where George the time traveler rescued Weena—one of the Eloi and the time traveler's eventual love interest—from drowning.

"So Weena's screaming for help—"

Dave broke out in laughter.

"Sorry," he said, rubbing his eyes. "The name just struck me as funny. Who names their kid Weena, anyway?"

I stared at him. "It's thousands of years from now, remember?"

"So what? It will always be a stupid name."

The one thing Dave never laughed about was when I started talking about Filby. Dave seemed to grow impatient if I gushed too much about what a great friend Filby was, an ideal friend whose friendship was unparalleled.

"Nobody's that perfect," Dave would argue, refusing to look at me.

"But he supported George no matter what other people thought."

"So? George was an eccentric inventor. Of course everybody thought he was crazy. Who wouldn't?"

"Filby," I countered.

Dave didn't respond.

Why Filby was such a sore point with Dave I didn't know. I guess he thought that kind of unwavering friendship was impossible, while I still hoped to find my own Filby someday.

Dave's mom and dad are nothing like Dave. Nothing. He didn't even particularly resemble either of them, especially in width or height. If I didn't know better, I would have thought he was adopted, and sometimes I still wonder. Dave's parents are a matched pair of always well-groomed, well-dressed optimists who just laugh at Dave's cynicism, as if he can't possibly be serious. Oddly, Dave takes it all in stride.

"What did you expect? They're old people," he would say, even though they were both younger than either Onion's mom or my dad. "I'm related to them, but I can't relate," was his mantra.

Dave lived even further away from The Big Brown Box than I did, in a neighborhood with sprawling homes on spacious lots with fancy street names like "Diamond Court" and "Country Club Lane." Me, I live on Third Street. I don't know if Dave's cynicism is due to his embarrassment at his parent's wealth or his rejection of their preppy "sold on suburbia" attitude. Either way, it sure seemed like he was trying hard to be and do the exact opposite.

Something of a physics scholar, Dave once referred to where he lived as "the anti-neighborhood. If it ever came in contact with a real neighborhood, they would explode."

I wasn't all that familiar with the inside of Dave's house because Onion and I were seldom invited over. Not because Dave or his parents were ashamed of us or anything like that, but because Dave's parents led very active social lives and were always hosting fancy dinner parties that Dave avoided like the plague, which was why he was usually available to drive us wherever we wanted to go. The few times I've been there, it almost seemed like Dave didn't belong, as if he were an imposter in his own home. With his usual rumpled, untucked shirt and big, baggy jeans with tattered cuffs, he looked like a lost soul wandering the wide hallways and spacious rooms with their tasteful, expensive furnishings and pricey wall art. His bedroom was the only place that was a reflection of the Dave I knew—strewn with papers, books, a couple of acoustic guitars he barely knew how to play, and piles of unwashed clothes on the floor almost identical to the ones he was wearing.

The first time I saw his room, I had to call him on his hypocrisy.

"And to think you make fun of how Onion lives."

He shrugged as if that wasn't a valid comparison. "This is just one room. With them, it's their whole *house.*"

The last time I was there, Dave's mom smiled and said, "Isn't he such a silly boy? But we love him anyway," which gave Dave a scowl for the rest of the day. Not surprisingly, Dave hasn't invited me back since.

The last but most important thing you had to know about Dave was his car.

Dave's car was old, large, and loud, and sucked up gas the way a boat with a hole in its side sucked up water. A kind of sickly green, it had a once-black vinyl covered top that was now a mottled gray, with scratches and gouges galore. And a radio with a cassette player, even though not one of us had ever owned a cassette to play in it. That kind of car.

"I tell you, they don't make them like this anymore. And it's a good thing, too," Dave liked to joke.

Over time Dave had personalized it with seat covers, bumper stickers, books, papers, clothes, and trash that seldom got taken out until it was a one of a kind, rolling home away from home you could spot a mile away in any parking lot.

"What, no fuzzy dice?" Onion asked him when she saw it for the first time.

"Too corny," Dave said, "although one of those flat pine tree air fresheners would be nice. It stinks in there."

For Dave's next birthday, unbeknownst to each other, both Onion and I gave him half a dozen. After we laughed about that, Dave unwrapped all twelve and hung them up like a miniature forest or something, making the inside of his car smell like Christmas every day of the year. A very potent Christmas.

The car was less his pride and joy and more an extension of who Dave was. When Dave slipped behind the wheel, he became the car; the two seemed nearly indistinguishable when he was in it.

I met Dave on the school bus the beginning of our sophomore year, just a few weeks after school began and a few months before he bought his car. Since I had barely made it to the bus stop before the driver closed the doors, the bus was packed. The only open seat was next to this intimidating-looking guy with a full beard who was so wide there wasn't much room next to him. But since I didn't need much room, I approached him cautiously. He sat staring out the window with kind of a stoic look, as if accustomed to sitting alone.

"This seat taken?" I grabbed the overhead shelf to brace myself as the bus roared around a corner.

He turned to me, seemingly surprised that someone was talking to him.

"Could be. Are you a nitwit?"

"No. No, I'm not."

He nodded and tried to scrunch over as far as he could. "All right then. Just so you know, I don't tolerate fools."

I was beginning to understand why the seat was available.

"Thanks," I said, and slid in next to him. "I'm a sophomore."

Why I felt it necessary to reveal that I'm not sure. It kind of sounded like an apology or something, but I guess I thought he would appreciate knowing.

"So am I." He looked away.

Two things happened when he said that. First, I was kind of startled. He looked old enough to be a fifth-year senior, maybe even older. And second, I wondered if he never had a seatmate on the bus because of his appearance, especially his imposing beard. If so, that was kind of sad.

We didn't speak for a while after that, and then we both spoke at nearly the same instance.

"I'm George."

"I'm Dave."

We both laughed a bit at the awkwardness. I racked my brain for something intelligent to say so he didn't think I was a nitwit after all and eject me from the seat.

"Man, I hate getting up this early. It's like death. How about you?"

That seemed like a safe conversation starter, since everybody on the bus looked like they hated getting up early. Some even looked like they were falling back to sleep despite the swaying, noisy ride.

Dave didn't answer. Instead, he just stared out the window again with a faraway gaze.

Complaining about the food in the cafeteria was another safe bet, I figured, since it was uniformly awful day after day. I had yet to have anything either nutritious or delicious from the place.

"Do you eat in the cafe? The food is just horrendous, isn't it? They seldom serve anything edible."

He seemed to stir a bit at that remark, as if he was overhearing me talk to someone else.

I sighed quietly to myself, determined now to either be accepted or labeled a fool.

"You know, you could try a few ice breakers yourself just to be a little friendly."

He turned his head slowly—very slowly—toward me.

"Do I look friendly?"

I accepted the challenge.

"Actually," I said, looking him up and down, "I was hoping there was a nice guy in there somewhere just waiting to bust out."

His grin was faint. "Good. You're sarcastic. That scores points. Yes, I hate getting up this early, and yes, the food in the cafeteria could kill you and might yet. Anything else you want to talk about? Anything . . . meaningful?"

Studying his cold expression, I had the feeling he was daring me be to friends with him, testing me to see if I was worthy. He struck me then as one of those perpetually dissatisfied souls, always angry at the world, always complaining about some injustice somewhere whether it affected him personally or not.

That was only a hunch, but I went with it. I could be a dissatisfied soul, too, at times. Besides, now he had me feeling feisty no matter how intimidating he looked.

"Sure," I said, "Let's talk about how were not just being educated, but indoctrinated by the powers that be, forced to conform to their idea of what it means to be a solid citizen, a contributing member of their society, as if that's all that really matters when what we should be learning is to embrace our individuality, only they'll never teach us that because then we could be a real danger to their regime. Should we talk about that instead?"

While his expression didn't change, his eyes betrayed him as they fleetingly registered his astonishment.

"You don't mean that," he said, and looked away again.

I knew right then my hunch was right.

"Sure, I do. Why wouldn't I?"

He turned back to me. "Come on. You're like everybody else," he nodded once to our fellow sleepy bus passengers. "Follow the rules, be a good boy, don't rock the boat whatever you do. That what I peg you for." It was his turn to look me over, only he didn't look so sure of himself—in fact, he almost looked like he wanted to be proven wrong.

"Yeah, I play along with the school's little mind games," I said. "The thing is, I know it's just a game. The truth is, I'd rather think for myself." I tapped the side of my head. "You can't take everything you read or hear at face value. I mean you can, but then you really would be a fool, wouldn't you?"

I did mean that, although I wasn't about to take up arms over it or anything. My mom had said to always keep an open mind, which seemed like good advice for anyone.

Dave's tough guy facade broke right then and he sat back relaxed, looking at me with newfound respect.

The bus lurched into the main drive to the school. People stood up to gather their belongings as the driver pulled behind a long line of buses parked by the main doors.

Dave and I got up, too. He tapped me on the shoulder as we inched our way forward down the aisle.

"Far corner of the cafeteria, last table. Meet me there at lunch. We'll talk more."

And that was the beginning of our friendship.

CHAPTER THREE
# KENNY AND MOM

I remember well the day my mom brought Kenny home, even though I was only six years old. Kenny was a good baby, meaning he slept most of the night and wasn't fussy like they said I was. It probably wasn't until Kenny was three years old that we started to notice he was kind of zoning us out, refusing to make eye contact and no longer paying attention to anything we did. When the doctor suggested he might be on the "autistic spectrum," I don't think any of us were really too surprised, although Mom still cried off and on for a few weeks and spent hours on the internet nearly every day looking for a treatment. Dad said that she had to be careful because there was a lot of snake oil out there, and I could see for myself that was true. They had magnets you wore on your head, herbal pills, weird potions and dubious injections, even though there was no real scientific evidence that any of them actually worked.

It seemed incredibly cruel to sell false hope like that to people who were desperate. I guess some people are willing to try anything, even though they probably know deep down that they're just throwing their money away. Maybe they figure that's better than doing nothing at all.

Mom didn't fall for any of the online bag of tricks, but she did realize we couldn't afford the kind of intensive tutoring that really could help Kenny to some degree. Mom and Dad talked about moving to another state where Kenny might qualify for some assistance, but Dad didn't think at his age that he could give up all his clients and start all over at some new insurance agency in some unfamiliar town. Instead, she taught herself some of the things that the tutors did, but then she died so Kenny didn't have a chance to get much better than he is. He seemed to come out of his shell for a little while after she was gone, probably because the daily routines we all had changed drastically. Kenny kept asking where Mom was and we kept telling him she wasn't coming back, but it took months for him to understand that our new routines were permanent and that none of us would ever see her again. Once he seemed to finally understand that he withdrew again, although at times he was incredibly perceptive about how Dad and I were feeling, telling us every now and then to "be happy like Kenny."

I think Mom would have been proud of Kenny for reminding us to keep our spirits up. At times, we needed Kenny's reminder—especially on holidays—and he seemed to know it even before we did.

Kenny is skinny, even skinner than I was when I was his age, and has this stubborn swirl of red hair that never looks combed no matter how much we try. He wasn't much for personal grooming except for showers. Kenny would stay in the shower all day if we let him, although he would run out of hot water long before then. Many a time I took a cool or lukewarm shower after Kenny was done because he had drained the hot water tank and I couldn't wait for the tank to do its thing. Still, it was hard to get mad at Kenny given how he was. The one time I got upset over something he did and snapped at him, he just stared at me with his distant, soulful eyes, and I realized that Kenny would never deliberately do anything wrong as far as he was aware.

One day my dad said something that seemed unbelievable, and made me glad I wasn't around back when he was young. He was reading the paper at the kitchen table on a Saturday morning when Kenny let out a laugh for some reason known only to him.

Dad put the paper down, shook his head, and said, "You know, when I was young, kids like Kenny were either bullied or beat up. Usually both."

I was shocked. "For being autistic?"

Dad shrugged. "We didn't know anything about autism back then. If you were different somehow, eventually someone would hit you, and that was it. People like Kenny were institutionalized or kept hidden away so nothing bad would happen to them." He went back to reading his paper. "But that was some time ago."

I was glad to hear that last part. It would be terrible if Kenny was punished just for being Kenny.

One thing I make it a point to do is not tell anyone that Kenny is autistic. I just tell them that I have a brother since that's all that really matters. When they finally meet him, I watch them closely for their reaction. If they're warm and friendly towards him right away, then I know we can be friends. If they avoid him or—worse yet—seem disappointed, then I know we can't. Needless to say, both Onion and Dave passed the test with flying colors.

One girl I dated last year didn't fare so well.

She was cute and witty and came from a nice family and all that, but everything fell apart when I finally invited her to my house. She took one look at Kenny, recoiled, and spun around to confront me.

"You didn't tell me there was a problem with your brother," she whispered confidentially, as if offended.

Engrossed in his Game Boy he had owned for years and played constantly, Kenny ignored us. I was grateful for that.

"Problem?" I asked, my anger rising. She didn't look so cute anymore. In fact, she suddenly looked downright ugly. "What problem is that exactly?"

"Well, look at him," she whispered. "He's obviously retarded or something." She wrinkled her nose as if Kenny smelled bad, too.

"No, he's autistic," I said calmly. "The problem is I've been wasting my time with you. I had no idea you were that heartless. Come on, I'm taking you home. We're through."

The only word that really rankles me is "retard." Both Onion and Dave learned real fast that I despise that word. They both stopped saying it when I told them I couldn't be friends with anyone that insensitive.

I still worry about what's going to happen to Kenny when he's an adult. Dad was putting aside some money for him and had a nice life insurance policy, so I figured Kenny would be okay financially, but unless he lived with me, Kenny would end up someplace with strangers. I didn't think Kenny would like that at all, even if they were nice strangers. I had my own life to live, of course, but I knew that I could never leave Kenny on his own, even if we found the best caregivers ever. Whatever my future plans might be, Kenny would always be included. I knew it was going to be hard to find a girl willing to accept both Kenny and me as kind of a "package deal," but that's all right. I could wait to find someone who will accept Kenny for who he is rather than wish he was something he's not. Like Filby, that girl had to be out there somewhere; I just hadn't found her yet.

The bottom line was that Kenny was my brother, and as far as I was concerned, brothers stick together no matter what comes our way.

On what would have been my mother's birthday, we always had a little celebration for her. I don't remember it, but my dad said that tradition started at my shrill insistence the day before her birthday just a few months after she died. That first year I made a birthday wish for her—out loud—wishing she hadn't died. My dad said he understood then why I wanted a party, and we've been celebrating her birthday ever since. My dad would either buy or bake a small birthday cake, and the three of us would sit at the kitchen table with the fourth chair "reserved" for my mom, as if she was with us in spirit or something. We'd sing "Happy Birthday," I'd make a silent wish, and then both Kenny and I would blow out the candles.

At the most recent party, I decided to let Kenny make the birthday wish.

"Go ahead, Kenny," I egged him on. "Make a wish for Mom. It's your turn this year."

Kenny looked confused a moment. "Why, George? Mom is dead."

Dad and I were silent. I glanced at the empty chair.

"That's right, Kenny. She's not coming back. But that doesn't mean we should forget her. We'll never forget her, will we Kenny?"

Kenny ignored me and stared at the cake instead.

"Cake for Kenny now, please," he said.

After I made a hasty wish and blew out the candles, we ate the cake in near silence. I decided I would make all her birthday wishes from now on.

As we cleared the table, I went to push the fourth empty chair back in place, then stopped with the eerie thought that maybe mom really was sitting there in spirit or something, watching and listening to us.

"Happy birthday, Mom," I said quietly, and just in case, left the chair right where it was.

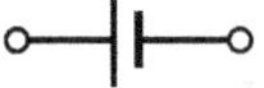

Mom had died at home in her sleep. I remember waking up late for school, wondering why I heard strange voices in the house. I went into the kitchen and saw the flashing blue and red lights of a silent ambulance in the driveway through the kitchen window. The lights looked festive, even kind of pretty. There was an unfamiliar clatter behind me, and when I turned around, two paramedics were wheeling a gurney out of my parents' bedroom. Whatever was on the gurney was covered with a sheet.

"What is it?" I asked them, more out of curiosity than fear. I was still sleepy, and so far this just seemed like another dream. They stopped where they were when they saw me, not answering.

"George? *George?*"

My dad came quickly out of the bedroom and stood between me and the gurney, too late to block my view. I wondered why he was still in his pajamas when he should have been dressed for work.

"Turn away, George," he said. There was something in his voice and eyes that told me I should do just that, and be afraid.

Just as I was about to comply, the paramedics jostled the gurney to get out of the house. As the gurney started to roll, my mother's right arm slipped out from under the sheet, her hand bouncing as if waving me to come to her.

I knew right then the awful truth and let out a little cry, then threw my arms around my dad. He held me tight.

One of the paramedics quickly tucked my mom's arm back under the blanket while the other looked at me with mournful eyes.

"It's all right. She can't hurt you."

Why he thought I was afraid of being hurt I'll never know. My mom had never hurt me, but that wasn't what upset me then. What upset me was that it seemed like with those waves of her hand she had wanted one last hug from me before they took her away, but I rejected her by cowering in fear instead. I was bothered for the longest time by that memory of her beckoning me and how I let her down, although I told no one.

And that was my last memory of Mom at home.

## CHAPTER FOUR
# THE TALE OF OUR TABLE

Dave was not at all popular with the cafeteria ladies.

It started one day last year when Dave asked for a burger at lunchtime and one of the ladies misunderstood where he was pointing and gave him a plateful of some kind of tomato sauce-covered pasta glop instead.

"What's *this*?"

While the question was reasonable, and it was only two words, it was the manner in which Dave said it that made all the cafeteria ladies behind the counter stop and stare.

"It's *lasagna*," said the woman who served him, Olga or Hilda or something like that, in her thick accent and in a sharp tone that mimicked his. "Did you want something else?"

Dave hesitated, his frown deep as he stared at the now identified dish. "Nah. I can probably choke it down." He put the plate on his tray.

The cafeteria ladies continued to stare.

Olga's eyes narrowed. "I'm going to choke you in about a minute."

Now you would think being intimidated by one of the cafeteria ladies wouldn't mean much, but Olga was a big, burly woman, nearly as big as Dave, with a hint of a beard of her own. Dave froze briefly, his jaw slack, probably at the thought of Olga's beefy, calloused hands squeezing the life out of him. After that, the cafeteria ladies gave Dave the evil eye whenever they saw him in line, and Dave always made it perfectly clear what he wanted to avoid any further misunderstandings, not to mention any more death threats from Olga.

We always sat in the far corner of the cafe, the farthest away from the serving area. Because of its distance from where the food was, "our" table was usually available during lunch hour. We didn't care if the table was dirty or clean, or if the chairs were shoved aside or even missing as long as our table was there. On those rare occasions we found it somewhere else, we would drag it back where it belonged, the tabletop chattering madly as it bounced across the terrazzo, making an awful racket that turned heads and drew curses and complaints.

Our table was more than just a place to eat—it was part lectern where we debated, part confessional where we poured our hearts out, and part home base where we could just kick back and relax. Once, Dave even did a little jig on it to celebrate a B he got on a Biology test he thought for sure he had flunked.

Like most of the stuff throughout the school, the square cafeteria tables were pretty much bomb proof—fake dark wood laminate on heavy pressboard with a steel center post and legs. Despite its prison-like heft, someone had managed to take a chunk out of the laminate on one of the edges of our table, the edge Dave always laid claim to as if assuming full responsibility for the ancient vandalism, the damage worn smooth from years of curious fingers and palms. That damage helped us identify it among all the others in the cafe. We became true creatures of habit at that table—Dave at his damaged edge, Onion to his right, and me on the left.

There had been rumors for years that the cafe was going to get updated someday, "refreshed," as they say, but we hardly ever gave it any thought. That is, until Onion noticed a bunch of guys bringing large boxes through the entrance closest to the cafe one morning when we arrived just as homeroom ended, too late for our morning breakfast or coffee.

"Something's happening in the cafe," she announced.

The sound of struggling electric drills echoed through the halls.

It didn't seem important enough to go investigate, so we just shrugged it off. But the truth became known at lunchtime.

Surprisingly, we didn't notice at first. We joined up in the hall and made our way to the not-too-long serving line, where we bought the usual junk food we lived on. It was only as we marched single file through the crowded dining area, trying to keep our trays level as we weaved our way to our usual corner, that we finally noticed.

Leading the way, Dave noticed first and came to a halt. I nearly crashed right into his back, averting disaster at the last possible second.

Onion came to a halt right behind me in similar fashion.

"Look!" Dave said, quite loud.

I blinked and turned my head in either direction, unsure what it was I was supposed to be looking at.

"The tables and chairs!" Onion said, just as loud.

Only then did I notice. We were surrounded by a sea of bright new cafeteria tables with light, cheery fake wood tops rather than dark, depressing fake wood tops.

And new brown vinyl-padded chairs, too, instead of the molded fiberglass bucket-style ones that made your butt fall asleep after a while.

Dave moaned. "Our table. It's gone."

We approached the new one warily. None of us put our trays down on it just yet, as if unsure we wanted to accept the impostor.

Dave grimaced. "Well, it'll have to do, I guess." He set his tray down first.

Onion and I tentatively followed suit then we all stepped back.

Dave's arms flew up in the air. "So what. It's just another table. Nobody cares." He sat down and started to eat.

Both Onion and I sat down stiffly.

"We didn't even get to say goodbye," Onion lamented.

"I wish they had told us," I said. "We could have had a going away party for our table this morning."

"Maybe we could have offered to buy it!" Onion exclaimed.

We looked at each other, intrigued by the thought.

"Just eat," Dave commanded.

We ate in silence. I noticed that Onion was being careful not to touch the new table, like me.

Dave dropped his burrito. "For crying out—

Onion put her fork down. "Well, it's just not the same, is it?"

Dave wiped his mouth, wagged a finger at us. "Wait. I'll make it the same."

And with that vague promise, he got up and went to one of the vending machines on the far wall and came back carrying one of those fancy iced teas in a heavy glass bottle. I had never seen him drink iced tea before and wondered what he was up to.

"Stand up. Take everything off the table. Off."

We complied, setting all on the empty table next to our impostor.

"Now get out of the way."

"What for?"

"Just do it. You'll see." He raised the bottle over his head.

Onion and I scrambled back. My new chair fell over on its side.

Dave stared at the table with a phony bright expression. "I hereby christen thee 'Table Two.' May you serve us well in our final year here in The Big Brown Box."

And with that, he swung the bottle down full force to the edge.

There was a loud bang. Tea and shards of glass flew everywhere.

"*David!* What are you *doing?*" Onion said. She shook her hands free of tea splatter.

A few nearby people glanced our way.

"Hey!" Dave positively beamed now, staring down at the table's edge. "I took a chunk out of it!"

I wiped my tea-wet neck with my sleeve and moved forward to look.

Sure enough, there was a semicircle of missing laminate where thick glass bottle had met fake wood top.

Dave pointed proudly. "There! Doesn't that look like the ding in our old table?"

"It does!" Onion said, marveling at the sight.

I righted my fallen chair and moved in for a closer look.

Except for being rough rather than worn smooth, the semicircle Dave created was nearly the exact same size and shape.

"Now we know what might have happened to the old table," I said.

Onion nodded. "And now we'll always know which table is ours, just like before."

Dave grabbed a fistful of paper napkins and wiped the table-top dry, then pulled up his chair and sat behind it, still beaming. "Watch out for chunks of glass on the floor," he warned. "Sorry about that. I'll clean it up when we're done."

We returned our trays and backpacks and sat down to finish eating.

Strange to say, but after Dave's impromptu christening, I felt a lot better about the new table. Even Onion started eating again with her usual gusto.

*Such is the power of ceremony*, I thought, understanding now why ships were christened, and people, too, and why mayors and governors and presidents were sworn into office.

And we never questioned the legitimacy of our new table again.

# CHAPTER FIVE

# MY DAD, THE POST, AND OUR LIVES WITHOUT MOM

My dad said he took part in Operation Desert Storm, but mostly he spent the time cleaning and restocking his supply ship with his shipmates. He never shot at anybody or had anybody shoot at him, although he said he saw the aftermath of a land battle once, something he refuses to discuss. He climbed the ranks and, when he was discharged, married my mom. My mom and dad met when he was on shore leave in New York. After they got married, they moved so Dad could join a Navy friend's insurance company, where he still works. I came along ten years later and Kenny six years after that. Dad said that decade without kids were the happiest in his life, but Mom always said he was kidding.

Sometimes I think my dad wasn't kidding, and good for him. He deserved that time alone with her, considering.

When Mom died, it was a huge shock to everybody, especially her doctor. She had always been so vibrant and healthy. They think she had a stroke or something, but Dad didn't see the point of doing an autopsy so we'll never really know for sure. As the years go by, I seem to remember her less and less. I've got pictures and videos of her, of course, but those moments not on film seem blurry now, and try as I might, I can't quite remember exactly what she said or exactly when she said it. It's odd, but when you stop seeing and talking to someone every day, that person kind of fades away in your mind, and you begin to doubt how true your memories are of that person, as if you need that daily contact to keep all the details fresh.

My dad used to say to me, "If your mother were still alive, she would be very proud of you" or "furious with you" or "happy for you" or whatever fit the occasion. But as time went by Dad would just say, "If your mother . . ." and let it go at that. I didn't need to hear the rest to know what he meant.

Maybe the best way to describe it is that my mom was in charge of scooping me up and my dad was in charge of sitting me down. Now, while I understand and appreciate why my dad had to sit me down when I did something dumb—more often than I care to admit—it was the scooping up part I missed the most.

I've often thought about how we would react if she suddenly returned, walked through the door like it was all some gigantic mistake, a big misunderstanding. I think we've moved on so far with our lives now without her, it would be really difficult to go back to how we were, to return to those old days and routines. It would be—well, *awkward,* to say the least—and as much as I loved my mother and still cherish the memory of her, we said goodbye just by moving on with our lives without her, whether we liked it or not.

This may sound cruel, and even ungrateful in a way, but the more time goes by, the further and further we're leaving her behind. She belongs to another time and era in our lives now, one I know will never return.

One thing Dad did was to join a Veterans of Foreign War post right after we moved into town. Not many vets do nowadays, but my dad says that's a mistake. The post has a number like they all do, of course, but Dad just calls it "The Post," like it's not only the best one, but the only one. Our little family joke is that I've got "The Movie" and my Dad has "The Post." I've been going to The Post for as long as I can remember. Dad first took me there to help spruce the place up before meetings. Early on he had to drag me, but now I love to go. It's a great place because it's hardly changed since the day it opened in 1952. Stepping through the door is probably the closest I'll ever come to really travelling into the past—the green and black linoleum floor, the ancient appliances and countertops in the kitchen, the pastel drapes and tables and chairs with chrome legs. None of it has changed, and while there are older buildings in town, The Post is the one constant in my life, a portal back to the middle of the last century. And all you had to do to get there was open the door and step across the threshold, no time machine needed.

There used to be small weddings and other events held there—dozens every year, the older veterans told me—but as time went by, the young brides-to-be turned up their noses at the dated decor and eventually the weddings stopped, as did the other rentals. There was some talk of renovating the place to bring in more revenue, but as membership shrank, they couldn't afford it, so now The Post is frozen in time like a small museum.

Dave came with me once and said afterwards, "Why do you like that crummy place? Even the air is old and stale," but he doesn't see it the way I do. It's not a crummy place; it's a preserved monument to the past, a different way of life. There's a big difference.

If I ever join the service—not that I'm planning to—I would definitely join The Post as soon as I was discharged.

Once, there was an open house at The Post in an effort to boost its dwindling membership. My dad managed to get some free publicity on the radio and newspaper, so the hope was there would be a decent turnout. Two really young-looking Army guys who served in Afghanistan came by right away, chatted a while with the older vets, then left with their applications and a promise to return. They looked disappointed in the surroundings, just like those who hoped to rent the place, but seemed very interested in what Dad and the others had to say about their military careers, probably the only reason they stuck around for as long as they did. No one else showed up until the open house was about to end.

The restless man seemed only slightly older than the first two soldiers and had served three tours of duty in Iraq. Unsmiling, he not only refused to give his name, he refused to sit down, preferring instead to pace as they talked.

"The Post was built not long after World War Two, when the town boomed with returning vets," my dad said. "Lots of guys have benefitted from being VFW members over the years."

"Like how?" the young pacing soldier asked. His jaw went from side to side as if he were chewing gum, although I was pretty sure he wasn't.

"Well, we've helped with job searches, veteran benefits, medical issues, that sort of thing," one of the Vietnam vets said.

"Medical issues," the soldier repeated. "Like mental health?"

He stopped pacing, but his jaw kept going.

"That, too," my dad said.

He resumed pacing. "What kind of jobs?"

"All kinds," my dad said. "What are you interested in?"

He looked away. "I don't know. What else goes on here? Why are you recruiting new members? I didn't even know this place existed until I read about it in the paper yesterday. Seems odd that you have to advertise." He looked at them with suspicion.

"Well, frankly, our numbers are down and we could use some fresh blood to stay afloat," my dad explained. "We had funerals last year for our two oldest members. That's another thing we do, offer funeral assistance with honor guards and all that, even though at our age we look kind of raggedy when we try to come to attention."

The Post members laughed.

The young soldier froze, his face turning pale. His left eye winked twice thanks to what could only have been a nervous tic.

"I don't want to hear about it," he said, looking away again. The speed of his pacing increased.

No one said anything for a few uncomfortable seconds.

"Did you need . . . some kind of assistance . . . with a health issue?" My dad asked haltingly. "We can make some recommendations. That's not unusual, you know."

He vigorously shook his head. "No, I'm just fine. What else do you do here? Is that it? I hope it's not just bingo or something boring like that."

"Nope. No bingo here. That's for old people."

The Post members laughed again.

My dad continued. "Really, it's the camaraderie we have that's important. It's just nice to talk to others who've had military experiences similar to your own."

The young soldier's chewing stopped as his face hardened. "*Similar?* They're not similar! You shoot some random kid, a young girl in the wrong place, the worst possible place . . . you have *no* idea what I've been through!" His voice was sharp.

My dad stepped forward, his expression sympathetic. He spoke softly as if to counter the young soldier's bitterness. "Actually, we do. We've all seem some terrible things in our military careers, disturbing things. Haven't we, men?"

All the men nodded, some staring down at the floor as if remembering only too well.

"See? You're not alone," my dad said.

"So why would I want to come here and relive them? What good is that going to do?" He practically shouted now. "I'm trying to forget what happened, not remember! I'm sorry, but I'm afraid I won't be joining your happy little group!"

And with that, he turned and stormed out without so much as a goodbye or farewell.

The Korean vet sighed. "That went well, didn't it?"

My dad looked at me. I was standing by the kitchen just hanging back, not saying a word.

"How about it, George? Think he'll change his mind?"

The other Post members laughed uneasily.

For some reason, the rest of the day I couldn't shake the image of that unknown, pacing soldier and his distress. That evening, I wrote a short poem about it, even though I normally don't write poetry. Here it is:

FOREIGN WAR
Imagine traveling
So far away
To deliver a bullet
In person
And you never even
Knew his name.

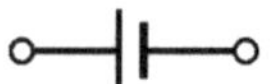

One evening Dad, Kenny and I went to a dance on The Post's back patio. The patio is actually pretty nice. It's a huge brick-paved area with a knee-high wall surrounding it, one deep enough to sit on. The dance was on a perfect summer evening, one of those cool, cloudless days with hardly a breeze. The veterans wore their old formal military uniforms—if they could still fit into them—and their wives or girlfriends wore long summer dresses. Since we had everyone from Korean War vets to the two young soldiers who kept their promise and came back and joined The Post—and even a few members from other VFW posts nearby—the music covered everything from the big band era to Lady Gaga, which was pretty cool. As darkness fell, we lit several Tiki torches in the corners of the patio. The night was so still, the flames barely flickered in the growing purplish twilight.

My dad danced with probably every woman there at least once. Both my mom and dad used to dance. They were very good at it. I remember watching them twirl around the living room after my dad moved the coffee table out of the way. They never missed one of these patio parties, and when my mom got tired, Dad would find another dance partner, so he was used to cutting in.

Kenny was fairly restless through the night and sat on the patio wall playing with his Game Boy. But whenever they played a Beatles song, Kenny would put his video game aside and start dancing right there by himself. For some reason, Kenny just loves The Beatles—or as he calls them, "John Paul George Ringo," the names strung together like a single word.

When the Beatles' song "A Hard Day's Night" started, Kenny kind of yelped and ran to the middle of the patio to dance. At first not too many people noticed, but he was dancing so vigorously and bumping into so many other dancers that they cleared a big space for him. Some of the dancers smiled, but others looked annoyed.

My dad came over to me where I sat watching everyone having fun.

"George, can you do something about Kenny?"

I didn't understand. "Like what?"

"Like get him to stop."

"Dad, he's just dancing. That's Kenny."

My dad looked back at him and sighed. "I know. Still, it's disrupting."

It was my turn to sigh. "Fine. I'll get him."

I went over to when Kenny was pumping his arms up and down, eyes closed, half bent over, shaking his rear end back and forth.

"Kenny," I said. "You have to sit down now." I felt kind of bad having to say it.

Kenny opened his eyes and shook his head. "No. Kenny's dancing."

"I know you're dancing, but Dad wants you to stop."

"No. George dances with Kenny."

"What?"

Kenny knew I never danced, or at least had never seen me dance. I was a really pathetic dancer, so I avoided dance floors at all costs, except for the few times when Onion dragged me out to make a fool of myself so she and everybody else could have a good laugh at my utter lack of coordination.

"Kenny, I don't know how to dance."

"Doesn't matter," he said. "Have some fun. George needs it. If Kenny can dance, George can dance."

For an autistic kid who had never offered such sage advice before, that was pretty hard to ignore.

I glanced over at our dad, who stood there arms folded, waiting for me to pull Kenny back to his video game.

I gave Dad an exaggerated shrug to let him know it was no use, and then turned back to Kenny.

"Okay, Kenny. You want me to dance? I'll dance. I'll dance way better than you."

And with that, I mimicked Kenny's every move.

A roar of laughter came from the crowd, even from the dancers who moments earlier seemed annoyed at the intrusion.

We danced face to face, arms going, our skinny butts swaying side to side.

"Now George is dancing," Kenny said.

"Yes, I am. Better than you."

"No, George isn't. George is not better than Kenny."

It was one of those rare near-normal conversations with Kenny that came all too infrequently. That really made it special.

The song finally ended and Kenny abruptly stood up straight and walked off back to his Game Boy. I followed right behind him to the sound of applause from the other dancers.

Dad looked only slightly amused. "Well, I'm glad that's over."

I looked at him. "I'm not. That was fun."

My dad looked away. Some slow big band song started and the dance floor quickly filled in again.

I sat down by Kenny. Dad sat down next to me on the other side.

"Thanks, George. I never know quite how to handle Kenny in situations like that without looking like an overbearing jackass."

I knew exactly what he meant. Kenny could kick up quite a fuss, making you look like . . . well, an overbearing jackass when you tried to get him to calm down.

"Glad to help."

"George," he began softly, "you know your mother and I often talked about what would happen to Kenny when we were gone. I'm not going to live forever, you know. I hope he can count on you when I'm gone. I know it's a burden, but you'll be all he's got."

I turned slowly to look at him, anger rising up my throat. "A *burden*? He's not a burden. He's my *brother*. I've told you a hundred times I would take care of him. Weren't you listening?"

A few nearby dancers glanced our way as my voice rose despite my efforts to keep it down.

My dad raised his hands as if to fend me off. "Okay, okay. It was just a question. I was just hoping that Kenny was still in your plans for the future, that's all. I'm glad he is."

The problem was, I hadn't made any plans for the future, at least not yet. It occurred to me then that maybe I had better start making plans if Dad thought I already had them. I felt my anger drop to nothing as I wondered what those plans should be.

Dad patted my knee. "Well, let's go home. We'll come back tomorrow to clean up. They won't miss us. It's getting late."

Kenny yawned as if in agreement.

It was then I noticed that one of the Tiki torches had gone out, and two others were taking their last gasps, their flames sputtering and low.

On the way home, Kenny put his head on my shoulder and fell asleep. I took his Game Boy out of his hands and turned it off. The night air had gotten cooler, and it felt good rushing by me, especially after trying to outdo Kenny on the dance floor.

When riding with my dad, I always sat in the back with Kenny, never in the front passenger seat where my mom used to sit. After all these years, somehow it still didn't seem right to take her place up front.

My dad cleared his throat and glanced at me in the rearview mirror, one of those rare times when he made direct eye contact before he spoke.

"Sorry if I insulted you back there. I guess I should have known you would always watch after your brother. I can't help but worry about him, you know."

"I know."

"Ever since your mother died you've really assumed responsibility for Kenny, like you felt you needed to take over for her. That means a lot to me."

That comment made me a little uneasy for some reason. I didn't reply.

"You might as well know one other thing, George. I named you the executor of my estate. You'll be the one financially responsible for Kenny when I'm gone. You're the only one I really trust."

"Thanks, Dad."

Unlike Dad, I wasn't worried about Kenny's future at all. Whatever it took, whatever I had to do, Kenny was going to live as normal a life as I could possibly give him.

And maybe, I thought, that was the only plan I really needed.

# CHAPTER SIX

# HOMECOMING HORROR

I have no idea whose idea it was to schedule Homecoming on the same Saturday as Halloween. Homecoming is crazy enough without throwing ghouls and goblins into the mix. Guess I was alone in my apprehension, though, because all the student groups loved the idea, especially the cheerleaders and pompon squad. They've had an informal competition for years as to who could make the biggest and best Homecoming float. Sometimes they had a hard time coming up with ideas—and a few of their floats have been really poor—but the Homecoming theme this year was "Keep the Spirit Alive!" (as usual, pretty lame) so you would think the floats would practically design themselves.

I mean, honestly, if they couldn't create a decent float with a Halloween theme handed to them, they might as well get out of the business.

First up on Saturday was a pep rally, followed by a football game, followed by a cookout, followed by a bonfire, followed by a costume party and dance in the gym. The alumni have a formal dinner somewhere later in the day and cut out right after the game, but that's okay since the rest of us have our proms at the end of the year. It was going to be one of those overbooked days that seemed to go on so long, by the time you finally got home you collapsed into bed without even bothering to get undressed, that's how exhausted you are. We all knew we would have to steel ourselves if we were going to make it through the day.

For a week leading up to Homecoming we were bombarded with mutants and monsters and all manner of "scary" decorations on the hallway walls and hanging from ceilings, most of which were just annoying, especially the fake spider webs. If the webs were too low, they got tangled in your hair and felt just as disgusting as the real thing. And the announcements over the intercom system that week all started with a blood-curdling horror movie scream that always made me jump, much to Onion's and Dave's great amusement.

"That's it! They're taking this Halloween theme too far," I said after spilling coffee down the front of my shirt when the intercom let out one of its ear-piercing shrieks before announcing some boring bake sale the chess club was having later that day.

"No, they're not," Dave said, still laughing at me. "I love it."

I glared at Onion, who was laughing just as hard.

"Oh, I'm not laughing at you, George, I'm laughing with you. No, wait," she said, glancing away to reconsider. "I *am* laughing at you!"

And they both laughed all the louder.

The pep rally Saturday was in the gym. Less than half the crowd wore Halloween costumes, mostly freshmen who looked young enough to still go trick-or-treating. There was a lot of loud, piped-in dance music and the usual energetic routines from the cheerleaders and pompon girls. The guy cheerleaders in their matching uniforms—way too perky, in my opinion—shouted at us in the bleachers through little plastic megaphones. You could hardly hear what they were saying over the music and yells from the prancing girls behind them, but I guess that didn't really matter. It was the spectacle that counted, not the message. The pompon girls went through a long routine with a military precision that would have made the Marines proud, and the cheerleaders—not to be outdone—formed a pyramid so high, it was a wonder the girls at the bottom didn't get crushed to half their height. And when it was time for the pyramid to come apart starting from the top, the girls just fell to what looked like certain death, only to be caught in the nick of time by the cheerleader guys who kept their perky smiles going as they raced to save one life after another until the pyramid was gone.

And then the music stopped, and we all headed out the doors to see the floats and watch the football game.

Our football team was not exactly competitive, which is a polite way of saying they were zero-and-something for the year, as usual. They won a game so infrequently the four years I was there that whenever they did manage to eke out a victory, it would actually make the local news, which seemed to me only added to their humiliation.

Coach Steener, our head football coach, was one of those brawny guys you would immediately peg as a coach of some sport or another. I never saw him without his baseball cap, which led to speculation that he had worn the cap for so long, his skull had grown around it like a chain left wrapped around a tree. The coach always had this kind of shell-shocked look whenever I saw him, as if he was all too aware of the team's dismal record and didn't have a clue what to do about it. I know he had tried to get Dave to rejoin the team—many times—but Dave was steadfast in his disinterest in playing football again no matter what. It got to the point where Coach Steener finally recognized me as one of Dave's friends and starting giving me dirty looks, as if I was responsible somehow for Dave's refusal to reconsider.

One time, and one time only, did he confront me about Dave when our paths happened to cross.

"Wells! Your buddy, Dave. Why did he quit the team? Why doesn't he want to play for us anymore? He was a natural."

There was a look of bewilderment on his face and more than a hint of dismay.

"I don't know, Coach. If he doesn't want to play, he doesn't want to play. What more can I tell you?"

His shoulders slumped as if he knew all along what my answer would be.

"We need a big, talented guy like him," he said. "What a waste."

And his lower lip actually trembled as he turned away.

I felt sorry for the coach right then, but I couldn't do anything to help.

Some people wondered why the administration didn't look for a new coach since the team had been so awful for so long, but Coach Steener had been with the school ever since it opened and was as much a part of The Big Brown Box as the walls and the windows and the doors. The place just wouldn't be the same without him. Each year that went by made him more entrenched here, that much harder to kick out.

Or as Dave explained it scientifically: "It's inertia. A body at rest tends to stay at rest unless acted upon by an outside force. And nobody wants to act."

Spoken like someone who really knew his physics.

So Dave and Onion and I take our seats in the bleachers to watch the floats and then the game. With our team's record, Homecoming was the only time the bleachers were filled, and we had to hunt to find a place where we could sit together.

At one end of the eight-lane running track that surrounded the football field were two wide gates that were seldom opened. As the school band played a medley of Halloween-themed songs, the gates swung inward and two enormous floats barely squeezed through, pulled by lawn tractors driven by two of the guy cheerleaders. Decorated with thousands upon thousands of different colored tissues, they looked like gigantic wedding cakes or something, only with ghosts and goblins and whatnot sticking out.

It must have taken both groups endless hours to create their floats. If they had spent all that time studying instead, I thought rather sarcastically, they would all be straight A students.

Behind the floats was a big old Cadillac convertible with the Homecoming King and Queen in the back seat, wearing their cheesy crowns. This year they were the traditional boy and girl, their bleached-bright smiles nearly blinding in the sunlight as they waved regally to the crowd. Okay, so maybe their smiles weren't *that* bright, but as Dave once said about Homecoming royalty, "They're everything you thought you wanted to be when you were growing up, but thankfully not anymore."

As the floats approached the front of the bleachers, it seemed to me that the tractors were pulling the floats way too fast, since the tops of the floats were swaying. Standing on the bottom platform of each float were the cheerleaders and the pompon squad, waving to the audience.

Just as the first float with all the cheerleaders on board went by, I saw the tractor swerve and the driver fighting for control. It went left, then right, then left again, as if it had a mind of its own. Seconds later, one of the front tires on the tractor broke free and went rolling away under the bleachers. The tractor went nose down and the float came to an abrupt halt. The cheerleaders lurched forward, grabbing the float and each other to steady themselves. The crowd gasped.

The tractor driver of the second float, waving to the crowd with one hand while driving with the other, seemed oblivious to the stalled float in front of him as he raced forward.

"*Look out!*" half the audience yelled, most of us rising from our seats.

The tractor driver looked at us perplexed, and too late, turned forward to see the back of the stalled float just a few feet ahead. I could see him brace his arms, mouth wide open in a silent scream, and then he disappeared completely into the back of the float, tractor and all, as if swallowed up.

There was a loud thud as the floats collided, and cheerleaders and pompon girls alike went flying off their platforms.

It was a good thing they were so athletic, I thought, since they all went either cartwheeling or handspringing end over end down the track as if in a race, landing firmly on their feet as if the accident had been planned. The two floats now looked like one, only missing most of their tissues, which littered the track ankle deep. Their chicken wire frames, visible now and mangled, kept shedding tissues back and forth until the shock of the collision finally dampened out.

The girls stared in frozen disbelief at their now-wrecked creations, and there wasn't a sound from anyone for what seemed like an eternity.

Then one of the girls laughed, a single loud snicker. That started another one laughing, then another, and another, until they were all laughing so hard they had to cling to each other for support.

As if relieved to know that they were all right—and because the collision and its aftermath was, well, just awesome, really—the entire audience stood up and started hooting and hollering like we had all just won the lottery.

When the football team burst through the paper banner set up for them at the other end of the field, they slowed and stopped at the sight in front of them, hands on hips as the crowd continued to cheer—only not for them, as they now realized. Together with the cheerleaders and pompon squads and a bunch of volunteers from the audience, they swarmed to clean up the mess so the game could begin. But when the wrecked floats were pushed apart to set them aside, they all stopped what they were doing when the driver of the second tractor came staggering out.

The crowd immediately fell silent again, mainly out of guilt, I figured. We had forgotten all about him.

In the new silence, he stopped to face us, arms apart, a look of horror on his face as if he had encountered a real Halloween ghost. He stared at us with pleading eyes, as if begging for forgiveness for destroying a Homecoming tradition.

"Oh, let's give him a big hand," Dave said, and began to clap. "That was *highly* entertaining."

The clapping spread, slowly at first, until we were all back on our feet, whistling and cheering again.

His expression slowly changed from horror to bewilderment. When he feebly raised a hand to acknowledge the cheers, we cheered all the louder.

Still unsteady on his feet, a couple of cheerleaders supported him on either side and led him away, and that was that.

The football game seemed anticlimactic afterwards. Practically before we knew it, the score was 7-0 visitors, then 10-0 visitors, then 17-0 visitors—all in the first quarter.

Dave shook his head. "Look at us on offense. We're going backwards."

While not a great student of the game, it was plain to see what Dave said was true. There were fumbled snaps, incomplete passes, tackles well behind the line of scrimmage, and frequent quarterback sacks—our quarterback, of course—until we were thirty or forty yards behind where we started and facing fourth down.

When the team finally made its first first down of the game right before the half, the crowd stood up and cheered. I wasn't sure if the team appreciated that or if they thought we were being cynical.

Halftime came none too soon, with the score 28-0.

"Come on," Dave said. "Let's get something from the concession stand. I'm dying of thirst here."

Onion wasn't interested, so Dave and I made our way down to the front, where those of us trying to file out of the bleachers were stopped by the marching band director to allow the band access to the field.

The marching band wore these spiffy dark blue and gold uniforms with tall frilly hats. I thought we wouldn't have to wait too long for the band to file in, but they just kept coming and coming.

"How big is this band?" I asked Dave as they continued to pour on to the field. I knew the line had to come to an end eventually, I just wasn't sure when.

"Oh, it's huge. At least four or five times bigger than the football team."

It occurred to me if enough of the bigger band members had played football instead, we would probably have a pretty decent team.

The second half was just as brutal as the first half. Towards the end, I noticed that most of our team was sitting on the benches while nearly everyone on the other team was still standing.

"They're exhausted," Dave said, as if he read my mind. "We don't have nearly as many players as they do. Some of our guys were out there for nearly the whole game."

Only then did I notice that for every player we had, the other team had at least two, maybe more. Our entire team sat motionless, some with heads bowed, as the clock ticked down.

Final score: Visitors, 42. The Big Brown Box, 0.

The other side of the field erupted into cheers, which I thought was really rubbing it in, although our team looked resigned and didn't much seem to care. They lined up at midfield and shook hands with the other team in a perfunctory fashion.

As the three of us headed toward the exit, we were stopped again, this time to let our team off the field. We stood there respectfully as they went by, their eyes hollow and expressions empty, as if they had nothing left to express. I think most of us wanted to say a few words of encouragement—anything—but what could you say at a time like that that wouldn't sound phony and contrived? So we said nothing as they filed by, the uncomfortable silence ending only when the last player left and it was the coaching staff's turn to leave.

Someone in the crowd hissed when Coach Steener went by. I saw Dave stiffen when Steener looked up and saw us.

The coach paused. "We sure could have used you out there today, Baker. Thanks for nothing."

Dave turned slightly red as several people nearby looked at him inquisitively, and then the coach was gone.

Dave lowered his head and bulldozed his way out. Onion and I had to hurry to keep up. We didn't speak for a while. I felt compelled to finally address the issue after avoiding it for years.

"So why did you quit football? Steener said you were a natural."

He looked at me almost as if he expected the question.

"Because I don't want my bell rung on a regular basis, that's why. I like my brain the way it is, believe it or not. I don't want it turning to mush later on. After games and contact practices, I was getting these nagging headaches. That was my warning to quit. There's just no way to make the game safe unless you eliminate tackling, and what kind of football would that be?"

"Flag football?" Onion suggested.

"Exactly," Dave replied. "Good luck finding a big fan base for that."

Because we had charged out ahead of the crowd, we weren't too far behind the football team as they made their way slowly back to their locker room, helmets off and held loosely at their sides, heads still bowed. A few were limping and some already wore ice packs on their legs or arms. All their uniforms were muddy, and several had torn jerseys. I couldn't help but wonder now what kind of hidden toll the game was taking on them, what price they were going to pay for all those vicious hits.

"Hope they'll be okay," I said as just kind of a general observation.

"Me too," Dave said softly, looking up at them with concern. "Me too."

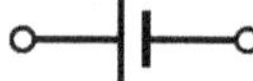

The cookout was a nice change of pace after the sour ending to the football game. It was one of those times when you're so preoccupied, you don't realize just how hungry you are until food appears. I ate nearly as much as Dave, which took some doing, then regretted stuffing my face minutes later when I had the overwhelming urge to immediately take a nap.

Dave saw me yawning and shook his head.

"Amateur," he said. "If you're going to pig out, you have to learn how to pace yourself. See?"

He took a dainty bite from his second burger and chewed politely. My plate was already empty.

It was nearly time now for the bonfire. I could tell because the crowd was starting to gravitate toward the ravine at the end of the parking lot where the enormous pile of scrap wood sat waiting to be lit. Building the bonfire was to certain guys what the Homecoming floats were to the cheerleaders and pompon squad—an intense labor of love. It didn't matter if you were a geek or a nerd, popular or unpopular, a mighty jock or an eighty-pound weakling, there was just something about building the biggest, baddest pile of wood for the sole purpose of burning it all to the ground that just couldn't be explained to those who had no interest in sending flames sky high, the higher the better. But while I liked bonfires just as much as the next guy, I had no desire to spend my weekends and after school hours hunting and begging for scrap wood throughout town as the dedicated bonfire builders did. Guess that meant I wasn't quite pyromaniac enough, but that was all right by me.

One guy who definitely was pyro enough was Sam, the Fireworks Man, our Senior Geek Supreme. We called him the fireworks man because if you ever wanted to buy fireworks, Sam was the guy to call. He could get you just about anything, legal or not. For the past three years, Sam had a tradition of setting off fireworks right before the bonfire was lit. It nearly rivaled the town's Fourth of July display, even if not for all that long. Why the school administration didn't put a stop to it after the first year, I'm not sure—maybe because they liked it just as much as any-one else, and because it added a really nice touch to the whole Homecoming experience. After his first successful Homecoming show, he added halftime at home football games to his repertoire. The one time he was sick and missed a game, some students ac-tually complained that the fireworks were "forgotten," as if the school were responsible for providing them.

Dave, Onion, and I found a good place near the ravine to watch the show. Just as we sat down, there was a flash, followed by a dull thump next to the small mountain of wood scrap waiting nearby. Something whistled faintly as it traveled high up in the air, then there was an explosion and corkscrew streamers of multicolored lights raced away from the center in a huge floral display directly over our heads.

"Outstanding," Dave said, his head craned back like the rest of us in the sizable crowd.

I looked around as everyone *oohed* and *aahed*. It was moments exactly like these that I knew I would miss most about high school, and wished I really did have a time machine so I could return to this moment whenever I wanted to revisit my good old high school days.

After about five minutes, the pace of explosions in the air picked up for the grand finale, with overlapping streamers and rapid-fire crackling. When the last streamer faded and all that was left were faint traces of drifting smoke, the crowd gave Sam a standing ovation, even though we couldn't see him down in the dark ravine.

As we settled back down for the lighting of the bonfire, prepared to literally bask in its warm glow, I saw someone rising up out of the ravine and head our way. Gangly and with a purposeful gait, it could only be one person.

"Great job, Sam," I said as he strode by.

Sam stopped and turned around, searching for who it was who called out to him.

"George!" he said when he finally spotted me. "Didn't see you there, my good man. Glad you liked it. My last Homecoming," he said with a wistful note. Then he came closer to confide something in a low voice. "Hey. I hid an explosive device in the bonfire. You'll hear it shortly after they light the pile. Just wanted to throw a little scare into people since its Halloween and all that."

"Thanks for the heads up. Now I won't pee in my pants when it goes off."

Sam laughed and strode away.

"What did he say?' Onion asked over the general murmuring of the crowd.

"He said he put a bomb in the bonfire."

That caught Dave's full attention.

"*What?*"

The next few seconds were a bit foggy, but here's the best I can recall.

I turned my head toward Dave, laughing lightly, to tell him it wasn't actually a bomb but just an 'explosive device,' whatever that meant. Out of the corner of my eye I saw someone in the ravine light a red flare to start the bonfire.

"Relax," I told Dave. "Sam wouldn't actually—"

I never got to finish the sentence because just then, I saw a streak of flames leap from the flare into the pile of wood, followed by a blinding flash and near deafening explosion. As the massive pile flew in all directions, I felt a hand hit me in the chest and push me back, flat on the ground.

"Get *down!*" Dave yelled, the owner of said hand.

Not a fraction of a second later, I saw a flaming board fly just a few scant inches over my face, right where my head had been.

As you might imagine, utter pandemonium ensued. People were screaming, running, shouting, doing everything a panicked crowd does.

All three of us sat up together to see what had happened. The enormous pile of wood that had taken days to painstakingly assemble was gone, strewn from one end of the ravine to the other. Fortunately, all the heavy stuff—old furniture, shipping pallets, logs—had stayed in the ravine. The lighter stuff, though, was scattered not only among the crowd, but in the parking lot behind us. Smoldering sticks and pieces of plywood were on top of cars or in between them, with dozens of car alarms wailing.

"Thanks for the push, Dave."

"Don't mention it. After all, that's what friends are for, right?"

And he stared sternly at me as if expecting an answer.

From the ravine, I saw the guy who only wanted to light the bonfire come zigzagging his way out, stepping over smoldering wood scraps, the burning flare still in his hand. It looked like smoke was rising off his clothes and hair, but I couldn't be sure. He stood speechless before us, observing the chaotic scene, wondering like everyone else what the in world just happened.

Everyone, that is, except me.

"Sam," I said, over the sound of a siren drawing near.

"Yeah. Sam," Dave said, looking around. "Where is that guy? I'd like to have a little chat with him."

"So would the police," Onion added, nodding towards the squad car that came racing down the main school drive.

The fire department arrived *tout suite* and doused the few scattered fires, and everyone pitched in to clean up. Fortunately, there were only a few slight injuries— scrapes and bumps mainly—and minor damage to the cars. Since most were high school beater cars like Dave's, no one much seemed to care.

I'm not sure if Sam had told others about his 'explosive device,' but pretty quickly the rumor spread that it had to be sabotage. Most of the jocks were blaming other teams, especially our conference rivals. A few people thought it was an inside job.

Finally, someone mentioned Sam's name, and faces brightened as if that must be the answer.

Sam was nowhere to be found. I figured he had either meant to blow up the bonfire—which seemed inconceivable to me—and he was in hiding, or it was an accident because his 'explosive device' was way more powerful than he had calculated and he was in hiding. Either way, all I knew for sure is that he had some explaining to do when he finally came around.

Principal Morgan soon came by with a megaphone that had the fire department's logo on it.

"Ladies and gentlemen, please head to the gym so the fire department can conduct its investigation. We will start the dance early tonight. Thank you for your cooperation."

He repeated the message until the crowd turned away and slowly headed toward the gym, some of the girls still clinging to each other nearly in tears.

"That's Morgan for you," Dave said as we trudged along with the others. "Grabbing the spotlight as usual."

As we should have expected, the gym was plastered top to bottom with Halloween decorations. I saw that the few upperclassmen who had worn Halloween costumes had ditched them and looked like themselves again. Frankly, by this time I was sick of Halloween and doubted I was the only one. And after being outside in the dark, the harsh fluorescent overhead lights were a bother.

"These lights are way too bright," Onion said, rubbing her eyes and confirming exactly how I felt.

Over in a corner of the gym on a stage, the band seemed surprised that the crowd was streaming in already; I guess no one told them we were on our way after the bonfire disaster. They scrambled to plug in mics, tune their guitars, and adjust the volume on their amplifiers as the gym filled up. I had never heard of the band and wasn't even sure what type of music they played. All I knew was that they were local and new, which didn't bode well for the quality of music we were about to hear.

Set up at last, the lead singer of the band signaled one of the Homecoming volunteers to turn off some of the gym lights. The room dimmed considerably, which was welcomed relief.

"*Hello, people!*" the lead singer yelled into his mic.

After the events of the day, no one seemed to have the energy to respond.

The singer tried again.

"I said *hello, people!*"

The response was weak; I think the only reason we responded at all was so he wouldn't yell at us a third time.

The singer shrugged and the music began.

They were a cover band, singing all the songs the radio stations had just stopped playing because they had fallen out of favor. The band wasn't bad, but they weren't great, either. "Serviceable" was probably the highest compliment I could give.

"Mediocre," Dave said, far less charitable.

He danced a couple of songs with Onion—which was a sight to behold since Dave danced worse than I did—then the three of us kind of wandered around.

"You dance like Frankenstein," I told him.

Dave shrugged. "Why not? It's Halloween."

Instead of dancing, most people stood in little groups here and there, still discussing the bonfire explosion. One group of guys looked particularly angry about it. I realized they were the ones who had spent countless hours planning and building it.

"Wells!" one of them called out as we went by them. "Where's Sam?"

"I have no idea, Mike."

"Come on. You're friends with him, aren't you?" He stared at me as if I really did know where Sam was but wouldn't say. The others in the group glared at me with the same anger.

"Yeah, I talk to him. He's okay." I thought that was a fair assessment.

"Okay? *Okay?* You mean as in okay to destroy something we spent weeks working on? That kind of okay?"

He came right up to me, daring me to answer. The others behind him pressed forward, too. Mike was one of those thin, wiry guys who were a lot stronger than they appeared.

Dave stepped between us.

"Is there a problem here?" he asked.

"Not with you. Stay out of it."

Dave shook his head. "No can do. If you've got a problem with George, then you've got an even bigger problem with me. You *capisce*?" Dave glowered down at him.

Mike winced a bit, then held up his hands and backed away.

"Fine. No trouble."

Dave gave his usual exaggerated smile. "Great! You take care now, hear?"

Dave's dark expression returned as we walked away.

"Thanks, Dave."

"Not a problem. Jerks."

"All right, everyone!" the band singer announced. "We're told it's time for the awards for the best Halloween costumes! If you're wearing one, come on up!"

All the freshmen in their costumes crowded in front of the stage, making it look like a middle school party.

"Let's get out of here," Onion said as the names of the costume winners were announced, followed by the shrill, excited shrieks from all the short ghosts and vampires. "I've had enough of Homecoming." She rubbed her forehead.

"Fine by me," Dave said.

"Me too," I said, making it unanimous.

It wasn't until we left the gym that I realized how loud the band had been. My ears were ringing, and I wondered if that was from the music or the bonfire explosion. Probably both.

The outside air was refreshing, and our moods improved as we traipsed down the road to Dave's car in the far parking lot. Far behind us we could see the flashing lights from all the police cars and fire trucks as they continued their investigation, the whole ravine condoned off now with yellow and black caution tape.

"*George.*"

We stopped and looked around, trying to pinpoint where the soft, ghostly voice came from.

"*Over here.*"

I looked at a row of bushes on the other side of the dimly lit street. They rustled, and then a shadowy figure came out from behind them. I thought I recognized the gangly shape.

"Sam? Is that you?"

I felt Onion's fingernails dig into my arm.

Sam came forward, looking either way down the road to make sure we were alone.

"I didn't do it, George. I didn't do it!"

"That's not what people are saying," Dave replied.

As Sam came closer, I saw the frightened look on his face and actual beads of sweat on his brow.

"I know they are, but what I put in the bonfire couldn't possibly have released enough joules to blow that massive pile apart. Here, look, this is what I put in there. One of these."

As he reached out to hand me a short tube with a long wick sticking out of one end, I noticed that Sam's hands were shaking.

I heard myself gasp and stumbled back at the sight. Why, I wasn't sure.

Dave took the tube from Sam instead.

"What is this? A quarter stick?"

"Just about," Sam said.

Dave handed it back to Sam.

"If that's what you really put in there, then you're right. All it would have done was make everyone jump when it went off."

"That's what you said you were trying to do, wasn't it, Sam?" I asked, trying to put my unintentional snub of him aside. "Just scare us a little, for Halloween."

He nodded, breathing hard. I still couldn't take my eyes off his hands as they shook.

"Well, you better hope the fire department finds some other cause for the explosion," Onion said. "If not, they're going to drag you in for questioning."

He nodded again. "What should I do in the meantime? The longer I stay away, the guiltier I look."

"Yeah, that's a problem," Dave said. "I would just lay low. Let people think what they want. If you're innocent, all the talk will be gone."

Sam looked resigned. "I guess so."

"Good luck, Sam," Onion said. "Hope things go your way."

And with that, Sam darted back across the road and disappeared into the darkness.

We hardly spoke as Dave drove us home, Onion first. When I made my way into the house, it finally hit me how bone weary I was.

To my surprise, my dad was still up. I didn't think he was waiting to make sure I got home safe since he hadn't done that in years. Instead, I had noticed recently that he was having trouble sleeping. Dad had said that was a common problem as you got older.

He lowered the volume on the TV.

"So. How was Homecoming?"

Now, I'm not one of those teenagers who can't or won't talk to their parents, I'm really not. I don't give one word answers or sulk or claim they just don't understand me. But as tired as I was, and with all that had happened, I really didn't know what to say or even where to begin.

"Fine. Really. It was all good," I said, hoping that would suffice.

"Great. Glad to hear it," my dad said, and turned the volume back up to continue watching his show, apparently satisfied with my simple answer.

I collapsed on my bed when I got to my room, shoes still on and all, and didn't wake up until almost noon the next day. I was glad my dad let me sleep since I needed every minute of it to recuperate from the horror that was Homecoming.

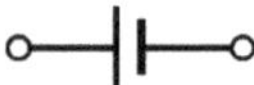

On Monday morning, back at The Big Brown Box, word spread that the fire department had figured out pretty fast why the bonfire exploded. It turned out that Mike's dad, of all people, decided to "speed things up" when they lit the bonfire by filling an old dresser drawer at the bottom of the pile with several gallons of gasoline. When the flare was struck, that streak of flame I saw leaping from the flare to the bonfire were the gas fumes igniting, and when the flame reached the drawer, the gas had more than enough energy—"joules" as Sam called it—to blow everything to kingdom come. Sam returned to school mid-morning on Monday—looking mighty relieved—and it was Mike who was red-faced the rest of the day and had to endure the ridicule, not Sam.

"Serves him right," Dave said when he heard the news. "Jerk."

No charges were filed or anything like that since it was determined to be an accident, not a deliberate act, so that closed the final chapter on Homecoming.

"Tell you one thing," Dave said when all the buzz about Homecoming finally died away. "They will never, ever hold Homecoming on Halloween weekend again. Not if they know what's good for them."

I could only hope Dave was right.

# CHAPTER SEVEN

# KENNY'S MAGICAL NIGHT

Kenny was always garbage-picking. He found the most mundane things interesting—wrapping paper, rubber bands, ribbons, paper clips. He was really creative with the junk he scavenged and fashioned all kinds of models out of them—airplanes, birds, you name it. When my dad finally bought some matching appliances for our kitchen to replace the ones that were here when he bought the house, they arrived the old-fashioned way, in enormous boxes. Well, when Kenny saw those boxes he practically went nuts. The delivery men tried to take them back to their truck, but Kenny refused to let go of them. Not only did the men let him keep them, they went to their truck and gave him a bunch more. Kenny laughed and twirled around right there in the street, he was so happy. There were so many boxes they filled the garage, meaning Dad had to park in the driveway. My dad was probably waiting for Kenny to forget about them so they could be tossed, but Kenny got busy right away building something, and Dad finally realized he would be parking in the driveway for quite some time.

The funniest thing is that Kenny wouldn't let us see what it was he was creating. Whenever he worked in the garage, he would lock himself in. When he was done, he would move a chair to block the garage door off the kitchen, as if that could really keep us out. Dad could have used his remote in his car to open the overhead door, of course, but I think both Dad and I not only wanted to respect Kenny's wishes. We kind of liked the mystery of not knowing exactly what it was.

"I'll bet it's a big cardboard boat," I said.

"Could be," Dad replied. "He is taking a lot of rope into the garage. Maybe it's a sailboat, with old bedsheet sails."

Having been a sailor a good part of his life, Dad's face seemed to glow with satisfaction at the thought.

Kenny didn't make a whole lot of noise building whatever it was he was building—I mean, how much noise can you make working with cardboard?—but he sure spent a lot of hours in that garage.

And then Kenny stopped, and the kitchen chair sat for days in front of the garage door.

"What's he waiting for?" Dad said one day after running through the pouring rain into the house because he still couldn't park in the garage. "Usually when he's done building something he's anxious to show us."

There was another thing that had grabbed Kenny's attention that month, even before he got all his boxes. The electric company had come with a big blue bucket lift to work on some overhead electrical lines nearby. They worked on the lines for a couple of days and then parked the lift in the middle of the empty lot between two houses halfway down the block. It sat there for weeks, bucket high up so nobody could mess with it.

"I wonder if they forgot about it," Dad said as we drove by it on our way to the grocery store one day.

Kenny kept getting in trouble for poking around the lift instead of staying and playing in our backyard like he was supposed to. Mrs. Loomis—whose house was right next to the empty lot—told me that she saw Kenny in the bucket one morning, but he had climbed down before she could call to tell us. I didn't dare tell Dad about that because I knew he might have told Kenny to stop working on his secret project and throw all that cardboard out as punishment, something I didn't want to happen.

Kenny's project was too important now not to let him complete it. In a way, it had taken on a life of its own.

Around midnight that same night, I heard a strange noise coming from outside. It was a motor of some kind—not a car or a motorcycle exactly, but some kind of engine. It revved a few times, but otherwise it was a steady, rather annoying drone.

After a few minutes of listening to it in the dark, I dragged myself up to investigate what it was.

It was then I discovered that Kenny was gone.

I searched the house in near-panic mode, wide awake and kind of scared, hoping that I would find him so I wouldn't have to wake up Dad to let him know.

Not in his usual places, I wondered if he was out in the garage, working again on his creation. A few times I've gotten home late from somewhere or woken up in the middle of the night only to find Kenny quietly involved with something, even if it was just his Game Boy at the kitchen table.

The chair was gone from its usual spot in front of the door to the garage, so I took that as a good sign I would find him there.

I threw open the door, less frightened and more annoyed now. "Kenny, what are you—"

The garage was empty, the overhead door wide open. I stood there in disbelief, then in the faint light from the streetlamps and full moon that night I saw someone much too tall to be Kenny coming hurrying up our driveway, around my dad's car.

"Kenny?" I asked anyway.

"No. It's Mrs. Loomis."

To my surprise she looked wide-eyed, almost happy, despite what time it was. Wearing a pink fuzzy bathrobe with matching slippers and white pajamas, she motioned me to follow her as if inviting me to a slumber party.

"Hurry. It's Kenny. You've got to see this."

If it involved Kenny, I could believe just about anything. Just the fact that Mrs. Loomis seemed eager to show me what Kenny was doing was both reassuring and yet unsettling at the same time.

As soon as we passed her house, I realized the sound I had been hearing was the electric company's bucket lift. We turned the corner and I came to an immediate halt, stunned by what I saw.

"Can you believe it?" Mrs. Loomis asked.

Kenny was high up in the lift, manipulating two boards attached to ropes. And attached to the ropes on the other end was what Kenny had worked so hard and long to create in the garage and now revealed to the world.

A giant cardboard robot, dancing slowly by itself under the glow of the moon to some unheard song.

I moved closer, passing two guys who looked to be in their twenties. They must have been driving by when the spotted Kenny's oversized puppet show and stopped for a better look.

One of the guys looked at me. "Nice, isn't it?"

"That's my brother up there," I said, not sure if I was proud of that or if I was just offering an explanation.

"Nice," he repeated.

As I got closer, I saw that the robot had two old hubcaps for eyes, and an open mouth cut like a smiling Halloween pumpkin. The nose was an old plastic flowerpot.

If I had to estimate, I'd say the robot was about three times my height, maybe taller. The closer I got, the taller it looked, until my head was craned back almost as far as it would go.

It was amazing how well Kenny made the robot dance. It moved smoothly, its arms and legs swinging in unison as it did a kind of happy, soft-shoe shuffle. I had never seen Kenny manipulate a marionette before. It was almost if he knew instinctively how they worked.

The robot stopped and its giant head came down as if to take a closer look at me. Someone behind me gasped, as if I were in real danger. When I glanced behind me, I saw there were over a dozen people there now, with more crossing the street, most in bathrobes like Mrs. Loomis.

The robot tilted its head first one way, then the other. I felt like there was an intelligence behind those hubcap eyes, even though I could see through the gaping mouth that the robot's head was hollow.

When it stood back up, the robot offered me its cardboard hands, each hand with four stiff fingers and an inoperable opposing thumb. I held onto the thumbs and the robot began to dance again. I understood then that the robot wanted me as a dance partner, or at least Kenny did. I followed the robot's lead, and together we shuffled through the weeds and overgrown grass, the robot trampling them down with its giant cardboard boots that looked like the ones astronauts wore.

The growing crowd behind me laughed and then applauded.

We swayed back and forth for a while and then someone tapped me on the shoulder. It was Mrs. Loomis, grinning.

"My turn now," she said

I let her take my place.

A few others danced with the robot, and in about twenty minutes I saw the robot begin to droop as if growing weary, its shuffling slower and less precise.

I looked up and realized that it was Kenny who was tired now. It must have taken all his strength to manipulate the robot like that— even though it was hollow, it had taken so many cardboard boxes to create it that it had to be fairly heavy.

The robot stopped, the lift engine revved and the bucket began to descend. As it did, the robot laid down on its back as if to take a well-deserved nap.

The crowd applauded again, the performance clearly over.

When the bucket reached ground level, the engine went off and Kenny got out.

The two young men who had stayed to watch the robot dance came forward.

"Hey kid, how did you get the lift started? Did they leave the key in the ignition?"

Kenny shook his head no. "Kenny made one."

He handed it to him.

The young man stared at it in disbelief. "You made this? It's nothing but a couple of thin strips of sheet metal glued together and cut like a key! How did you know how to do this?"

Kenny stared blankly at the young man as if the answer should be obvious.

"Hey, everybody! Look at this! He made his own key for the lift! Isn't that amazing?"

The two of them seemed more interested in the key Kenny made than the enormous robot, which was now surrounded by about a dozen of our neighbors. Mrs. Loomis lifted one of the robot's arms by the wrist as if she was taking its pulse and someone else lifted one of the robot's legs.

Kenny wordlessly held his hand out for the key. The young man seemed reluctant to give it back, but then returned it.

"Nice," said the other young man, as if that was the nicest word in his vocabulary.

The two of them turned and strode away.

"Come on, Kenny. It's almost two o'clock in the morning. Dad would have a fit if he saw us out here."

The moment I said it, I wondered if that was really true, if Dad wouldn't have liked to have seen Kenny's robot in action. At the very least, he would have finally known what it was that kept him from parking the car in the garage for weeks on end.

Kenny nodded and we headed back to the house, leaving the robot to further examination by the neighbors, who ignored us as we walked away.

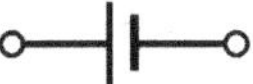

I woke up late Saturday morning. Dad was up already, reading the paper in the kitchen. I didn't see Kenny.

"Where's Kenny?" I asked, wondering if he was planning a daytime demonstration of his robot.

"He's in the garage. He was up even before I got up. I heard him banging around in there."

Since there was no chair against the garage door, I opened it a crack and peeked in. The overhead door was wide open, and it appeared that something large had been dragged across the dusty floor.

I immediately thought of the Morlocks dragging the time machine into their underground workshop shortly after the time traveler's arrival in the far distant future, only our garage was empty. No time machine and no cardboard robot either.

Kenny finished stuffing something into the recycling bin, which was so full the lid wouldn't close. He turned around and beamed at me as if tremendously pleased with himself.

"Kenny, where's your robot?"

Kenny pointed to the recycling bin.

"You *recycled* it?" I nearly staggered into the garage. "Why? It took you weeks to make it!"

Kenny stared with his usual lack of comprehension. "Kenny was done."

I looked in dismay at the bin, which held neatly cut cardboard panels that were once a magnificent, towering robot. Then I saw the two hubcaps and plastic flowerpot back in the corner of the garage where Kenny had found them. It was as if the robot had never existed, as if the events of last night were just a pleasant dream.

It was silly to mourn a cardboard robot, of course. What would we do with it? Where would we keep it? We couldn't keep it in the house or the garage, and outside it would be ruined with the first rain. Still, it was sad that the robot hadn't lasted at least another day or two, but since it was Kenny's and not mine, how long he robot lasted was up to him.

I had a sudden thought.

"Did Dad see it?"

Kenny shook his head no.

The only thing I could think of was that Dad would be disappointed, and that Onion and Dave would have liked to have seen it too.

"Oh, Kenny," I said, for no particular reason.

"George?"

I looked into the bright sunlight and saw Mrs. Loomis standing on our driveway, holding her cell phone. She was in her usual sweatpants attire now instead of her nightwear.

"Look. I took a picture last night of you with Kenny's puppet."

"You did?" I hurried to see it.

It was a dim picture of me dancing with the robot, but at least now I had proof it wasn't all just a dream. You couldn't see the robot's head in the picture or anything below my knees, but you could see me holding the robot's hands, my head craned upward to look at my gigantic dance partner.

"Could you send this to me?" I asked her. "I'll give you my number."

"Of course. I thought you might want it. Sorry I only took one picture. I would have taken a few more, but when I looked outside this morning the puppet was gone. Kenny must have gotten up really early."

Kenny yawned mightily as if to prove her correct.

"Thanks, Mrs. Loomis."

As she left, Kenny tugged on my shirt. I looked down at him and saw he was trying to hand me something. I took it from him.

It was the key he made for the lift.

"Are you done with this too, Kenny?"

He nodded and yawned again.

"Maybe you should go back to bed. I think you only slept like three or four hours, didn't you?"

Kenny walked around me and back into the house, apparently not needing to be told a second time.

I looked closer at the key and marveled at how well made it was, just as the young men had done last night. Kenny must have spent hours cutting the smooth, precise grooves with a tiny file. How he knew the pattern and depth of those grooves I had no idea and probably never would. Like the robot itself, despite all Kenny's work the key was meant to have a single purpose and a short life.

"Dad?" I called out. "You can park your car in the garage again."

I heard footsteps from the kitchen and Dad appeared at the door.

He looked around. "Good. It's supposed to rain again next week. I'm tired of making a mad dash for the front door. Say, what was it Kenny made with all those boxes, anyway?"

I looked at him. "It . . . wasn't a boat."

He looked surprised. "No? Then what was it?"

"It was a big robot. Kenny cut it up and recycled it this morning." I pointed at the recycling bin.

"Oh. Well, Kenny always cleans up after himself, I'll say that. Too bad I didn't get to see it." He didn't sound particularly disappointed.

"Yeah, too bad." I would have told him more about it, how the neighbors came out one by one to see it and how Kenny used the lift to make the robot come alive, but I was afraid he would only regret not having seen it for himself.

Dad returned to the kitchen. I looked again at the overstuffed recycling bin, the robot's final resting place, still sorry it was gone.

As I pressed the button to close the garage door, I held tight to the key as something to always remind me of that magical, mystical night when I danced with a giant robot by the light of the silvery moon.

# CHAPTER EIGHT

# MY ARREST

Dave always parked in the school lot by the football field. He was too cheap to pay for a prime parking spot right by the school, so instead we had to hike two blocks through all kinds of weather just so Dave could save a few bucks.

Onion and I offered several times to help him pay for a parking sticker—usually as we were hiking in the pouring rain—but Dave refused "on principle" because he thought all the parking lots should be free, not just the distant ones. So we got soaked, and we got cold, and still we walked those two miserable blocks every day.

As I mentioned before, Dave is very protective of his car, even though it's basically a rolling wreck. That's why I'm not sure exactly what possessed me to do what I did. Dave would have liked an explanation, that's for sure. So would Coach Steener and Principal Morgan, only I couldn't give them one. They say teens act irrationally because their brains aren't fully developed; unless I come up with a different reason someday, I'm going with that.

So here's the sequence of events. Dave and Onion were standing in front of Dave's car, which he had parked backwards as usual next the field. He and Onion were disagreeing about something while I sat in the back seat waiting to go home. When five minutes went by and there was no sign that their animated conversation was going to end anytime soon, I had the idea to crawl into the driver's seat and start the car. Dave had put his car key in the ignition before getting out to argue with Onion, and the key ring hung there as if daring me to give it a twist.

I did just that. The car started up smoothly.

To my surprise, Dave hardly reacted. He glanced over his shoulder, but that was all. Honestly, I think I was the first one to not only sit in the driver's seat but actually start Dave's car ever since he bought it the middle of his sophomore year.

So I wondered what would happen if I put the car in reverse and backed up a few feet to the edge of the field. I put my foot on the brake, quietly moved the shifter to "R" and lift my foot off the brake pedal.

The car began to slowly inch away, making that soft, peculiar scrunching sound as the tires rolled on the asphalt lot. I felt the back of the car drop slightly as the rear tires rolled into the grass.

I stopped. Dave and Onion hadn't noticed that the car was now several feet away. Wondering now how far back I would have to travel before they finally did, I took my foot off the brake pedal and let the idling engine continue to creep the car backward.

The front of the car dropped a bit as the front tires hit the grass. Completely off the asphalt now, I had to give the car a little push on the gas to get it rolling again. Dave and Onion still didn't notice.

I rolled backwards across the sideline, then on to the field it-self between the thirty and forty yard lines. For some reason, the car seemed to bog down a bit and I had to give it yet more gas to keep going.

As I approached midfield, I saw Onion—now half a block away—point in my direction. When Dave turned around, his arms shot up in the air as if he was surrendering, and he ran toward me faster than I've ever seen him run before.

I had the crazy thought that maybe he should have kept playing football. Coach Steener would have been very impressed with his forty-yard dash.

I stopped and turned off the car when I realized he was yelling something at me.

I poked my head out of the window as if nothing was unusual. "Yes? Can I help you?" I asked.

Out of breath, Dave grabbed the door handle and gasped to speak.

"What . . . do you think . . . you're *doing*?"

I looked around as if I had no idea what he was talking about.

"Is there a problem, sir?"

Dave glared. "Out. Get out. *Now!*"

I meekly did as he said, unsure why he was so mad. I thought it was a harmless, funny prank, but he was acting as if I had driven his car off a cliff or something.

"Look, you idiot! Look what you did!"

I looked where he was pointing. To my surprise, there were two deep tire ruts from the parking lot all the way to the front of the car.

I scratched my neck, not sure what to say. "Huh. I did that?"

Dave looked incredulous. "You see any other cars out here? It rained all night last night, remember? What did you think would happen when you drive a heavy car across a soggy field?"

I gasped and stepped forward, realizing something. "Hey! This is just like the scene at the end of The Movie when George dragged his time machine out of his garden and back into his lab, leaving ruts behind! See?" I pointed at the ruts as if Dave hadn't seen them first.

Dave grabbed his head and spun completely around. "Oh, no. Oh, no no no no no. Don't tell me you were trying to imitate that stupid movie. It's *stupid!*" He stomped a foot on the ground.

"Well, no it's not. And I wasn't trying to imitate it. I was just making a valid comparison, that's all."

The incredulous expression returned to Dave's face. "That's all? That's *all*? I don't think you realize how much trouble you're in. You could be *expelled* for this. Now do I make myself clear?"

I considered that possibility. "Expelled? For this?"

"George, this could be hundreds of dollars' worth of damage. They've expelled people for a lot less."

Onion tentatively approached me, but not too close, as if associating with me now would somehow taint her. "Dave's right, George. You might have to finish high school at an alternative school now."

I looked away. Things felt like they were spinning out of control in a hurry. All I had wanted was to play a little joke on them, and all of a sudden they were talking like I was public enemy number one.

Dave ran his fingers through his hair. He looked frightened now, as if somehow he were to blame. "Let's get the car off the field. I'll drive it straight forward so it doesn't make any new ruts." He gave me a dirty look before opening the car door and getting in.

As Onion and I watched, Dave put the car in drive and gently stepped on the gas. The car lurched forward, then the rear wheels spun and the car settled down as if it decided to take a seat right there.

Dave slapped the steering wheel with both hands and turned the car off. He glared at me again.

As Dave got out, we saw three buses pull into the parking lot. I could see dozens of faces turned our way, but they were too far away to identify.

Onion gave me a piercing gaze. "You better hope that's not the football team," she warned. "If it is, you're going to wish you ran yourself over instead of the field."

The buses stopped by the gym entrance and people started streaming off. A handful broke away from the crowd and headed toward us. As they got closer, I could see it they were cheerleaders, still in uniform.

"Lucky you. You get to live another day," Onion said.

The closer they got, the more I realized they were furious.

Onion backed away several steps. "Oops. I might have been wrong about that 'live another day' thing, George."

There were five of them. They marched up to us and stood in a straight line with their hands on their hips in front of us, eyes dark, as if ready to start some sinister cheerleader routine.

"Are you out of your mind?" one of them said.

"Yeah, wait 'til Porter sees this," said another. "You're a dead man walking."

Porter was the biggest, strongest dude on the football team, and by far the best player. Despite the team's dismal record, he had at least a dozen football scholarship offers from big name colleges. As much as it pained me, I had to admit that if anyone on the team could kill me with hardly any effort, it was Porter. The only thing that might stop him was the possibility of losing those scholarships. But even then I feared that if he went ahead and killed me anyway, that might only enhance his reputation somehow.

"What have you got to do with this, Baker? You protecting him?"

Dave put his arm around me and squeezed harder than necessary to show them we were chums.

"Take it easy now, ladies. George was just playing a little prank on me, weren't you, George? I'm sure the field will be as good as new in practically no time at all after he helps fix it. Isn't that right, George? He'll do whatever it takes to make things right."

He squeezed my shoulders again. I nodded wordlessly with a big smile like I was Dave's sock puppet or something.

The girls relaxed a bit, but not much.

"Well, he better fix it if he knows what's good for him," yet another cheerleader said, and their dark stares returned.

The thought of being mercilessly pummeled by the cheerleading squad seemed so wrong on so many different levels that I was grateful Dave had managed to calm them down.

And then I saw Principal Morgan casually heading towards us, right between the two ruts, as if merely out for a stroll.

The cheerleaders stepped aside, knowing full well their presence paled in comparison to that of Morgan.

He stopped a respectable distance away, unlike the cheerleaders who had gotten up close and personal.

"Good afternoon, gentlemen," he said in voice that told me he was less than pleased. "It would appear there's been a little accident here with Mr. Baker's car." He casually gazed behind him at the long, twin tire ruts. "It was an accident, wasn't it? Because if this was deliberate, I'm afraid I'm going to have to call the police. You've caused considerable damage, you know. This is vandalism."

"Oh, not at all, Principal Morgan. This was just a silly little prank that—"

I raised a hand to stop Dave from assuming any responsibility. That spinning out of control feeling returned as I sputtered to explain what happened.

"Honest, I was just trying to—didn't think—didn't know I was damaging anything."

A little "gotcha" glimmer appeared on Principal Morgan's face.

"That's right, George. You didn't think. So you're the culprit here. Excuse me a moment, would you?"

He pulled out his cell phone and began to call someone. I wondered if he was making good on his threat to involve the police.

"Hello? Stanley? Are you in your office? Good. Would you mind coming out to the main field? I'm afraid there's been . . . an incident. Right. Thanks. See you soon."

He put his phone back in his suit pocket. "Coach Steener will be here shortly. I'd like to hear what he has to say about this."

Dave slumped as if all hope was lost.

Soon, Coach Steener was hurrying towards us, letting out loud cries of disbelief as he followed the ruts to where we waited.

"What happened, Charlie? What happened?" He held his arms out as if imploring him for an explanation.

"Take it easy, Stanley. Apparently, George here was just playing a little prank that got out of hand, didn't it, George?"

Coach Steener gasped. "Out of hand? He destroyed my field!"

He looked at me wild-eyed, as if it were inconceivable.

And then another figure appeared heading toward us between the ruts, an imposing figure even from a distance. I had to wonder how many more people were going to show up, if I was going to be surrounded by an angry mob before I knew it.

Behind me, a safe distance away, I heard Onion gasp as she recognized who was coming. Even Principal Morgan stepped aside.

Coach Steener looked behind him to see who I was staring at with apprehension. He let out a gleeful laugh.

"Well, well. Here comes Mr. Porter, our team captain. Let's hear what he has to say about this."

Dave stiffened and stepped forward, as if expecting Porter to blame him for the damage. Then I realized that Dave was just acting as my bodyguard should things get really ugly.

"Hey, Coach," Porter said when he arrived. "What's going on?"

He put his hands on his hips just like the cheerleaders did, only there seemed to be no malice in the gesture—he was just asking a question out of curiosity as he gazed around.

Coach Steener immediately pointed at me.

"Ask him. He's the one who wrecked our sacred ground here, our home turf. He has to answer to *you* now!"

Porter looked at me. "Hey, George. Dave. How are you guys doing?"

"Could be better," I said, hoping that didn't sound too flippant. "How are you?"

"Doing okay," Porter said.

Coach Steener let out cry of exasperation.

"Enough with the introductions! He ruined our field! What do you have to say about that, Porter? Tell him!"

Morgan raised his hands as Dave took another step forward, putting me in his shadow. "Now boys, let's settle down here."

Porter stared at Coach Steener with a blank expression.

"Well, Coach, I guess we'll just have to fix it, that's all." He shrugged as if there was no other possible answer.

Coach Steener went limp, as if someone had pulled a plug on him and he partially deflated.

"But . . . our field . . ."

"Coach, our season just ended. We've got a whole year to fix it. Besides, I've seen the field in worse shape than this."

Coach Steener deflated a little more, apparently unable to disagree.

"So what happened, guys?" Porter asked, looking now from me to Dave.

That feeling of losing control went away and I could finally speak in complete sentences.

"I was just playing a prank on Dave, seeing how far I could back up his car before he finally noticed. I made it to midfield." I glanced back at Dave's car. "As you can see."

"Ha!" Porter's head went back in mild amusement. "That's pretty far!"

As he surveyed the scene again, he had a calm, almost angelic look about him, which made me wonder if that was why our team seldom won. If they were all like Porter, they were way too nice.

"Well, I gotta get going, Coach. Just wanted to let you know all the jerseys are clean and folded and in your office like you wanted. See you tomorrow in class. Bye Principal Morgan. George, Dave."

As he shook Dave's hand, he grew serious.

"Sorry you left the team, Dave. It was fun playing with you. You were an awesome lineman."

"Thanks," was all Dave said. He shook Porter's hand again.

And Porter walked away.

Morgan cleared his throat, as if uncomfortable with how that went.

"This doesn't get you off the hook, George," he said when Porter was gone.

"Yeah," Coach Steener chimed in. "There's still this little matter of vandalism, whether you meant it or not."

Morgan nodded, standing next to the coach as if to present a united front and undo Porter's kindness.

"What do you think, Stanley? What should we do about George here?"

Coach Steener didn't hesitate. "Call the police." He said the words without looking my way.

The five cheerleaders, standing behind them, nodded solemnly.

"All right. I'm afraid I have to agree. That's the way it goes, George. This can't go unpunished, you know."

Morgan pulled his phone out again and pressed just three numbers.

"Hello? Could you send an officer to the main football field at five fifty-five North Lombard Road? That's right, the high school. No, just the police. It's not an emergency. This is Principal Morgan. I have an . . . issue with a student. Fine, we'll be here. Thank you."

He put his phone away with a defiant look, and I realized he was going to call the police no matter who said what.

"Sorry, man," Dave said.

Onion was next to me again on the other side. How long she had been standing there I didn't know.

She briefly put a hand on my shoulder. "Oh, George," she sighed in a mixture of sorrow and pity.

This was yet another one of those times when I wished I had a time machine so I could go back fifteen minutes and stay in the back seat of Dave's car where I belonged. Just fifteen minutes, that's all I asked.

I looked up at Mr. Morgan as a police car came up the drive. Coach Steener flagged it down.

"Things can change drastically in the blink of an eye, can't they, Principal Morgan? In the blink of an eye."

His jaw grew slack and his gaze softened a bit before they hardened again. "Very profound, George. But that still doesn't get you off the hook."

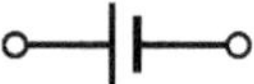

Have you ever been arrested? It's scary, but also very interesting if you can stay detached like I did. Strange as it might seem, it was almost as if I was just standing in for someone else through the whole process, like I was observing rather than participating, if that makes any sense. The youngish-looking policeman who showed up didn't seem particularly concerned about anything; in fact, he seemed greatly disinterested, as if he had much better things to do. He didn't even put handcuffs on me. Oddly, in retrospect, I kind of wish he had. If you're going to get arrested, you might as well go whole hog and do it up right, I say. All he did was read me my rights and hold me firmly by the arm as he walked me to the squad car, where he helped me into the back seat so I didn't bang my head.

I had quite an audience for that. I think the cheerleaders who confronted me ran and told everyone still around what was happening and they all came out to see me get hauled away. It was almost like one of those celebrity busts where the reporters and paparazzi get tipped off and surround the celebrity, only nobody was clamoring to ask me any questions. A few of them took some pictures with their cell phones, but mostly they stood there in silence, as if not sure what to think. Like me.

Onion waved goodbye as the squad car turned around to take me to the police station. For a moment it looked like she was going to cry, but I wasn't sure.

Dave just stood there stoically. I thought he was going to salute or something the way he was standing there at attention, but he just watched.

On the way to the police station, the youngish police officer finally said something that could have come right out of an old detective movie.

"So why'd you do it, kid?"

"It was just—"

I stopped. I was going to tell him it was just meant to be a prank, that I didn't know I was damaging the field as I traveled backwards in Dave's car, but then I remembered I had the right to remain silent and decided that was probably a real good idea.

"I better not say. Sorry, officer."

He gave me a quick backward glance. "Suit yourself. I wasn't trying to trick you or anything. I don't really care why you did it. Just making small talk."

I believed him, but still thought it best not to say anything.

The police station had a secure area behind a heavy metal door that reminded me a little of the entrance to the Morlocks' underground lair, but instead of a dark, foreboding cave filled with noisy machines, I was escorted into a brightly lit, sparsely furnished cinder-block room that was eerily silent. I was left there alone for a few quiet minutes while the officer went to do some paperwork. When he returned, he was holding a small plastic sign filled with numbers. He set that aside and took my fingerprints, rolling each finger and thumb of my right hand across an ink pad and then a white card marked for each digit.

The officer looked almost apologetic as he gave me an alcohol wipe to clean my hands. "Sorry about the ink. We're supposed to go digital soon. We still do it the old-fashioned way, I'm afraid."

Truth be told, I preferred this old fashioned way since it was traditional and just what I expected.

Then I had to stand against a wall that had height markers so they could take my mug shot. It was then I noticed what looked like a two-way mirror in the wall across from me.

"Do you use this for lineups?" I asked, still in my calm observer mode.

The officer looked down at his digital camera and fiddled with the controls. "Sometimes. Not too often. Oops, I almost forget."

He set the camera down and handed me the plastic sign.

"Hold this under your chin."

I complied. He held out the camera and peered at the display on the back.

"It's upside down," he said.

"Huh?"

He lowered the camera with a look of mild exasperation.

"The booking sign. It's upside down."

"Oh!" I scrambled to turn it around. "Sorry."

He held the camera back up and took two quick pictures, one of me facing forward and one facing to the side. I tried to look totally innocent, whatever that's supposed to look like.

The officer laughed when he reviewed the pictures.

"You look like a little lost . . . well, never mind. Bond is set at one hundred dollars. That's pretty standard for something like this."

Once again the officer looked disinterested, as if he were disappointed I wasn't a safe-cracker or some other kind of more exciting criminal.

"Do you have that much cash with you?"

I shook my head.

"Well, then, you'll have to call someone to get it and bring it here, or else you'll be spending the night in a cell."

I immediately had an image of being held in a dank room full of Eloi skeletons like George the time traveler, and my observer mode came crashing down, even though I knew the cell was probably clean and bright like the room I was in. All I wanted was to get out of there just as fast as I could, as if I had suddenly discovered I was claustrophobic and couldn't breathe. It was then I realized my pockets were empty. I had left everything in my backpack in Dave's car.

"Where's the nearest phone?"

o—|⊢—o

As it turned out, I didn't need to make that call. Dave and Onion were already at the station and had pooled their money to bail me out. Between them, they had just enough.

We hardly spoke as Onion drove me home in her mother's boxy yellow Volvo, Dave's car still at midfield and waiting to be towed. It was odd to see their roles reversed up front, odder still to drive in silence with them. Usually it was hard to get a word in edgewise.

Both of them looked at me with apprehension as I got out of the car.

"Good luck explaining it to your dad," Dave said. "Hope he doesn't kill you."

"Get a good lawyer," Onion called out the window as she promptly pulled away.

I slunk into the house without a clue how to tell my dad I had been arrested. I mean really, what do you say? Do you wave your hand to minimize the whole thing and say, "Hey, big guy, just so you know, I got in just a little bit of trouble with the law today," or maybe break the news laughing like it was no big deal and say, "You're not going to believe it, but I had this huge, silly misunderstanding with Principal Morgan!" Or maybe act shocked and dismayed and say, "It's so unfair! There was no reason to call the police!"

How my dad actually found out was quite different.

He was in the kitchen with Kenny, making our dinner. Kenny was playing with his Game Boy at the kitchen table. Kenny looked up at me for maybe two, three seconds tops with his usual vacant eyes, then returned to his game and announced in a loud voice, "There's something wrong with George. What's wrong, George?"

How he knew I have no idea, but then again, I never understood how Kenny could be so perceptive at times when he seemed so distant in his own private world.

My dad stopped stirring a pot of something on the stove and looked at me. "What? Is that true?"

He turned down the burner and faced me when I didn't answer right away.

I wish I could have felt like a calm observer again as I broke the news, but my heart was pounding and my mouth felt dry as the words came tumbling out.

"I had an accident at school today, Dad. I damaged the football field with Dave's car, trying to play a stupid joke on him. Morgan called the police and had me arrested. Here's my bail bond receipt with my court date."

I held up the receipt the officer had given me, as if a confession like that really needed any written proof.

Dad looked at me like I had just announced I was pregnant or something.

"An accident?"

"Yes, sir." I braced myself, waiting for him to start reading me the riot act.

"Morgan had you arrested because of an *accident*? Are you kidding me?"

You know, it's funny how you manage to convince yourself sometimes that things are going to play out a certain way, only to be stunned when they go in the complete opposite direction. I didn't want to go overboard and start blaming Principal Morgan too much for my arrest since my dad might have had second thoughts if I did, but if my dad wanted to blame Morgan I sure wasn't going to say anything to dissuade him either. It came across a little as that sad, old, "but officer, my son's a good boy!" coddling some parents resort to whenever their Dear Little Boy gets in trouble, but then I remembered that Dad didn't like Morgan. At all. That went back years ago when Morgan publicly complained about the "bloated military establishment" taking too much money away from education at a packed school meeting one night. I remember my dad seething back then at that remark, frantically waving his hand in the audience, hoping that Morgan would allow him to speak. Morgan ignored him instead.

His anger now seemed focused somewhere up over my right shoulder, as if Principal Morgan was lurking behind me. I actually glanced behind me to see what he was looking at; nothing out of the ordinary was there.

"You didn't mean to cause any damage, did you, George?"

"No, sir."

"But Morgan had you arrested anyway, didn't he?"

"Yes, sir."

"Didn't he realize this could go on your permanent record?"

"Well, I don't—"

"Of course he did! And you know why that didn't matter to him?"

"Um, well—"

"Because he doesn't care, that's why!"

"Dad, Kenny hungry," Kenny said.

Dad turned the burner back up under the pot and resumed stirring its contents, only much more vigorously than before.

"I know a really good lawyer," he said to the simmering pot. "I'll call him first thing in the morning. We'll get this resolved."

It was just like Dad to take charge of something if he felt it was his duty, just like he did for twenty years in the Navy. Nice as it was to let him handle things, I still had the uneasy feeling he might change his mind about my innocence when he found out what really happened and how much damage was done.

Dad finished making dinner, and we ate it in silence. I couldn't help but notice him chewing his food rapidly, his angry gaze still focused on the empty corner of the room as if Principal Morgan were there, still visible only to him.

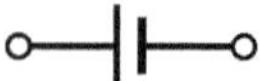

The lawyer's office was kind of crummy, with old, creaky furniture and tattered, ancient magazines in the waiting room. It reminded me of dentist's office, only dumpier. I thought that lawyers all had posh offices, but then I realized that this lawyer had probably been practicing law forever if Dad knew him, so he must have been really experienced, which was clearly a good thing.

We had dropped Kenny off at Mrs. Loomis's house on the way there. He liked her, and she was glad to watch him whenever Dad and I had someplace to go.

My dad tapped his foot impatiently, apparently angry again at Morgan for making us go through all this work to prepare for my court date in three weeks.

"We'll get you out of this mess, just you wait," he said. "Morgan's in for the surprise of his life if he thinks I'm going to take this lying down."

You would have thought all this was something personal between Principal Morgan and my dad and that I was just a pawn in their little game of one-upmanship.

When the lawyer appeared at his office door, Dad popped right up. I got up as fast as I could and stood nearby.

"Harold! Good to see you again. This is George."

Dad grabbed me by the shoulders and pulled me front and center as if I were on display.

"Hi, George. I'm Harold Turner. Your dad and I go way back."

We shook hands. Mr. Turner looked to be my dad's age, which didn't surprise me at all.

"Come right on in. Your dad tells me you had a run-in with old Principal Morgan, is that right?"

Mr. Turner sat behind his desk, and Dad and I squeezed into two chairs across from him.

"Well, yes," I began. "But really—"

"The whole thing's a joke," my dad interrupted. "Nothing but a joke."

He then proceeded to give Mr. Turner his own version of events, which varied considerable at times from the real story. I had told my dad exactly what happened, but he seemed to have ignored just about everything that made me look bad and embellished Principal Morgan's harsh reaction. Not that my dad was a liar or anything; I think he really believed that everything he was saying had to be true even though he witnessed none of it. He didn't exactly make me out to be completely innocent, but he sure made it sound like Principal Morgan either badly overreacted or had it out for me all along.

Mr. Turner took notes like a madman, writing faster than I thought was humanly possible, all the while nodding as if in complete agreement. When Dad finished, he dropped his pen on the notepad and leaned back as if ready to pronounce the verdict himself.

"It's obvious to me there's been a grave miscarriage of justice here. This matter could have been handled much better without any police involvement at all."

To my surprise, Mr. Turner pointed to my dad as he said that, not me. I was beginning to wonder if I was the one on trial or Dad.

"Hah!" My dad turned to me, finally smiling. "What did I tell you?"

Mr. Turner glanced at his notes. "I think I've got more than enough information here to prepare your defense, George. Were there any witnesses you would like to call, anyone who could corroborate these events?"

"No, not really," was all I could say. I couldn't think of anyone who could back up my dad's slanted story, not even Dave or Onion.

"That's all right. We'll go with what we've got." He stood up and stuck out his hand. "Don't worry about a thing, George. I think everything's going to turn out fine." He beamed at me.

As soon as he said that, I had a feeling that things might actually turn out not so fine, and regretted not offering just a few slight corrections to my dad's version of events if only to avoid looking like a total jackass should someone who actually witnessed what happened show up in court and tell the truth, the whole truth, and nothing but the truth.

Thanks to my dad, what Mr. Turner had written was not quite the truth, which worried me most of all.

# CHAPTER NINE

# TRIAL AND TRIBULATIONS

Maybe I watch too many old movies, because court wasn't at all what I expected.

There was a metal detector we had to pass through when we entered the building, just like at school, but after that we just sat a packed room with all kinds of people coming and going, waiting and waiting for my name to be called. Nobody sat in a witness chair and there was no dramatic testimony or lawyers jumping up to yell "Objection!" like I thought there would be. Instead, everybody just stood right in front of the judge and talked so softly I could barely hear what was being said. And even though there were a lot of cases to be heard, they didn't last very long. People went up, kind of whispered back and forth with the judge, and then either left the court immediately or stopped to pay a fine. That was it.

Mr. Turner sat next to me, my dad on the other side. Dad had contemplated wearing his old Navy dress whites to impress the court—which I thought could backfire badly—but fortunately decided at the last minute to wear a suit instead. I didn't own a suit, so I just wore a dress shirt with my nicest tie.

Dad said I not only looked fine, I looked Not Guilty. I wished I had the same confidence, but I didn't.

I leaned over to whisper to Mr. Turner. "It's not as exciting as I thought it would be."

He laughed quietly. "This court is for misdemeanors like yours," he whispered in return. "All the excitement is in felony court across the hall where the stakes are a lot higher. Believe me, you don't want that kind of excitement. I know this judge well, by the way. He's a fair one, so I think you'll do fine."

And then my name was called.

After all that waiting, I was more nervous than I thought I would be as the three of us strode up the aisle. It's one thing to watch people stand before a judge and another to stand there yourself.

Up close, the judge looked almost as disinterested as the young police officer who had arrested me. Someone handed him a thin manila file folder; he opened it and scanned the top sheet.

"George Wells," he said, and looked at me through his really thick glasses. "Is that you, young man?"

"Yes, Your Honor." My voice sounded dry. I tried to swallow, but didn't have enough spit.

He set the folder down and looked on either side of me. "So. Are these two old guys your bodyguards, or is one your father and the other your attorney?" He winked at Mr. Turner. "Hello, Harold," he said.

"Good afternoon, Your Honor," Mr. Turner said.

"Yes, I'm George's father," Dad said. "You guessed right, Your Honor."

The judge grinned and picked up the folder again.

I was shocked that a judge would actually joke around in court like that and decided I liked him already. All my nervousness disappeared, which might have been his intent.

The judge picked up the folder and scanned it again.

"So. A single charge of damage to school property. Any additional information for the court, Prosecutor?

"No, Your Honor. Nothing further to add. Vandalism to the athletic field grass."

It was only then I noticed her. A young woman, she stood off to the side with a bored expression as if yearning to be across the hall in the felony court where "all the excitement" was as Mr. Turner described it. She gave an impatient sigh as she brushed back her long blonde hair, like she the wanted the trial over with already.

"I see transcripts from two oral depositions here. David and . . . Nancy. Are these friends of yours?"

"Yes, Your Honor."

The judge grunted. "Apparently, both indicated they were involved in a 'heated argument' and didn't witness exactly what happened. They further claim no one else was present at the time. Is that your recollection, Mr. Wells?"

"Yes, Your Honor. It is."

The judge gave a weak smile as he closed the file and set it aside.

"All right then. How do you plead to the charge, Mr. Wells?"

"Not guilty, Your Honor," I said, as instructed by my attorney.

I remembered what Dave had said—"You see any other cars around here?"— and felt nervous again.

The judge nodded. "Very well." He gave the open folder back to the man who had given it to him. "Bailiff, see if there's anyone here from the school district."

The bailiff stood up, open folder in hand. "Is there anyone present representing the school district? The school district versus Wells? The school district?"

No one answered. As Mr. Turner had anticipated, the school district had sent no one to contest my plea. And without anyone to contest my plea, there would be no choice but to dismiss the case and I would go free.

It didn't feel quite right to me to do things that way, but I guess that's why you hire attorneys, to follow their advice.

Just as the judge leaned forward and was about to speak, I heard the courtroom door bang open on my right and glanced to see who was coming in.

I felt my heart jump.

Coach Steener flew into the room, looking flustered as if annoyed for arriving so late. When he saw me standing before the judge, he marched straight toward us, his right hand raised as if ready to be sworn in.

*So much for that plan,* I thought with a sinking feeling, wondering if I should immediately plead insanity or something like that.

"Your Honor, I'm here to represent the school district," Coach Steener said, breathing hard.

"Please remove your hat in the courtroom," the bailiff loudly announced.

"Oh. Sorry."

Couch Steener yanked his cap off. To my surprise, not only did the cap come off easily, I saw he had a glorious, full head of hair. I guess I had always assumed he was bald or balding, and knew I wasn't the only one who assumed that.

The judge didn't look too happy to see him. I knew exactly how he felt.

My nervousness grew when I glanced at Mr. Turner and saw his mouth drooping as if not only surprised, but totally unprepared for this turn of events. Even my dad was looking at him, puzzled.

"Please state your name for the record," the judge said.

"I'm Coach Steener, Your Honor. Stanley Steener. The head football coach."

"And you are currently employed by the school?"

"Yes, Your Honor. I was asked by Principal Morgan to give my testimony."

"Will counsel from the school district be arriving soon?"

Coach Steener's face was a blank. "Excuse me, Your Honor?"

"Will an attorney from the school district be joining us today?"

"Oh! No, sir. Just me. You know, budget cuts and all that. Principal Morgan thought I could handle things just fine since I'm in charge of the football field."

"Very well."

The judge scribbled something down. It might have been just my imagination, but he seemed to avoid looking at me after Steener arrived, as if he knew like I did that the jig might be up. He opened up the file again.

"Were you a witness to what happened in this case?" the judge asked." I don't see that you gave any prior testimony. Just Mr. Morgan, the school principal, and he arrived after the damage was done."

That seemed like a question my attorney should have asked. Instead, Mr. Turner just stood there flipped back and forth through the meager papers in his hands as if searching for a clue as to what to do next.

"I saw the damage Mr. Wells caused to the field, so yes, Your Honor."

"So you actually saw it happen?" the judge persisted.

"I was informed of the vandalism by Principal Morgan. I went out immediately to see for myself as he requested."

The judge took a deep breath. "I'll ask you again. Did you actually see the damage occur?"

Coach Steener frowned as if he didn't quite understand the question. "Your Honor, the damage I saw was fresh. Mr. Wells was standing right by the car."

"So you didn't actually see it happen, did you?"

"I saw it."

"You saw it happen?"

"Yes, sir. Right afterwards, like I just said." He beamed as if the judge should finally be satisfied with that answer.

The judge leaned forward and took off his glasses, tossing them on the bench. His beady eyes looked out of focus and out of patience.

"I'm going to give you just one more chance to answer my question, Mr. Steener. It's a simple question, really. A one-word answer will suffice. Did you or did you not witness what happened *as it was happening?*"

Coach Steener looked thoughtful. "Well, if you put it *that* way, then no, Your Honor, but what diff—"

"*Thank* you, Mr. Steener. That will be all."

The judge slipped his glasses back on and wrote something down.

I opened my mouth to confirm that Coach Steener didn't see me in the car, figuring that might help my cause.

"*Don't* speak," the judge warned, jabbing his pen in my direction. "Counsel, please advise your client to remain silent."

"Be quiet, George," Mr. Turner said softly.

At least my attorney finally said something useful. I realized then that the judge didn't want me to say anything that might get me in trouble, which seemed awfully nice of him.

"Your Honor," Coach Steener said, "it should be obvious that Mr. Wells here is guilty, whether I saw it happen or not. Neither of his two friends claimed responsibility. Who else could have done it?"

"Do you have written confession from him by any chance?"

"Well, no, but he didn't deny it either."

The judge sat back. "Mr. Steener. Unless you can produce a witness who actually saw Mr. Wells drive the car on to the field, or a signed, written confession from him that was witnessed and signed by others, then nothing is 'obvious.'"

Coach Steener reddened. "Your Honor, all I know is that the field was vandalized and that the damage is considerable. Considerable!"

The judge slowly shook his head. "The amount of damage is immaterial to the outcome of this trial if you have no evidence that Mr. Wells is responsible for that damage."

Coach Steener looked almost frantic. "But Your Honor! It must be in the thousands of dollars! Didn't you see the pictures we gave as evidence?"

The judge's eyebrows went up.

"Pictures? No, I didn't." He held up the file folder and shook it. Several photographs slid out in front of him.

"Oh! Here they are."

Mr. Turner stirred uneasily. So did my dad.

The judge held the pictures at arm's length, flipping through them one at a time.

He set them down. "So that's it? A pair of tire ruts? Is that what we're talking about here?"

Coach Steener looked aghast. "Is that it? I mean, yes, Your Honor. Tire ruts. Two of them, both about a hundred and twenty feet long. I paced them off myself." He seemed oddly pleased about that.

"And that's your 'thousands of dollars' worth of damage?"

Coach Steener wavered. "Well, yes, Your Honor. I mean, it could be."

"Do you have any written repair estimates stating such an exorbitant amount?"

Coach Steener seemed to shrink a bit. "No, sir. I don't."

"I didn't think so." He put the pictures back in the folder, closed it and slid it aside as if he had seen enough. "So how do you intend to repair the damage?"

"We have our own groundskeeper, Your Honor." Coach Steener's voice was small. "We'll probably . . . repair it ourselves."

The judge gave another weak little smile. "So really, we're talking about a few wheelbarrows of dirt and some grass seed, now aren't we, Mr. Steener? That's maybe what? Thirty dollars? Fifty dollars? Be honest with me now. It's not 'thousands of dollars,' is it?"

Coach Steener shrank a little more. "No, sir. I guess not."

"Do you have any other evidence to present at this time, Mr. Steener? This is your last chance before I render my verdict."

"No, Your Honor." Coach Steener's voice was smaller still.

"All right. Based upon the evidence presented, or lack thereof, this case is dismissed."

Both my dad and Mr. Turner shook my shoulders and patted me on the back.

"Just a moment, gentlemen. I didn't say *you* were dismissed. I'm going to make a little suggestion for young Mr. Wells here."

My dad and Mr. Turner both came to attention.

His stare was piercing, and I knew whatever he was going to suggest I was going to go along with it.

"It would be nice if you would show some school spirit, Mr. Wells, and volunteer to help repair the damage to the field, regardless who was responsible since you seem to have been, shall we say, in the vicinity at the time. Now I can't order you to do that since you haven't been found guilty of anything, but I'm sure it would be much appreciated by Coach Steener here as well as the football team. Wouldn't it, Mr. Steener?"

Coach Steener nodded obediently.

"Good. So, Mr. Wells, are you willing to state now before this court that you'll help fix the damage that . . . *somebody* . . . caused?"

From the intensity of his gaze, I almost felt like he had found me guilty after all, or knew I was.

I swallowed hard, out of spit once more.

"It would be an honor, uh, Your Honor. Sir Honor, sir."

Mr. Turner gave a faint little cry of amusement.

*Could I possibly sound any more like an idiot?* I thought, hoping the judge didn't think I was making fun of him. Instead, the judge looked pleased at my response. "Good! Then it's settled. You're dismissed."

He sat back and was handed another file folder for the next case. Turning to leave, I saw the prosecutor stifling a yawn, as if utterly unimpressed.

As we silently headed for the exit, I could tell from Coach Steener's wide-eyed look of disbelief that the outcome of the trial wasn't what he expected at all.

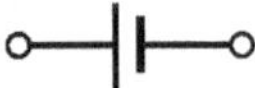

Dad drove me to the football field early on Saturday to help the school groundskeeper repair the damage I caused. It was comfortably cool and sunny, with only a few wispy clouds in the sky. Of all the things I could be doing on such a beautiful day, this would have been at the very bottom of my list.

"I knew Harold would get you acquitted, especially since it was just an accident." My dad seemed buoyant and not at all bothered by my having to "volunteer." "He sure is a good lawyer, isn't he?"

"Uh, sure, Dad," was all I could say. I didn't have the heart to tell him that Coach Steener irritating the judge to no end was the real reason why I didn't now have a criminal record.

When we pulled into the parking lot, I saw the groundskeeper already hard at work filling in one of the ruts, shoveling dirt out of a wheelbarrow.

There was another wheelbarrow full of dirt waiting by the other rut. I could only assume that one was for me. A pile of dirt was right at the edge of the lot, presumably to refill the wheelbarrows. It looked like more dirt than what we would need, but then again, what did I know about groundskeeping?

I winced when my dad pulled into Dave's usual parking spot, right where I had begun my little prank. The groundskeeper glanced up at me as I got of the car and then resumed working.

"Call me when you're ready to be picked up," my dad said pleasantly enough out his window, then drove away and left me standing there to face the task ahead.

I walked as casually as I could toward the groundskeeper, who seemed to be ignoring me. He was one of those ruddy, always tanned kind of guys who looked like they belonged outdoors.

"Hi! I'm here to help you today." I tried to look as helpful as possible by grabbing the shovel out of the wheelbarrow waiting for me on the other side.

A few clumps of dirt flew off the end of the shovel blade and landed on the groundskeeper's boots, hardly the best introduction I could have made.

I winced again as he stopped working and looked up slowly to face me.

"So. You're the idiot who did this?" His voice was flat, his gaze one of annoyance.

I remembered that Dave had called me that very same word at the far end of the ruts, and wondered if that was just the default description for someone who pulled this kind of failed prank.

I jabbed the point of the shovel into the ground and held my head up high, knowing there was no point in denying it any longer.

"Yes, sir. I'm the idiot."

A look of surprise along with the hint of a grin came and went from his face.

"All right." His voice was softer now. "Get that shovel going. We've got our work cut out for us today. Let's see if you can keep up with me."

I watched how he took a few shovelfuls of dirt to fill in about a foot of the rut and then tamped it down with the backside of the blade, crowning it slightly in the middle since—as he explained it—the dirt would eventually settle. Then he would repeat the process. Working fast, I caught up to where he was.

We didn't talk again for several minutes. When he saw I was keeping pace, he finally spoke.

"Tell me something. What made you think it was a good idea to drive a heavy car across a wet football field?" He didn't pause with the shovel.

I took as deep breath. "I just wanted to play a prank on a friend," I said for the umpteenth time. I kept working too. "I wanted to see how far away I could drive his car before he noticed it was gone."

He grunted and dropped another shovelful of dirt into the rut and tamped it down. "Too bad he didn't notice right away. That would have saved us all this work, and you a bunch of trouble."

"I know." I paused to rub my neck, which was already feeling a little hot and stiff. "It was a stupid idea."

He grunted again. "Glad you think so."

We fell silent again for a while as we worked.

I caught a whiff of something awful and realized the smell was coming from the wheelbarrow. "You know, this dirt smells funny."

He laughed once. "That's because it has compost in it."

"Sure stinks."

"Well, manure usually does."

I paused. "You mean we're shoveling . . ." I didn't say the word.

He laughed again. "You bet. Best thing in the world to make seed sprout and grow fast."

More silence followed. After that revelation, I tried not to touch the compost or spill any on me.

"As you probably know, my name is George," I said to break the silence. "What's yours?"

"Frank," he said. "Mr. Franklin Fields, but you can call me Frank. Nobody calls me by my last name."

I wondered if he was upset about that or just preferred his first name.

"Okay . . . Frank." It still seemed a bit awkward to me to call an adult I just met by his or her first name. "You have any hobbies or anything you like to do when you're not groundskeeping?"

The question made him break his work rhythm.

"Hobbies? No, not really. I like to watch old movies, but that's about it."

"You do?" I struggled to move my wheelbarrow closer to where I was working so I didn't have to walk so far for more dirt. "So do I. What's your favorite movie?"

He shrugged. "Oh, I don't know. Guess I don't really have a favorite. What's yours?"

I didn't hesitate. "The 1960 version of *The Time Machine*." I stuck the shovel into the wheelbarrow and pulled out another shovelful.

He nodded. "Great old Metro Goldwyn Mayer film. Rod Taylor, Alan Young, Yvette Mimieux. Sebastian Cabot too. George Pal's second full-length movie after *Tom Thumb*. Won an Oscar for special effects. I've seen it several times. Wouldn't mind seeing it again."

It took me a few moments for me to realize I was staring at him with my mouth open. I closed my mouth and finally dumped the dirt waiting on my shovel into the rut.

"But how . . . I mean, you know it that well?"

His grin reappeared, and this time stayed awhile.

"I know lots of old movies from that era. They're the best if you ask me. That was back when Hollywood really knew how to tell a great story."

"Like *The Time Machine*?"

He looked up at me, nodding in agreement. "You bet."

We worked and talked about movies for the next two hours until the ruts were filled. Frank knew a lot about George Pal's career, something I hadn't really looked into and now wondered why I hadn't. Then Frank showed me how to top dress the dirt filled ruts with grass seed, working it lightly into the soil with a rake. Finally, we watered both ruts gently so as not to wash the seed away, and the job was done. After calling my dad to come and get me, I helped Frank put everything away back in the storage shed near the gym.

I had always wondered what was in that shed since we drove past it every day. Now I knew—all of Frank's gardening stuff.

Frank turned towards me when my dad arrived to pick me up.

"Hope you learned a lesson today, George." There was no bitterness in his voice. Instead, he spoke the words as if he wanted to, not because he felt he had to.

"Yeah, I learned a lot. Especially about George Pal."

Frank laughed. "Well, take care of yourself," he said, and walked away before I could even offer to shake his hand.

I never talked to Frank again, although I saw him on occasion. We would wave at each other from a distance, but that was all. Still, I was grateful I had met him. It was rare to meet someone who appreciated the great old movies, especially The Movie.

As for school punishment, I had to serve a boatload of detention with other miscreants who came and went, but I wasn't suspended or expelled, and even Morgan seemed to treat me with something approaching respect for having taken my medicine like a man, even if my dad still said that Morgan was full of . . . compost.

For quite a while after that, every time we parked by the football field, I took a few seconds to see how well the grass was growing in the two filled-in ruts, especially the one I had filled. In a few weeks' time, you could no longer tell exactly where the ruts were, as if they never existed and the prank was all just a bad dream. My failed prank and its aftermath never achieved the kind of notoriety other events our senior year did, but it was one of those experiences you cherish if only because it was an adventure you never would have had otherwise, a path you would have rather avoided if you could but came out stronger in the end for having traveled.

CHAPTER TEN

# THE HOUSE PARTY

So I got invited to one of those house parties where the parents go away for a few days and tell the kids not to do anything stupid but they're stupid anyway.

Why I went, I'm not sure. I guess because both Dave and Onion said they were busy, so at least it was something to do on a Saturday night. Still, I was a little wary of the company and what I might be getting myself into.

It took me half an hour to ride my bike there. Had I known it was going to take that long, I probably wouldn't have bothered going.

The house was old but nice, way out in the original part of town. It was one of those tall Victorian things with a big front porch, a fancy paint job, and intricate woodwork. Had it been decrepit instead, from the outside it would have looked like a typical haunted house.

Two things hit me right away when I went in. First, the furniture and decorating looked straight out of the 1920s, which I thought was just excellent. It was like going back in time without a time machine—just like The Post, only older yet—and could easily have served as the time traveler's house had there been a lot more clocks in the parlor. Second, the smell of beer was overpowering, as if the place had been soaked in it, which was exactly what was happening.

Not surprisingly, nobody looked old enough to drink. One of those parties.

Since I don't drink, I immediately felt like I didn't belong. If the house hadn't been way out in the boonies, I would have worried about the police raiding the place and beaten a hasty retreat.

"No. No, thank you," I must have said a dozen times as people kept trying to hand me a beer.

"Oh, come on, man," one glassy-eyed partygoer implored. "Just one little beer. Join the crowd." He motioned back to the unsteady horde behind him, their slurred voices louder than they had to be in the packed room.

It occurred to me then that Dave and Onion probably knew what kind of party this was going to be, which was why both of them claimed to be too busy. If that was true, I wished they had warned me. I didn't intend to stay long, but since I had gone through all that trouble to get here, I figured I would check the place out first since it was a pretty cool house.

Other than Jason—the guy who invited me—and his younger brother Josh, I didn't know a soul there. There were a few vaguely familiar faces from The Big Brown Box, but I didn't know their names.

Josh was the bartender, although I use that term lightly. His whole job consisted of opening the refrigerator, pulling out a beer bottle, popping the cap off and handing it to whoever asked for it. Keeper of the Cold Ones was probably a better title.

Josh was kind of a blond emo kid, minus the heavy makeup. If I had to guess, I'd say he was no older than fourteen, fifteen, tops, dressed in tan baggy cut-offs and a too-long, matching tan T-shirt. He didn't seem to particularly enjoy his job since he also wore a frozen scowl.

Some bartender.

I just kind of wandered the house, poking my nose everywhere it didn't belong since there was nobody to stop me. Besides, in their inebriated state, nobody seemed to care.

As I passed by a washroom on the first floor I caught an overpowering whiff of puke. There was yet another reason not to drink—why heaving your guts out is considered a fun time I have no idea.

I made my way up the narrow stairs near the kitchen and found what had to be a guest bedroom. I thought so because while the room was tidy, when I opened it door it had a dusty, abandoned smell to it, as if the perfectly made bed hadn't been slept in for ages. There was an overstuffed wing chair in the corner, which looked comfortable despite its gaudy Victorian stripes, so I sat down. Even that smelled like it needed cleaning, or at least a vigorous vacuuming. I liked the room because it seemed frozen in time, like an Egyptian tomb or something, even if not that old.

Besides, it was the one place in the house that didn't reek of beer. At least, not yet.

Just a couple of minutes later, Josh stepped into the room and glanced at me, a Mountain Dew in his hand. I figured he was taking a break from his bartending duties—that, or they finally ran out of cold ones. He wordlessly went to a window and looked out, taking a sip from the can. I wondered what was really in it since Josh now seemed a bit unsteady himself.

Then I was struck by how much he resembled the robed Eloi from The Movie and wondered why I hadn't realized it immediately.

More out of boredom than anything else, I decided to go into movie mode, and picked the scene where the time traveler questions the Eloi at their dinner table. Besides, I figured, saying something to someone was a whole lot better than saying nothing to anyone after all the effort it took to even get to the party.

"Perhaps you . . . do you have books?" I asked.

Jason turned and looked at me. "Books?" He blinked. "Yes, we have books." He took another sip from the can, his expression otherwise blank.

I sat up straight in the chair, surprised at his movie-perfect response.

"Oh, wonderful!" I gestured widely, just like George the time traveler did in The Movie as I continued the reenactment. "I can learn all I want about you from books! Books will tell me what I want to know. Well, well, could I see the books?"

He shrugged and silently lead me into another bedroom, possibly his, where a lone bookcase sat by the closet door. Only two of its five shelves had books, and even those shelves were less than half full. The books were dusty, as were the shelves.

Secretly, I couldn't have been more pleased.

I pretended to pull back a curtain that fell apart before selecting a decades-old copy of *The Guinness Book of World Records*, opening it with the same eager anticipation the time traveler did when he examined one of the Eloi's books. Then I changed my expression to one of dismay as if the book was decayed and unreadable, just like in The Movie.

I looked up at Josh the emo-Eloi with practiced disdain. "Yes, they do tell me all about you."

And with that, I let the book drop as if it had disintegrated and swept a hand across an empty shelf, pretending to destroy a dozen brittle, useless volumes, their words of wisdom lost forever. A cloud of dust sprang into the air, as if on cue.

"What have you done? Thousands of years of building and rebuilding, creating and re-creating so you can let it crumble to dust!"

I slapped the empty shelf for emphasis just like the time traveler.

"A million years of sensitive men dying for their dreams. For *what*?" I flicked my fingers in his face and imagined—real or not—that more book dust sprung from my fingertips. "So you can swim and dance and play!

Like the unnamed Eloi in The Movie, he barely reacted except for a puzzled look.

I pretended to hastily dust off my arms and then hurried back downstairs.

"You!" I said, pointing randomly around the crowd. "All of you! I'm going back to my own time!"

No one paused their conversation or even glanced in my direction.

I continued the time traveler's soliloquy. "I won't even bother to tell of the useless struggle and the hopeless future! But at least I can die among men! *Aaah!*"

And with that, I strode out the front door in proper disgust.

The next thing that should have happened, of course, is that Weena would have opened the door to watch me leave in search of my time machine. But no one appeared, and the loud party chatter continued unabated.

I hopped on my bike and headed home, imagining that each push of the pedals was propelling me back through time, back to my world and home.

# CHAPTER ELEVEN

# A LITTLE ROMANCE

When Dave picked me up for school Monday morning, he seemed preoccupied and subdued, not at all his usual swaggering, roly-poly self.

"You okay?" I finally had to ask.

He flinched as if caught off guard by the question.

"What do you mean?" He sounded a little panicked.

"I mean you're really quiet this morning. Something wrong?"

"No! I mean, of course not." He kept his eyes on the road. "Everything's fine. Just fine."

I chalked it up to the Monday morning blahs and didn't ask again.

Things got stranger when Onion joined us for breakfast in the cafe. I was glad to see she was wearing a new outfit. Actually, a couple of them, as usual.

"Good heavens," I said. "That's a dress?"

That's what I always said whenever Onion showed up wearing something new; it was a line out of The Movie and our standard routine.

"Yes," was all she replied. No customary exaggerated eye roll, no "That was only funny the first time" usual response.

And she sat down without another word—not even a hello—ignoring both of us as she unwrapped her plastic fork and knife.

I was beginning to wonder if I were turning invisible, or if both Dave and Onion were turning into zombies.

I played along with the silence for a while and finished my morning coffee, waiting for some crack in the armor, for somebody to break down and tell me why the three of us were suddenly strangers.

I smashed my empty paper cup flat to get their attention. Onion jumped.

"All right. I don't know what's happening here, but this is ridiculous. Somebody say *something*."

Dave sighed. "Onion and I went to a movie Saturday night."

While that news wasn't startling, I hadn't expected to hear that Dave and Onion went somewhere without me. That was a first. In some small way, I suddenly felt neglected.

"Oh. That's it? Is that why you were both too busy to go to the house party with me? Why didn't you say something? The way things went, I would have rather gone to a movie with you."

Onion reddened slightly, her gaze averted.

I sat up straight, the obvious truth finally sinking in.

"Wait a minute! You mean you two went on a . . ."—I had trouble just saying the word—"*date?*"

I hadn't meant to make it sound so disgusting, but I did.

Dave slumped as if the horrible secret was out.

"Yeah. Kind of. Sort of."

Onion said nothing, gazing at her breakfast as it grew cold.

After all these years, it never even remotely occurred to me that there would ever been any kind of romantic interest between Dave and Onion. We were just buds, good friends, chums, the three amigos, those three people who always sat by themselves in the far corner of the cafe. It would have been easier for me to believe that Dave and Onion actually were zombies rather than interested in each other in quite that way.

"So, like, why now?" I had to ask.

Dave stirred as if not sure himself. "Well, I've always liked Onion."

She reddened slightly again.

"I like Onion, too, but we would never go on a date, now would we?" I looked directly at Onion. "Do you like Dave too the way he likes you?"

She shrugged half-heartedly. "Sure. I don't know."

Now, instead of feeling left out, I had this overwhelming curiosity to know more about their supposed date.

I tried to act casual about it but knew I was failing miserably. "So . . . what happened, if you don't mind me asking?"

"I already told you. We went to a movie."

"And?" I asked, beginning to hate myself for prying but fascinated by this totally unexpected turn of events.

"And nothing. I picked her up from home, we went to the theater I bought the tickets and snacks, and when the movie was over I took her home. The end."

I blinked, trying to think of a suitable response to what sounded like the most boring date ever.

"So how was that any different from when the three of us hang out, except for the fact that you paid for everything?"

Dave threw his hands up, seemingly exasperated by my questions.

"We just had to know, that's all! And now we do."

I knew he didn't want to hear yet another question, but I just had to ask.

"What do you know?"

"That we were just meant to be friends," Dave replied without any hesitation.

Onion nodded.

No one spoke.

It was my turn to express my exasperation.

"I hope this isn't the way it's going to be from now on, the two of you sitting there like uncomfortable strangers and me starting all the conversations."

"No, not at all," Onion tried to assure me. "We'll get over it."

"Are you sure? I sure hope your 'date' didn't permanently spoil our friendship here."

I was almost sorry for being so blunt, but that was exactly how I felt, even if it did make me sound like kind of a jerk.

"It's not always about you, George." Dave said. He glanced at Onion, who still refused to look directly at us. "We just thought there might be something more between us. There isn't. End of story."

"Fair enough. Let me know when you're 'over it.'"

Again, no one spoke. I fiddled with my smashed paper cup and then had an idea.

I flicked the cup aside. "Okay, let's come to an agreement here. To return everything back to normal, we're going to pretend that your date never happened and solemnly swear that we'll never mention it again. If one of us forgets and brings it up, the standard answer will be 'Date? What Date? I have no idea what you're talking about.' Agreed?"

Onion looked up at me for the first time that morning. Dave seemed intrigued by the idea.

"Could it be that simple?" Dave wondered out loud.

"Is what that simple?" I asked, already upholding my end of the bargain.

"I don't know . . ." Onion said, looking like she wanted to be convinced but wasn't.

I decided to take a different approach.

"All right, then. Here." I picked up a spoon. "I'll hypnotize both of you so you'll forget all about it."

Onion started to laugh, cutting it short when she saw me waving the spoon.

"That won't work! Will it?"

"It will if you believe it," Dave said, leaning forward to focus on the spoon, more than willing to give it a try.

Onion hesitated, sighed, and then moved in closer, too, even if she still looked like she wasn't convinced.

I cleared my throat to prepare my best mesmerizing intonation as I rhythmically waved the spoon. I didn't know exactly what I was going to say but pressed ahead anyway, like a lame version of The Amazing Kreskin or something. All I had to go on were the bogus incantations of actors playing hypnotists in old movies and TV shows I had seen years ago,

"You are getting sleepy, very sleepy. Soon you will be under my control. The only sound you can hear now is the sound of my voice, commanding you to believe what I say. The events of Saturday night are quickly fading, fading from your mind. They were all just a dream, an illusion, a fantasy without any meaning. The overpriced tickets, the too-salty popcorn, the less-than-ideal seats, the endless coming attractions for bad movies you'll never bother to see, the whiny kids and the ringing cellphones that ruined everything are all gone now, all gone. They have been permanently erased from your memory now, never to return. You are and forever shall be only friends—with George, too, of course—and when you wake, you will feel refreshed, and everything will be as it's always been, as it's always been. That is my command that you shall obey, now and forever. You may both awaken!"

I put the spoon down and waited, not sure if anything I said had any affect.

Both Dave and Onion relaxed, as if a great burden had been lifted from them, even though it was painfully obvious neither had actually been hypnotized by my spur of the moment, rather pathetic performance. All I did was provide a way out of their awkwardness, and they wisely took it.

Dave stretched and looked around as if surprised to find himself in the cafe.

Onion picked up her fork to eat as if nothing unusual had just occurred.

I nodded, pleased that my plan had actually worked. But then I saw Onion glance up at Dave with the hint of a sly grin, just a fleeting look I sensed I wasn't supposed to catch. Dave coughed softly as if to signal her that I was watching.

I sat back, staring from one to the other. Onion took a sharp breath and tapped my arm lightly, then pulled away as if unsure how I was going to react, her eyes filled with concern.

"Nothing changes, George."

"Yeah," Dave said. "We're still just friends like always."

Feeling foolish now and naive, I nodded again.

"Maybe I should have just hypnotized myself."

Both Onion and Dave laughed a little, and then Dave reverted back to his old self, holding court now as was his custom at our table.

"Man, can you believe that stupid assignment we just got in Geography? Is Jorgenson kidding? It's like something you'd be asked to do in graduate school. Who's got the time for . . ."

And we never, ever spoke about their date again.

# CHAPTER TWELVE

# DEATH PAYS A VISIT

Paul was one of Dave's childhood friends. As sometimes happens to those friendships, when they grew up they grew apart. Dave became the cynical, sarcastic agitator we all know and love, and Paul became a "jock of all trades," playing nearly every sport our high school had to offer. Like Coach Steener, Paul tried in vain to get Dave to rejoin the football team—something Dave still had zero interest in—but other than those rather one-sided conversations, the two of them orbited different worlds now and hardly ever spoke. Despite the disconnect, Dave would still speak fondly of Paul in a past tense sort of way whenever we discussed our childhoods, which was more often than you might think.

One day Dave came to the cafe looking dire, and hardly said a word as he returned to our table with his lunch.

Onion gave him the once over. "So. You want to tell us what's wrong or do we have to drag it out of you?"

He didn't smile or laugh. "I got some bad new this morning."

Both Onion and I became motionless. "About what?" Onion asked. "You okay?"

Dave nodded. "I'm fine. It's not about me. It's Paul."

Neither of us could remember for a few seconds who Paul was. Then Onion came to the rescue.

"Oh, sure. Paul. Your old jock pal from grade school. What about him?"

Dave hesitated. "He has cancer." His expression grew pained. "It's on his face. It started in his mouth and spread fast. There's no stopping it. I wondered why I didn't see his name on the football roster. Now I know."

"You mean he's going to—"

"Yeah, I mean he's going to die," Dave said abruptly. He finally began to eat, ignoring us.

"Oh, no," is all Onion said.

I wish I had known Paul better so I could share in some small way with Dave's grief, but I didn't. And neither did Onion.

Dave washed down a big bite of food with his drink. "It's okay. You guys didn't really know him. Why should you care, right?"

"Hey," Onion said, sounding genuinely irritated. "That's not nice. Play fair with us, buddy."

Dave grimaced. "Sorry. I'm just lashing out about it and you're the only ones here. I know there's nothing you can do."

Onion nodded her understanding, her irritation vanishing.

I had an idea.

"Maybe there is something we can do. Would he like a few visitors? We could go see him, cheer him up a bit."

Dave gave me an appreciative look.

"Yeah, that's a great idea," Onion said. "Find out and we'll all go."

Dave looked thoughtful. "All right. I'll let you know."

After that and for the rest of the day, Dave seemed more like his normal self.

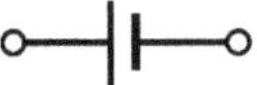

Paul's house was a small brick ranch where he lived with his mom. His parents had divorced when Paul was twelve, Dave told us, nearly the same age Onion was when her dad walked out of her life. Dave had lived a few houses down the block back then, and didn't move away until sixth grade. He said he still considered this his "true" neighborhood, not the upscale one he lived now. I think Dave would have moved back to his old neighborhood in a heartbeat if he could. He sure seemed sorry that he had ever left as we drove through it, what with him slowing down to stare wistfully at some familiar landmark from his youth.

Mrs. Humphries met us at the door. There weren't any decorations on the walls, and the home furnishings were old and pretty sparse, but the place looked really clean. Mrs. Humphries looked awful in a "haven't slept in weeks" sort of way, yet she still managed a wide smile when she let us in.

"Paul's in his bedroom." Her tired eyes flashed a warning. "Just be aware he's not like you remember him a few months ago. You're going to see what chewing tobacco can do to you, even someone as young as Paul."

With that warning, the three of us stiffened at the thought of what we were about to encounter.

Onion led the way down the hall. She knocked softly on Paul's door.

"Paul? It's Nancy, David, and George. Can we come in?"

That was one of the few times I heard Onion refer to herself by her real name and say "David" rather than "Dave" without being mad at him for some reason.

We heard Paul moving around in the room for a few seconds before he answered. "All right."

The words were spoken low, almost as if it wasn't really all right.

Onion opened the door slowly. It creaked like we were entering one of those carnival rooms of terror or something. It didn't help that the lights were down low and the window shades drawn.

"Paul?"

We entered cautiously. Paul was sitting on a chair by the bed, facing away from us.

Dave forced his way ahead, as if deciding he should take the lead. "Hey, Paul. It's Dave. How've you been, man? We've all missed you at school." His voice was solid and full of assurance.

Paul didn't answer. Instead, he slowly turned towards us, revealing in increments what the cancer had done to him, as if a slow exposure would be easier to take than a sudden revelation.

I felt my heart pounding as I tried to act as if everything was fine, just fine, when in reality Paul had no nose to speak of and barely any upper lip, the cancer having eaten its way up his face and around under his left eye, which seemed to hang out in space with so much flesh missing underneath.

"So how does it look like I've been doing?" he asked, the words slurred. His mouth hung slightly open, revealing a blackened mass where most of his teeth and pink tissue should be.

We said nothing for what seemed like ages.

"Honestly, not too goo—" Onion began, but didn't get to finish.

She didn't get to finish because Dave—big, strong, brave Dave— wavered a moment and then went crashing to the floor, the loud impact shaking the entire room. If Onion or I had fallen like that, we wouldn't have made half the noise.

Alarmed, Paul struggled to his feet just as Mrs. Humphries burst into the room.

"*Paul!*" she yelled, her voice sheer panic. "Paul?" she said again when she saw Paul standing there.

"It's Dave," said Onion. "I think he fainted."

Mrs. Humphries looked both relieved and worried at the same time.

"Should I call nine-one-one?" she asked, half turning to hurry to the phone.

"Wait. Let's see if he's okay. Dave would be really upset if we called an ambulance for him for nothing."

Dave was lying on his side. Onion tried to roll him over on his back, but he was too heavy for her to budge.

She looked up at me with impatience. "Give me a hand, will you? Just don't stand there."

Together we were able to roll him.

"Now what?" I asked.

"Anybody have any smelling salts?" Paul asked thickly. He tried to grin as best he could, but he didn't have enough mouth left to really make it work.

Mrs. Humphries laughed loudly, then covered her mouth as if ashamed of herself.

With that, I felt much better about the situation, except for the whole Dave passed out on the floor and possibly injured thing.

Onion tried tapping Dave's face, lightly at first, then harder when he didn't respond. "Dave! *Dave!* Wake up!"

Dave moaned low and his head went from side to side as if he were having a bad dream. Then his eyes sprang open, and with a gasp he sat straight up.

"What? What happened?"

"You fainted, you big doofus," Onion explained.

Dave looked bewildered. "I did? Really? I've never fainted before."

"First time for everything," Paul said before I could.

We all laughed, except Dave.

Dave struggled to his feet, refusing our help.

"Anything bruised or broken?" I asked.

Dave rubbed his neck. "Just my big ego." He looked sheepishly at Paul. "Sorry about that, man. Didn't mean to scare you or anything."

"Actually, I think I scared you, didn't I?" Paul lowered his gaze. "I have that effect on people now."

No one responded. Mrs. Humphries turned and left the room as if she had heard enough.

Paul gingerly sat back down, and I realized the cancer must have spread beyond just what was visible on his face.

Our conversation was more normal after that, with Dave and Paul doing most of the talking and me and Onion mostly there to provide a laugh track as they cracked jokes and reminisced about their shared childhood.

After about half an hour I saw Paul slump a bit, and his speech became even more slurred than it already was.

Dave—now fully animated with his head nodding left and right as he spoke rapid fire—didn't seem to notice.

"Paul," I interrupted. "You seem tired. You okay?'

He seemed relieved that I had noticed.

"Yeah. I get tired real quick now, that's all." He paused to catch his breath. "I think maybe I should rest."

"All right," I said, tapping on Dave's shoulder to signal him that we should leave.

Dave didn't budge or shut up.

I persisted for Paul's sake. "We better go now and let Paul rest. Right, Onion?"

"Right," she said, her answer directed straight at Dave.

Dave finally took the hint. "Sure. We're going. But we'll be back soon. Okay?"

Paul tried to smile again. "That's fine. Thanks for stopping by, guys. You're the first visitors I've had in months."

Dave's face reddened as he slowly rose to his feet, drawing himself up to his full height. "You mean no one from the football team . . . and you were the co-captain . . . none of the players, none of the *coaches*—"

"It's all right," Paul said, waving Dave's anger down. "Relax, Dave. Relax."

Dave slumped and immediately fell silent.

Onion and I could never have gotten Dave to calm down so quickly, and I realized how close Dave and Paul must have been at one time.

I shook Paul's hand. So did Onion. We both looked at Dave to see how he would say goodbye.

Dave hesitated in front of Paul, as if debating whether or not it was safe to throw his arms around him. Paul took the initiative and grasped Dave's hand with both of his.

"Thanks, Dave. It was good to have a few laughs again."

Then Paul leaned forward and whispered something in Dave's ear. Dave nodded once, swallowed hard, and then turned and strode from the room as if instantly dismissed.

Caught off guard, I watched Dave go, and then looked back at Paul in surprise. It looked like Paul was trying to smile again.

Onion grabbed me by the shirttail and pulled me backwards out the door.

Paul waved a faint farewell.

Mrs. Humphries thanked the three of us again for stopping by and soon we were back out in the bright sunlight. We piled into Dave's car.

"I'm really glad we saw him," Onion said.

"Me. too," I agreed. "Who knows if . . ." I let the rest go unsaid, more than a little sorry I even began to say it.

Dave pushed his key into the ignition, let go of it, and then lowered his forehead onto the steering wheel. He sat there motionless.

"Dave? Are you all right?" Onion asked.

Dave shook his head no, and then he started to sob—big, shoulder-shaking sobs that rocked the car up and down.

"Dave! What is it?" Onion asked.

The sobs quieted down and Dave sat back up.

"Paul and I . . . we used to play army guys when we were five or six. We would run through the neighborhood here after school, shooting terrorists everywhere with our toy guns and stuff. After each battle, before we'd go home to dinner, Paul would always say 'We live to fight another day!'"

"Is that what he whispered to you?" I asked.

Dave nodded. "I hadn't heard that in years. Not in years. And he told me to stay brave."

Onion and I said nothing.

Dave wiped his nose with the back of his hand, started the car and drove us home in silence.

Paul died later that month, before we could see him again. The funeral was family only, but on the day it was held, Dave didn't show up at school. I would like to think he had been secretly invited, although it's just as likely he found his own way and place to grieve. We never asked him where he went that day and he never told us.

Now, whenever I pass through Dave and Paul's old neighborhood, I find it comforting to know it's free of imaginary terrorists thanks to two brave boys who fought them off together so many years ago.

# CHAPTER THIRTEEN
# STICKS AND STONES

While it's generally agreed that the happiest time of the day is the final bell and the end of the school day, the second happiest is probably the start of lunch break. You can tell that by the sound of the crowd gathered in the cafe, what with all the laughter and shrieks and shouts and running around and other signs of chaos barely kept under control by the few unlucky hall monitors who have to try to uphold the law.

Onion and I got in line to get some grub one day just as lunch began. She was in an excellent mood, having just come from gym class where she had totally destroyed her opponent in badminton. Dave was nowhere to be seen, but as hungry as we were we decided not to wait for him.

"Where can he be?" I asked, scanning the crowd once more. "It's not like Dave to be late for lunch."

"Or any meal," Onion added. She shrugged. "I don't know. Maybe Olga finally strangled him after all. We'll find out."

The line moved forward at a steady pace. In front of us was a tall, skinny nerd whose name I could never remember. He tried to flirt a bit with Onion. Fortunately for him, fresh off her victory in gym class, she was willing to go along with his lame banter if only for her own amusement.

He pointed at me and snorted a little.

"Say, is he your boyfriend?" His voice was nasal and kind of grating.

Onion laughed. "No, just a friend."

"Oh, good," he said. "Then maybe I've got a chance."

Onion nudged me as if to let me know she was going to play dumb. "A chance for what?"

"You know, maybe ask you out and show you a good time." He snorted a little again.

Onion laughed again. "So what's your idea of a good time? Plotting graphs on your calculator?"

I tried not to laugh.

The nerd seemed puzzled, as if he didn't quite understand what was so amusing. "Well, that can be fun, of course—unless you're mocking me. But that wasn't what I had in mind at all, if you know what I mean." He tried to sound suave and debonair, which only made him seem even more of a nerd.

"No, I don't," Onion said, still toying with him as the line moved forward. "What did you have in mind?"

The nerd actual blushed a little. "Well, what I thought was—"

"Excuse me. Mind if I cut in front of you? I'm in kind of a hurry."

So focused on their conversation, I hadn't even seen her approach. She was one of the school's "Society Girls," as we called them, tall and shapely and fashionably dressed, with near perfect hair and complexion like a runway model.

The nerd stared at her with his mouth open, as if stunned that she would actually speak to him.

"Do I mind? Of course not! For you, anything!"

He motioned her in front of him.

She gave him one of those great big, plastic smiles that mean nothing.

"Great!" She stepped in line.

Onion frowned.

"No problem at all! Not for you! Say, what's your name? I'm Freddie, by the way."

Her plastic smile faltered a bit. "Hello, Freddie. I'm Veronica. Thanks again for the cut in line. Bye now."

She made a point of turning her back.

"Veronica," he repeated in a voice filled with admiration, oblivious to having just been snubbed. "That's a beautiful name."

She didn't answer.

Even though she had no real interest in him at all, I saw Onion kind of fuming that Freddie had turned all his attention to the Society Girl.

Onion cleared her throat.

"Anyway, as you were saying before we were so rudely interrupted."

"Huh?" He looked at Onion as if seeing her for the first time. "Oh. Nothing. Just forget it."

He turned to stare at the back of Veronica's head as if newly in love.

I could tell from Onion's dour expression that she wasn't going to let it go.

"You were starting to tell me how you were going to show me a good time."

Freddie looked back at her as if annoyed now. "That was before Veronica showed up. Frankly, she's hot and you're . . . kind of not. Not even close, you know." He snorted once more.

An odd look crossed his face then, as if he just remembered something.

"Wait a minute. Your nickname is Onion, isn't it? Yeah, I think it is! Onions are smelly, you know." He sniffed the air in front of her. "Hey, did you just come from gym class? Well, guess what? I think you're living up to your name!" He both laughed and snorted at the same time. "Isn't that right, Veronica?"

Veronica raised her head and turned around slightly, just enough to look Onion up and down.

"Whatever you say, Freddie," Veronica said with a little smirk.

Freddie snorted again, as if pleased with himself and happy that Veronica agreed.

To my surprise, Onion said nothing, her face pale. All I could think was that words failed her, which was a first for Onion. I would have spoken up in her defense but knew she was the type who insisted on fighting her own fights.

We got our food from the cafeteria ladies and headed to our table without another word. Only when we sat down at our table did I notice her eyes were misty.

"Everything okay?"

She shook her head.

"Turn around," she commanded. "Don't look at me."

"What? Why?"

Her moist eyes turned angry. "Just turn your chair around and face the other way. *Now!*"

"Yes ma'am."

I grabbed my coffee off my tray and did as I was told.

"And stay that way until I tell you."

"You got it."

Neither of us spoke. I listened but didn't hear her crying, probably because she didn't want me to hear. That was both reassuring and unnerving at the same time. I had never known Onion to cry about anything, but I guess everyone has their limits.

"Are you sure you don't want to talk about what's—"

"No, I do not." Her voice was firm, which at least told me she wasn't too terribly choked up.

As I drank my coffee, still concerned about Onion behind me, I looked around the cafe to see who might notice I was facing the wrong way and give me a puzzled look. No one did. Instead, everyone seemed involved in whatever drama or conversation was going on at their own table. The perspective I had was interesting if nothing else; it was like I hadn't really noticed what went on at lunchtime before. As I scanned the room I saw hugs and shoves, jeers and jests, tears and tirades. It was like being at the zoo and watching all the animals in their fake natural habitats.

Then I saw Dave trotting towards us from the other side, shaking his head as if disappointed, a couple of books tucked under his arm.

He came up to us a bit out of breath.

"Wow. Sorry I'm so late. I got in this big philosophical argument with Goodman after class and lost track of time. The good news is, I think I won!" Dave gave us one of his exaggerated smiles.

He said nothing about me facing away from the table, as if that's how I usually sat. I waited for him to notice and say something, anything.

Dave shrugged when neither of us responded, his expression pretty much blank.

He looked down at Onion. "So, like, what's cookin', good-lookin'?"

I stared up at Dave in disbelief, his blank expression still there. I had never heard him call Onion "good-lookin'" before, even if the saying was just a cliché—and as far as I know, he never called her that again—but if there ever was a time Onion needed to hear something like that, it was right now.

I risked a glance behind me to see Onion's reaction. She was staring up at him in even greater disbelief than me.

"Burgers and pizza," she finally answered. "Why don't you get some? The line is nearly gone now."

Dave looked over at the serving area and smiled. "Hey, great! Be right back." He dropped his books on the table and hurried off.

Onion turned her attention to me.

"What are you looking at?"

I shook my head. "Nothing. Can I turn around now? I'm kinda hungry and my food's getting cold."

She sniffed once and wiped her nose with a napkin. "Yeah, go ahead."

As I turned my chair back around, I noticed a bunch of crumpled napkins on her tray. I thought it best not to mention them.

We ate in uncomfortable silence a while as I struggled to think of something to say.

"At least you didn't kill them," I finally offered. "That was good of you."

She shrugged, as if they weren't worth the effort that would have taken.

"You know better than to let things like that bother you," I said, taking a chance on what I was about to say next. "Don't forget, you're a tough broad."

About to take another bite of her pizza, she paused and set it back down.

"That's the wisest thing I've ever heard you say about me."

I wavered a bit. "Well, actually, I didn't say it. You did."

Onion's face brightened as she sat back. "Oh yeah! I did say that, didn't I? No wonder it sounded so wise!"

And with that, we both laughed.

Dave came back with a tray heaping with food and plopped it on the table. We looked up at him.

"Hey," he said sheepishly. "I'm eating late, so I'm extra hungry."

Onion grinned up at him, her face nearly glowing.

"That's okay. Your gluttony is forgiven. This time, anyway."

Onion pushed his chair out for him so he could sit down, something I had never seen her do before.

"Well, thanks," Dave said, rubbing his hands as he sat. "So, did I miss anything?"

Onion and I glanced at each other.

"Not a thing." She patted his shoulder.

"Good," he said as he stuffed his mouth. He looked from me to Onion and back again. "Well, eat up, will you?" he said. "Times a-wastin'. I didn't rush here to eat by myself."

As hungry as I was, nobody had to tell me twice. And for the rest of lunch, Onion listened intently to Dave's usual boasts and complaints without ridiculing him at all.

# CHAPTER FOURTEEN

# OUR VERY OWN CHRISTMAS MIRACLE

There was a subset of students from all grade levels in The Big Brown Box who were really into fast cars. In another day and age they would have been called hot-rodders or something like that, but they tended to dress more like greasers from the 1950s, with leather jackets, white T-shirts, and hair combed straight back. I thought it was a pretty neat retro look, even if I didn't want to look like that myself. They didn't build their own cars like the hot-rodders of old, back when you could fix cars with just a screwdriver and a pair of pliers, but still they fawned over their vehicles almost as much as I fawned over The Movie, assuming of course that was actually possible.

Dave and I were out shopping for Christmas gifts for our families at the last possible moment, the afternoon of Christmas Eve. That was something of a tradition for us, wandering the crowded store aisles with all the other frantic last-minute shoppers, getting elbowed and crushed, picking stuff up and considering it as a gift then putting it back because it was either too expensive or maybe a little too tacky. We repeated that process store after store until—out of desperation—we finally bought something for everyone on our lists because time was running out, not because the gifts were perfect or even all that great.

It was hardly a perfect system, but we stuck with it because it got the job done.

Onion wasn't with us because she was way more organized than we were. She had all her Christmas shopping done ridiculously early, like September or something, and she bought nearly everything online so she didn't even have to break a sweat.

"You know, that's cheating," Dave said as we waiting in a long checkout line in an overcrowded store. "If you're not angry and miserable by the time you're done shopping, you've really missed the whole Christmas spirit thing."

As soon as we were finished, Dave and I stopped at the local drive-in for a quick bite to eat before heading home to wrap our gifts in a mad frenzy, just hours before they were to be opened.

The drive-in parking lot was full of shiny muscle cars, hoods open, with greasers milling around. Some of the cars were bright colors with racing stripes as if to draw the maximum amount of attention, while others were dark and stealth-like, as if trying to avoid detection.

"Awesome," Dave said, as we drove up in his old beater.

A few of the greasers pointed and laughed at Dave's car. He backed up and parked next to a shiny, low-slung car that looked fast just sitting still, then reached down and pulled the lever to pop his hood open.

"Are you serious?" I asked.

"Sure," he said. "My car is the comic relief here. We've got a few minutes. Let's go."

We went inside and bought something to eat. By the time we got outside, I was surprised to see nearly every greaser surrounding the front of Dave's car, looking at the engine.

"Oh, wow," Dave said, clutching his sack of food and oversized soda. "And here I thought I was only kidding."

As we approached the group, one of them waved us forward.

"Is this your car?" he asked.

"Sure is," Dave said, taking a sip of his drink. "Is there a problem?"

"Problem?" said the greaser. "Do you know what you've got here?" He pointed under the hood.

"A fuel-sucking engine?" Dave replied.

"Do you know why it's fuel-sucking?"

"Not, not really." Dave took another sip from his drink. "I seldom look under the hood."

The group stared at him with identical stunned expressions.

"Guy," the greaser said. "This is the big-block *supercharged* engine. Special ordered from the factory. Hardly any were sold. We've never seen one before. Do you know what this means?" He held his hands out, imploring Dave for the answer.

Dave gave a weak little shrug. "It can go really fast?"

The greaser's face brightened and he raised his arms in the air.

"Right! When this car was new, it could do zero to sixty in under *four seconds*. Nobody could touch it. It's probably still fast, even though it doesn't look like you've taken very good care of it," he looked down at the engine with some dismay as he slowly shook his head. "Man. This was back in the day when the average Joe could afford a car that roared, full of fury and fire in its belly. Now they just purr, kitty-cat like, as weak as they are meek." His expression turned wistful.

I found that surprisingly profound and even poetic, and understood his sense of loss.

"Well, gosh and golly," Dave said, shattering the mood. "That's great to know. Excuse us now, gentlemen. We're kind of in a hurry since it's almost Christmas Eve and all that." He stepped forward and closed the hood.

The group looked disappointed that they couldn't continue to gawk at Dave's fast engine.

As they all stood up straight, I noticed that the greaser who spoke to Dave was quite a bit taller than the rest, which made me wonder if that was why he seemed like the alpha dog of the pack and did all the talking.

"Wait!" The greaser said. "I'll race you. I gotta know if I can beat your car."

The others in the group stood behind him, faces serious, waiting for Dave's response to the challenge.

"Sorry, gents. Duty calls. Besides, I don't race."

"Why? Are you too chicken?"

Dave looked scornful. "Come on. You're not gonna shame me. I just don't have the time, that's all." He pulled out his car keys. I went around to the passenger side door to wait to be let in.

"What's your name?" the greaser asked Dave. "You look familiar. Aren't you on the football team?"

"Not anymore. I'm . . . Dave." He sounded reluctant to reveal his name.

"I'm Johnny."

"Nice to meet you, Johnny. Take care now." Dave unlocked his car door.

"Wait!" Johnny said. "I'll make it worth your while."

He pulled a surprisingly huge wad of cash out of his pocket, holding it up for Dave to see.

Dave stared at it, silent a moment. "How much?"

"Tell you what. If I win, you pay me nothing. If you win, I'll give you a hundred bucks."

Dave took another sip of his drink, contemplating the offer.

"Make it two hundred and you got a deal."

"Dave," I said, more than a little alarmed. "I thought you said we didn't have the time?"

Some of the other greasers glared at me.

"Deal," Johnny replied.

"And fifty bucks for my friend." Dave pointed to me.

Johnny's face contorted a second, and then he looked resigned. "Fine. And fifty bucks for your friend. Follow us."

Dave opened his car door, got in, and unlocked the passenger door.

"Are you out of you mind?" I said, scrambling into my seat. "You're going to get us killed! What do you know about drag racing? Besides, it's illegal! Do we really need more trouble?"

The greasers all piled into their own cars and started them up. With a collective rumble, they poured into the street. Dave's was the last car out.

"What's to know? You mash the gas pedal and drive straight ahead until you cross the finish line. Simple. Besides, it's two hundred bucks if I win. That's just about what I spent today. It would be nice to get that back."

"Why do you do these things to me? What am I supposed to tell my dad? 'Sorry I missed Christmas Eve, Dad. I was out drag racing with Dave.'"

"Relax. This shouldn't take too long. You don't even have to ride with me and you'll still get fifty bucks if I win."

We followed the muscle car caravan out of the city limits to the middle of nowhere where the roads were most flat and straight. The caravan parked on the side of a deserted road as if this was their usual place to start a race.

Johnny pulled over to the left lane. He was driving a yellow car with black racing stripes that made it look like a gigantic bumblebee. Dave stopped next to him on the right.

Dave looked at me. "You can bail if you want. I understand."

I took off my seat belt and reached for the door handle. Dave looked at me with a weak little grin.

"Just be careful. Okay, you big dummy?" I said.

"Sure," was all he replied.

I stared at him a few seconds more, wondering if this was the last time I was going to see Dave alive. Then I got out and stood next to his car a short distance away.

One of the other greasers came over to talk to Dave.

"Here's what you do. You step on the brake and rev the engine when I raise my arm. When I drop my arm, take your foot off the brake and punch it. The finish line is the red one we drew across the road about half a mile from here. We'll be waiting there to see who wins. Got it?"

"Got it," I heard Dave say over the noise of Johnny already revving his engine.

The caravan pulled out and headed down the road.

As the greaser who gave Dave the instructions took his place between the two cars, I felt this growing anxiety not for Dave, but for having abandoned him. It was like I was despicable, the worst friend ever. There I was, hoping to find a friend as loyal as Filby someday, and I couldn't even manage to show some loyalty of my own to one of the friends I did have.

I let out the deepest heartfelt sigh I could, then got back into the car against my much better judgment.

"You sure, man?" Dave asked as I hurried to put my seatbelt on.

"Yeah, I'm sure," I mumbled, angry now for risking my own life, too, yet feeling like I had little choice. "This is the stupidest thing we've ever done. Ever."

"And we're doing it together!" Dave said with a fist pump. "Yeah, baby!"

"Yeah, great. We're gonna die on Christmas Eve. Terrific."

The greaser in the middle of the road raised his arm. Dave revved his engine with his foot on the brake. Both cars bucked like large animals pawing at the ground, ready to leap.

The greaser dropped his arm.

I was immediately pushed back in my seat, astonished by the acceleration. Both cars gave off throaty roars as they sped side by side. Soon we were going faster than Dave had ever driven me before, faster even than on the open highway. Dave's car continued its impressive acceleration as the other car seemed to sputter and falter a bit, as if trying to catch its breath. It gradually fell behind.

"We're winning! We're winning!" Dave repeated over the engine's roar. He sat hunched over the wheel, focused on the road ahead.

I turned to watch Johnny's car and saw it begin to sway side to side then rise up in the air, nose first, as if the bumblebee had decided to fly. We zoomed across the finish line just as Johnny's car did a kind of graceful mid-air pirouette.

"We did it!" Dave shouted over the noise.

As Dave slowed, pumping a fist in victory, I watched in horror as Johnny's car came plummeting down into the ditch on the side of the road. There were loud metallic booms as the car tumbled end over end, ripping itself apart.

"*Stop!*" I yelled at Dave, who seemed oblivious to the destruction behind us.

Dave braked hard. His car squatted down as the tires screamed on the pavement. Even before we came to a complete halt, I jumped out and ran to the scene of the accident.

Johnny's car was unrecognizable except for a few parts—a door, a fender, the trunk lid. Pieces were stretched out in a long line, some of them smoldering although there was no fire. I picked my way through them, looking for Johnny, afraid of what I was going to find.

I stopped.

He was at the bottom of the ditch, away from most of the wreckage, flat on his back with his arms and legs outstretched and his head turned to one side, eyes shut.

"Oh, no," I said.

I hurried closer, wondering what I should do.

"Call an ambulance!" I yelled toward the finish line, wondering if anyone heard and if it wasn't already too late.

I got on my hands and knees next to him and peered into his face.

"Oh, no," I said again, unable to think of anything else to say. "Johnny."

With that, his right hand twitched and his eyes sprang open as if I had summoned his return. Startled, I fell backwards.

"Oh, man," he said, and sat straight up. "That was something."

I scrambled back as he stood up and stretched as if waking from a peaceful slumber. Surrounded by pieces of his wrecked car, he pulled out his comb from his back pocket and started combing his hair as if that was the most important thing he had to do.

"What?" he said down at me, arms outstretched, as I sat there in amazement that he was not only alive, but apparently just fine.

"Nothing," I said, still disbelieving what I was seeing, as if I were staring at the greaser ghost of Christmas present, our very own Christmas miracle.

He reached down and flicked a little piece of dirt off his otherwise spotless T-shirt, then finished combing his hair.

There was the sound of rapid footsteps, and then Dave appeared. He came up to us warily, looking from me to Johnny and back again.

Dave stood there wordlessly, mouth slightly ajar.

"I know, I know," Johnny said. "You won."

He took his wad of cash out of his pocket and pulled some bills from it.

"Here. Two hundred bucks for you and fifty for your friend over there, just like I promised."

Dave made no effort to take the money.

"You were driving," Dave finally said, pointing to the wreckage, "that car."

Johnny glanced behind him. "Yeah. So?"

"Nothing," Dave said, and took the money.

"Hey! It's six o'clock," Johnny said, glancing at his watch. "We better get going. It's Christmas Eve, you know."

Dave nodded slowly and we followed him up out of the ditch to the road.

The caravan of muscle cars had reformed and was driving towards us. Johnny waved them down. They beeped their horns as if nothing unusual had occurred.

"Hey, Mikey!" he said as the first car drove by slowly. "Merry Christmas."

"Merry Christmas," Mikey said.

"Merry Christmas, Tommy!"

"Merry Christmas," Tommy said as he drove by.

"Merry Christmas, Jimmy!"

"Merry Christmas," Jimmy said as he drove by.

"Merry Christmas, Billy!"

"Merry Christmas," Billy said as he drove by.

"Merry Christmas, Joey!"

"Merry Christmas," Joey said as he drove by.

"Merry Christmas, everybody!" Johnny said to all the other drivers as they paraded single-file down the street.

"Oh, good. Bobby! Merry Christmas! I need a ride." He opened the door of the last car in line. He looked back at us. "Have a Merry Christmas, guys."

"Wait!" I said, before he could get in Bobby's car.

He looked at me, puzzled. "What?"

I opened my mouth to ask if this sort of thing happened all the time, and what we should do about the wreckage, and why he wasn't upset about what just happened to his car along with a dozen other questions that were all begging to be asked, but the late hour and the annoyed look on Johnny's face told me they didn't really matter.

"Nothing. Merry Christmas, Johnny," was all I said.

He smiled and gave me a little punch on the arm.

"Merry Christmas . . . you," he said, and then got in the car.

The caravan sped away, leaving me and Dave by the side of the road.

And the smoldering wreckage behind us.

We turned around and looked at it. Neither of us spoke.

"So what exactly happened?" I finally asked, hoping Dave knew.

Dave looked down at the money in his hand. "Don't ask me. I just work here." He peeled off fifty dollars and stuffed it in my shirt pocket. "Let's go."

We walked back to his car and got in. As Dave swung his car around and drove past the wreckage, he pulled over and stopped.

"Wait right here," he said, and got out and ran down into the ditch. When he came back, he was holding the steering wheel from Johnny's car.

"Here's a memento for you," he said, handing it to me. "Merry Christmas, Georgie!"

I stared at the steering wheel, wondering what I was supposed to do with it.

"Well, thanks . . . Davey. Merry Christmas."

By the time I got home, my dad and Kenny had eaten Christmas dinner without me. I found my dad in the kitchen, cleaning up.

"Sorry I'm late," I said sheepishly. I held the packages in their shopping bags in front of me along with the steering wheel.

Busy loading the dishwasher, he barely looked my way.

"That's all right. I figured you were still Christmas shopping. You really should start doing that days earlier, you know. I don't know why you always wait until the last possible minute." He shook his head.

He froze, dirty plate in hand, when he finally noticed the steering wheel I held with the bags of gifts. "Where did you get that?"

"Huh? Oh." I held it up to look at it again. "Dave gave it to me. It's . . . a memento."

"Oh," my dad said, as if that made sense even though it didn't. "Well, dinner's in the refrigerator whenever you're ready."

"Thanks." I turned to go wrap the gifts, then stopped and turned back around. "Oh. One more thing."

"Yes?" he said, putting the last cup in the dishwasher.

I held up the steering wheel. "Merry Christmas . . . Daddy!"

He gave me a bright smile as he closed the dishwasher door. "Merry Christmas, George!"

And I headed to my room, still marveling at the Christmas miracle both Dave and I had witnessed and still wondering what exactly happened.

# CHAPTER FIFTEEN

# THE POST NO MORE

It was late when we got home from The Post after yet another party one Saturday night, later still when we finally all went to bed. It seemed like I had been sleeping only for a few minutes when I felt someone shaking my shoulder.

I opened my eyes just long enough to realize it was barely dawn.

"Kenny, turn off the light and go back to bed," I said without looking at who was shaking me. "We've hardly had any sleep." Every now and then when Kenny woke up early he wanted me to wake up too, just to keep him company.

"George, it's Dad."

I sat up immediately. "What is it? Is it Mom?"

Where that question came from I had no idea, but in my groggy state it's no wonder I was confused.

Dad looked puzzled. "No. It's The Post."

I rubbed my eyes. "What about it?"

His expression was grim. "It's on fire."

It took a few seconds for that to sink in. I said nothing.

"Come on, get dressed," Dad said. "I'll wake up Kenny. We're going to see what's happening."

I scrambled into my clothes and we all piled into the car to investigate. In the distance was the sound of multiple fire truck sirens, which didn't bode well. The morning sky was an inky blue, lighter to the east where the sun had yet to appear. Most of the streetlights were still on, but as we drove whole rows of them went off as the sky brightened.

"How did you find out?" I asked as Dad pushed beyond the speed limit to get us there ASAP.

"The colonel called. The fire department had called him and said that all the smoke detectors were going off."

I realized he didn't say that "a" smoke detector was going off, but all of them. That didn't bode well either.

Kenny laughed like we were going on some new adventure as we sped down the block. Dad and I ignored him.

As we turned down the street where The Post was, I didn't see any flames up ahead, but we drove through an acrid gray cloud that had little bits of black soot, like tiny corkscrews that collided and stuck to the windshield. I rolled up my window to keep the stench out.

Bits of The Post were coming to us, and we were still more than two blocks away.

"Kenny, get your head in here and close your window," I said. "You shouldn't be breathing that."

I looked at Dad and saw his fierce gaze on the road up ahead. He drove like he was heading into battle and nothing was going to stop him. He didn't make a move to close his own window, and soon I noticed that peculiar soot on him and the dashboard.

A fire truck arrived on the other side of the street just as we pulled up. There were half a dozen trucks already there, some from neighboring towns. All their red and white flashing lights illuminated the scene in a kind of stop-action motion. The last fire hose turned off because it looked like there was practically nothing left to hose down. Except for a few waist-high sections of brick walls still standing, The Post was gone.

Dad got out without a word, and Kenny and I followed. It was then I finally noticed that Dad was wearing his dress uniform jacket, the same one he had worn to the dance the night before.

He marched up to a fireman who was giving orders to the others as they rolled up the hoses and carried gear back to their trucks. They all stopped in their tracks to look at Dad.

The fireman who seemed to be in charge saluted as Dad approached.

"What's happening here, Sergeant?" Dad asked.

"It's a total loss, sir. I'm sorry. The whole building was in flames when we arrived."

Dad nodded. "Is it safe to enter?"

The fire sergeant didn't answer right away. "I shouldn't let you go in, but the roof's gone and most of the walls have already collapsed. Just be careful you don't trip on something. A few things might still be hot, so don't pick anything up, either. It's a real mess in there."

Dad nodded again and waved at me to stay put. I stood there behind Kenny with my hands on his shoulders to keep him right where he was.

"Fire trucks," Kenny said. "Danger."

"That's right, Kenny," I answered softly. The smoke cloud had nearly dissipated, but the smell of burnt rubber and plastic still hung in the air.

Dad walked through the opening where the front door used to be and disappeared into the ruins. He emerged from the rubble a few minutes later and shook hands with a few of the firefighters, thanking them even though The Post was no more.

Dad walked up to me slowly, his shoulders drooping. "It's all gone," he said quietly. "Everything."

I pulled out my phone. "Can I walk around the outside to take a few pictures?"

"Sure. Kenny and I will wait here. I want to see if they know where the fire started and what might have caused it. Not that that's going to change anything. Might help with our insurance, though."

Despite the enormity of the situation, I thought Dad was taking it extremely well.

I took a couple of pictures of the collapsed entrance and then walked around to the back.

The brick patio behind the building was practically unscathed. The Tiki candles on their poles still lined the perimeter, having never been put away. A few folding chairs left out here and there seemed forlorn, as if aware they were the only survivors. Used paper cups, plates, and napkins were strewn about, waiting to be picked up and properly disposed of, as if that even mattered now.

I turned around. The glass patio doors had either blown out or were shattered by the firemen as they fought the fire. I glanced on either side of me, and not seeing anyone else, went quietly inside to the kitchen.

It was disconcerting to be able to see the sky above the now blackened countertop and cabinets. All the party supplies on the countertop were mostly wet cinders now, forming odd, melted shapes that took a few seconds to recognize. I snapped a few pictures then sloshed through about an inch of water to the old cast iron stove, still recognizable except for the knobs, which had partially melted and run down the front of the stove like giant red tears.

I was reminded of the scene in The Movie where the time traveler witnessed the nuclear destruction of London before escaping in the nick of time in his time machine. The Post now looked like it could have been in that scene.

Something about the oven caught my eye. I wondered what caused the odd streaks of black soot right above the oven door, and then with a gasp remembered the cookies we were making.

I tapped the stove handle and felt it was merely warm now. When I opened the door, a puff of smoke emerged. When the smoke cleared, I could see there were two warped aluminum cookie trays, one above the other on the oven racks, both with burned black cookies in neat rows.

When I looked at what was left of the oven dial, I saw it was still set at three hundred and fifty degrees. My mind raced as I logically connected the sequence of events.

I had suggested we make cookies for the party since we had the ingredients and all our other snacks were going fast. Dad agreed, and Kenny and I made them and put them in the oven at three hundred and fifty degrees.

The cookies were left cooking in the oven overnight because no one had turned the oven off.

I was the one who was supposed to turn the oven off when the cookies were done, only I forgot about them.

Ovens left on too long cause fires.

Therefore, the person responsible for starting the fire and burning down The Post was . . .

Me.

I dropped my phone in a puddle and buried my face in my hands. My forgetfulness had destroyed my dad's most sacred of places, one I cherished, too.

When I heard someone near, I retrieved my waterlogged phone and still hunched down, crept back out to the patio.

As soon as I stood up, Dad appeared around the corner.

"There you are. What have you been doing?"

Feeling numb, all I could think to do was hold up my phone. Water dripped out of it. "I . . . dropped it in a puddle. It's ruined."

I looked back through the missing patio doors to where the stove sat, too afraid to tell him the whole truth.

Dad's face hardened. "Sorry. Everything's going wrong this morning, isn't it? Come on, we have to leave. I have to make some calls and let people know what's happened."

I followed him, my legs suddenly wooden and my head spinning. There was only one fire truck left, and I paused when the fire chief's SUV pulled up on the other side of the street.

"Morning, Chief," my dad said, surprisingly chipper for a guy who just lost his home away from home.

"Morning, Mr. Wells."

The chief was a big guy, taller and wider than even Dave. He was huffing and puffing as if he had fought the fire himself instead of just walking across the street to join us.

"Sorry I missed all the excitement," he said. "My men said it went up fast. They weren't kidding, were they?" He shook his head and gave a low whistle, hands on his hips as he surveyed the rubble. "Too bad. Anything salvageable?"

"No," was all Dad said.

"I'm not surprised. That was a big fire."

"Did anyone say how it might have started?" Dad asked.

I stiffened, but said nothing.

"No, sometimes it's obvious right away and sometimes you've got to dig to find the answer. I'll let you know the cause as soon as we finish our investigation."

"Thanks, Chief."

My wooden legs carried me back to our car.

As we drove away, Kenny seemed to finally respond to what we saw.

"Big fire," he said. "A disaster."

I slumped in my seat and closed my eyes, fearful what the results of the fire investigation would reveal, that the fire was due to human error, and that the human who erred was me.

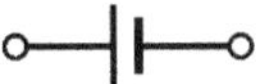

Despite how tired I was, I couldn't go back to sleep when we got home. Instead, I lay there wondering how I could have been so stupid as to forget that the oven was on and what the repercussions of my forgetfulness would be. I figured it would be something like a manslaughter charge, although not quite as serious since nobody died. All I killed was an empty building, a town landmark. Still, like manslaughter, somebody's has to pay a price for what happened; you can't just say it was an accident and expect to walk free.

I also wondered how my dad would react when he found out I burned the place down. Worst-case scenario, he kicks me out of the house and never forgives me. Best case scenario, I get to stay but he never forgives me.

I wasn't sure which fate was worse.

After a couple of exhausting hours tormenting myself, I finally got up to get something to eat, even though I wasn't all that hungry. This was turning out to be one of those times when I wished time travel was possible and I could go back and pull the cookies out of the oven on time, or at least turn the oven off.

For that matter, if I had my own time machine I would put a big, fat "rewind" button on it and fix all the mistakes I've ever made. I would be really busy for quite a while, but after a few days or weeks I would have prevented all the stupid things I've ever done. Like burning down an irreplaceable building.

Kenny was at the kitchen table playing his video game. He slept at the oddest times, so I wasn't too surprised to see him still awake.

"George is worried," he said with barely a glance up at me. "Why?"

Once again, Kenny's summed up the entire situation in as few words as possible.

"I'm worried about the cause of the fire at The Post, Kenny." I didn't elaborate.

"Yes. Post gone," he said. "Nothing left. Too bad."

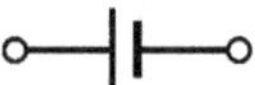

On Monday, Dave was taking me home after we dropped off Onion at her house. Usually we had a lot to say, but I didn't feel much like talking so all the conversations Dave tried to start went nowhere. Fortunately, he was in one of his buoyant moods, so for a while he did all the talking for us until he finally realized I wasn't adding much to the conversation.

He regarded me with suspicion. "You all right? You've been awful quiet today."

"I'm fine," I lied, although tempted to talk to someone—anyone—about my fear of having burned down the Post.

"No, you're not," Dave said. "Something happen at home, or at the Box? You can tell me."

Dave might not have been Filby, but he could be sympathetic when he wanted to.

"You just want to know what's wrong so you can blab it to Onion."

"Ah ha!" Dave's eyes widened and he sat up straighter behind the steering wheel. "I knew something was wrong. Now you've got to tell me. I promise I won't tell anyone."

"Like I would ever believe that."

He looked genuinely hurt. "Fine," he said. "Maybe I'm not as perfect and loyal as your precious Filby character—who's still make-believe, by the way—but I've still been a pretty good friend. Besides, confession is good for the soul, you know."

I decided he was right; keeping the secret to myself was slowly killing me inside.

"Okay. But you can't breathe a word of this to anyone, you got it?" I gave him the sternest glare I could muster.

"Scout's honor. My lips are sealed. So what's the big secret?"

I sighed. It took a few seconds for me to begin. "It's about the fire at The Post."

"Let me guess. You started it." He laughed.

I didn't answer, and didn't look at him either.

"Hoo boy," Dave said, and slowed down. "This is serious, isn't it?"

I nodded. "The party the night before. Kenny and I were baking cookies in the oven because we were running low on snacks. I forgot all about them. The oven was on all night. In the morning when the fire was out, I snuck into the kitchen and saw that the oven knobs had melted from the heat and there was all this black soot around the oven door. That had to be the cause."

Dave sat back, looking greatly relieved. "So it was an accident. Big deal. It's not like you tossed a Molotov cocktail through the front window or something. You weren't trying to burn the place down."

"No, I'm just waiting for the fire department to determine the cause, which shouldn't be too hard to figure out. I'm surprised my dad hasn't remembered I was using the oven. If he does, it's game over."

"Yeah, but people accidentally burn down buildings all the time, even their own houses. They don't go to jail for that."

"You don't burn down a building—especially a town landmark—without major repercussions."

"Take it easy. The building was insured, wasn't it? They'll build a new one."

"Yeah, but it just won't be the same. I loved that old building."

"Oh, no. This isn't more of that going back in time junk, is it? You know, that's getting really old. Let it go."

"It's not just that. I screwed up big time. Don't you get it?"

"You're always screwing up big time. So what's new?"

I laughed once in spite of myself. "Thanks a lot. This was a lot bigger than usual."

Dave shrugged. "Well, I still don't think you've got anything to worry about."

We drove along in silence for a while, and then I saw a mischievous grin appear on his face.

"What's so funny?"

"Hmm? Oh, nothing."

His grin remained. I wondered what he was up to.

He began to hum softly to himself, just a few notes that seemed vaguely familiar. That was fine until he finally said the song title, revealing what he had been humming.

"Light my fire."

"Stop. That's not funny."

I turned away to suppress a laugh, amused yet appalled at the same time.

His grin grew wider. "Yes, yes it is. What's the matter? Don't like The Doors? Well then, how about some words of wisdom from Billy Joel?"

"*What?* Billy Joel? What words of wisdom?"

Dave looked positively delighted I had asked.

"We didn't start the fire!"

"Shut up," I said, struggling not to laugh too loud.

"Okay then, at least remember what the Killer himself, Mr. Jerry Lee Lewis, had to say."

Now I was almost afraid to ask. "I give up. What did the Killer say?"

Dave turned to look straight at me, delighted again, while I would have much preferred he kept his eyes on the road.

"Great balls of fire!"

I much as I didn't want to, I threw my head back and laughed even louder.

"Will you knock it off?"

"Cookies," he said, eyes back on the road where they belonged. "The whole place burned down because you wanted...cookies. Imagine that."

"Stop," I said, but just kept laughing.

Dave gave me a sidelong glance, a smug little smile on his face.

"That's better," he said. "My job here is done."

We pulled into my driveway..

"Here we are. Don't thank me for making you feel better. That's what good friends are for, even if my name isn't Filby."

I got out of the car.

He backed out immediately, looking almost gleeful now. "I could always change my name, you know! Whee!" he said as he drove away.

I had to admit I did feel somewhat better thanks to Dave, even if I still thought I was in enormous trouble.

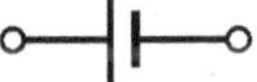

Two weeks later, when I could finally go a couple of hours at a time without worrying about the fire investigation underway, Dad got a phone call. I was watching TV with Kenny when he came into the living room and stood there grim-faced, staring at me.

It took me a few seconds to realize he wanted to say something, and from his stern expression I had a hunch what it was. I turned down the TV, not surprised to feel my heart start thumping hard in my chest.

"I just heard from the fire chief," he said, his eyes locked on me.

"They know the cause of the fire."

I waited for him to say "It was you," or more precisely, "You for-got to take out the cookies out of the oven, you idiot," or maybe "The police are coming for you any minute now," or words to that effect. Instead, he said nothing, and it finally dawned on me that he was waiting for me to say, "What was it, Dad?"

I cleared my suddenly dry throat. "What was it, Dad?"

He hesitated, almost as if he couldn't quite bring himself to say it. "It was . . . the electrical panel, just as I was afraid."

I shot up to my feet in stunned silence not just because it wasn't the oven that start the fire, but because my dad then buried his face in his hands and sobbed. I had never seen him cry like that before, not even when Mom died. The TV remote control fell out of my hand and hit the floor, and the batteries flew out in different directions. I paid no attention to where they went, focused instead on his astonishing breakdown.

Dad had always been our solid rock, our unwavering strength, and to see and hear him wail as if suddenly vulnerable was fright-ening, to say the least.

If he was that vulnerable, what did that make us?

He lowered his hands and explained himself, still weepy. "I had done some rewiring about a year ago. I thought there might be something wrong with it, but I never had it checked out even though we kept tripping circuits. If I had only hired an electrician to do about an hour's worth of work instead of pinching pennies and trying to do it myself, this never would have happened." He wiped his eyes. "It's all my fault."

I didn't know what to say. Finally, all I could manage was the too-familiar "Accidents will happen, Dad," which sounded lame even as I said it.

But my response did seem to help. He nodded and his voice

grew calmer. "The insurance will pay to rebuild it, but The Post will never be the same."

I opened my mouth to immediately say, "No, it won't," in agreement, then thought better of it and said nothing instead.

Despite the official report, I was still troubled by the oven business. And even though it felt like a confession, I had to know for sure that it had been ruled out.

"Dad, what about the oven? Did they consider it?"

He looked puzzled. "Consider it for what?"

It was my turn to hesitate. "As the cause of the fire. Kenny and I were making cookies, remember? I might have . . . left the oven on. All night." I looked away, knowing that wasn't quite true. "I did leave the oven on all night. The melted dial was still set at three hundred and fifty degrees in the morning. I saw it myself."

My dad laughed once. I wasn't sure if it was a good laugh or a bad laugh.

"George, we've left that oven on overnight by accident dozens of times. It was cast iron, build like a tank. The Post would have burned down years ago if leaving the oven on could have started a fire. Usually we find some soot around the oven door, but that just wipes right off."

"I saw that soot," I said in amazement.

"Well, there you go." He shrugged, and then looked puzzled again. "You mean you've been worried all this time that you might have burned the place down because you left the oven on and you didn't tell me? I could have told you right away that wasn't possible."

"I guess I thought I'd be in big trouble."

He nodded. "Well, you're not."

I kept waiting to feel a big sense of relief, but it never came. Instead, I felt numb. Hollow.

There was really nothing to celebrate.

I had an idea. "Hey! Maybe they can rebuild it the way it used to be," I suggested. "It might not be exactly the same, but it could be close."

"What? No, the old Post is gone, George. If we have a chance to rebuild it, it should have all the modern conveniences so we can start attracting outside rentals again. That's about the only good thing that will come out of this. We'll get a brand new Post." He looked pleased at the thought.

Dad was right, of course, but then again I knew he didn't cherish The Post quite the way I had. His view was more practical and pragmatic; mine was strictly nostalgic, like Dave said.

"Well, that's it. I thought you should know," he said, sounding and looking normal again. He pointed at something on the floor. "Don't step on the remote control. It's right behind you."

Still feeling numb, I found the wayward batteries and got the remote control into working order. But I didn't feel much like watching TV and gave the remote to Kenny, who shut the TV off and picked up his Game Boy.

"I'm going to bed," I said.

"So early?" my dad asked from the kitchen, where I heard him filling the dishwasher as if the cause of the fire no longer mattered, as if The Post itself no longer mattered.

In an odd sort of way, I felt alone in my sorrow and maybe even a little betrayed.

It wasn't easy to fall asleep. And when I finally did, I had the strangest dream.

The dream started out pleasant enough—in fact, it was great.

I dreamt I was home alone in the living room by my clock collection, eagerly waiting for all of them to sound at noon. But when noon struck, the clocks were silent, and I realized that they had all stopped ticking. Right then I sensed that I had caused time to stop somehow, and that I needed to go into my bedroom to find out how. To get in, I had to force the door open just like Filby did to the time traveler's laboratory door at the end of The Movie when George left forever in his machine to be with Weena. When I entered, I saw something large covered in a sheet by the window. I went over to whatever it was and pulled the sheet off.

It was the time machine from The Movie.

The machine was switched on and humming, lights and dials lit, and I wondered if that was why the clocks had stopped. I walked once around it like the time traveler had before he took his first trip forward in time, then climbed aboard, marveling not only at the machine but at my good fortune for having it somehow. I rubbed my hands together in anticipation and reached out and grabbed the operating lever, pushing it ever so slightly forward into the future, eager to see what was ahead.

The room dimmed but nothing else happened, as if the machine was broken. When I looked up, there was Dave standing in front of me, his expression grim, even a bit scary.

"What are you doing here?" I asked.

"There's no going forward yet," he said, in a voice that wasn't quite his. "This way."

I got off the machine and followed him out to the driveway, where my dad's car sat. There was no sign of Dave's car.

"Time for a ride," he said in his strange voice, then unlocked the passenger's side door.

For the first time since my mom died, I got into the front seat where she used to sit. For some reason, that felt perfectly natural. Dave started the car and drove us to The Big Brown Box. It seemed like we got there in just a few seconds.

When we entered, I saw that the clocks in the hall had stopped, too, only now it was midnight, not noon. We walked through the silent, mostly dark building to the empty auditorium, where Dave ushered me down the main aisle to the front.

"Watch," he commanded, and the stage curtains parted.

The stage set was an exact recreation of our living room around Christmas, back when I was nine or so and my mom was still alive. I knew that because not only was there a Christmas tree by the picture window, there was my mom, dancing with my dad to the Beach Boys' song "Little Saint Nick," one of her favorite Christmas songs.

As my dad twirled her around, it seemed for one brief moment she looked straight at me.

"Mom?" I said, but she didn't answer. "Mom?"

I raised my arms to let her know it was really me, that I was right there, when I saw that I was holding the lever to the time machine even though I didn't remember taking it.

I held the lever close to my face to examine it. The scene before me was multiplied within its multifaceted crystal knob, with a dozen images of my mom smiling and laughing as she danced, each image different like a different moment from her life.

Then the music faded, the lights went down and the curtains began to close.

I rushed forward, trying to make it to the stage before it was too late.

"*Mom?*"

I sat up abruptly in bed, wide awake now, my heart pounding.

Whether I had said that last "Mom" out loud or not, I didn't know. I sat a while in the dark, hugging my knees and wondering if there was some hidden meaning to the dream. The only explanation I could think of was that unlike the fate of The Post, which now had a tidy, logical explanation, there was none for my mom and there never would be. That, and the fact that losing The Post put her life even further into the past, yet another major event in our lives she didn't live to see.

I eventually fell back into a dreamless sleep, but that dream haunted me the next day like some dreams do. I never told anyone about it because the last thing I needed were a bunch of amateur psychiatrists telling me what it "actually" meant, especially Onion and Dave. The more I thought about it, the more I realized there really was a straightforward explanation for why it affected me as much as it did:

I still missed my mom, and no amount of wishful thinking or dreaming was ever going to bring her back.

Or The Post.

# CHAPTER SIXTEEN

# WHEN REENACTMENTS GO BAD

Dave says it's cosplay, but I say it's not nearly that nerdy. Every now and then we would do faithful reenactments of scenes from The Movie to show our profound respect for George Pal's masterpiece. Or at least, my respect, since I make all the arrangements.

"Humor him, will you, Dave? It won't kill you," Onion said more than once about our reenactments. Dave thought they were stupid, as you might imagine, but went along only because Onion and I insisted. To be honest, I don't think Onion like the reenactments any more than Dave did, but at least she was a good sport about it rather than a pitiful whiner like Dave.

I decided the next scene we were going to recreate was the one where George the time traveler goes forward in time to the year 1918. He breaks out of his abandoned, boarded-up house, sees who he thinks is his good friend Filby across the street, and then discovers that it's Filby's son, now a young man and the spitting image of his father.

Filby, George finds out to his great distress, is dead, killed at the front in World War One.

It's a great scene, one that always chokes me up a bit.

Naturally, we have to improvise a little when it comes to finding a location for our reenactments of The Movie. For this scene, we had to improvise a lot.

We were doing the reenactment on Sunday morning, The stores downtown were closed then, and after scouting for a good location the week before I had found a shop that vaguely resembled the one the young Filby was about to enter when approached by George, with exactly five steps like in The Movie. Across the street was an alley that would have to do for George's boarded-up property. It was hardly ideal, but the minute I saw the location I knew we could make it work.

We dressed for our parts, of course, although that could be difficult depending on the scene. I had found an old dark plaid suit in the Goodwill store that was kind of like the one that George the time traveler wore at the beginning of The Movie. It was a little too big for me, but good enough. I was able to wear it for several scenes we reenacted since that was what George wore throughout The Movie, although it was in tatters by movie's end. For this scene, Dave should have been wearing a British WWI uniform, but obviously not having one of those, Dave just wore his brown leather bomber jacket and a plain green baseball cap. That looked sufficiently military, even though it looked to be from the wrong world war.

Onion was going to be the driver of the car that almost hits the time traveler as he crosses the street after getting the bad news about Filby. For that, she had her mother's car and claimed she had an old-fashioned dress that was close enough to pass for 1918. Of the three of us, Onion's wardrobe was the most extensive. I think she liked dressing up for the reenactments much more than the reenactments themselves.

So Dave picks me up real early Sunday morning looking like he slept in his clothes, which he probably did. We headed downtown.

"You owe me big time for this," he said. His sigh afterwards turned into a loud yawn.

"Oh, come on," I said. "It'll be great fun."

"Barely. Maybe for you."

"Do you have your lines memorized?"

"Yes, yes." He seemed to bristle with resentment. "You'll see," he added a few seconds later, then gave me a smug look that made me wonder what he had planned.

Onion arrived just moments after we did. She got out of her car and posed to show us how she was attired. Wearing a long, flowing ankle-length dress with a high collar and wide-brimmed sun bonnet, she looked perfect for the part.

I looked at Dave, who stood there disinterested.

"And to think she has a small role today. Why can't you get that involved?"

"Well really, I just like the dressing up part," Onion confessed, as I suspected. "These reenactments . . ." she rolled her eyes and let the rest go unsaid.

Dave turned slowly to face me.

"Let's just get this over with, okay?"

"Fine. Get in your car. When you hear me break though the fence, that's your cue to slowly drive up to the shop, get out and walk up the steps. Onion, you wait in your car behind Dave. When I walk back across the street, you know what to do. All right, places, everyone!"

I rubbed my hands together; instead of Onion, it was Dave whose eyes rolled this time.

I hurried to the alley. Obviously, I wasn't going to break through a fence, but I had seen a tall wooden pallet that I could use as a stand-in for a fence. All I would have to do was kick out a couple of slats and crawl through.

The pallet was right where I saw it yesterday, next to an over-stuffed dumpster. I turned it to face the street.

"Ready, and action!"

I kicked at the slats. Nothing happened. I kicked harder.

"Hold on, we're having some technical difficulties here."

I kicked as hard as I could; my foot slipped between two slats and got stuck. Worse, the pallet had slid forward from my kicks and now leaned towards me. It took all my strength to keep from falling backwards under its weight.

"Uh, some help over here? Right away, please?"

I could see Dave sigh again. He got out of his car and lumbered across the street. I could be wrong, but it sure seemed to me he was taking his sweet time as I struggled mightily to stay upright.

Dave nonchalantly reached out with one hand and stood the skid up straight.

"Hold perfectly still."

With just two well-placed kicks from behind me, he loosened the slats on either side of my stuck foot. I pulled it free.

"There you go. Not that you deserve it."

He immediately turned and lumbered back across the street and into his car, not even waiting for me to thank him.

A bit rattled, I swallowed hard. I'm sure some of what I swallowed was my pride.

But the show, as they say, must go on.

"Okay now. From the top. Ready, set, action!"

I had no trouble kicking the slats off this time, sending them scattering. I crawled through the pallet frame and headed across the street.

Dave slowly drove up to the curb. I stared at his car as if I had never seen one before, just like George the time traveler had. Dave parked, got out and took four steps up to the closed shop.

"Filby!" I called brightly. "Well what are you doing, going to a masquerade party?

Dave turned around to look at me and came back down the steps. I cackled exactly six times, the last time on a high note just like in The Movie.

"You look rather silly without your mustache, old man."

Dave gave a big sigh, which was not in The Movie.

"Were you addressing me, mister?"

"It's 'sir,' not 'mister,'" I corrected him quietly. "Filby, it's George. Well, I must say I expected a little more enthusiastic a greeting."

Dave raised a finger into the air, much higher than necessary. "I think you're confusing me with my father, sir. Yes. There was quite a resemblance. I'm James Filby."

So far, so good; Dave's timing and inflection were spot on.

"Was?"

"Were you a friend of Father's?"

Even though he had delivered the line perfectly, he fluttered his eyelids and cocked his head in a much too obvious parody.

It was a struggle to remain in character. "Yes! Yes, I've been away."

"He was killed in the war. A year ago."

Dave briefly crossed his eyes and stuck his tongue out of the corner of his mouth, which finally made me scowl.

"Oh. Oh, I'm so sorry. What about the gentleman across the street?"

"Oh! Oh, him, the inventor fellow." Dave gave a little hop—again, not in The Movie. "He disappeared around the turn of the century."

"'Chap.' Not 'fellow,'" I said softly, now more than a little irritated.

Dave wagged a finger at me, much more vigorously than the scene called for. "Look here, if you're interested in that house, sir, I'm afraid you can't buy it. Can't even get inside."

Unlike other times when Dave had flubbed his lines and I had to help him along, this time he nearly had them down cold. It was the embellishments that were driving me mad. I would have insisted that we start over again but knew the outcome would probably be the same.

"Why is that?"

"Well my father was executor of the inventor's estate and father just refused to liquidate it. I often chided him on that account, but he felt positive the owner would return someday. People hereabouts think it's haunted, but, ha ha . . . who are you, sir?"

Dave put an index finger under his chin and curtsied, which made Onion laugh as she waited in the car. That didn't help my darkening mood.

"Just a stranger who once knew your father."

"Have you been at the front?"

"Front? What front?"

"Why, the war of course."

"What war?"

"Good heavens!" He slapped his forehead and staggered a bit, again not in the script. "You mean you don't know we've been at war with Germany since 1914? I thought you just returned from France perhaps, or perhaps . . . perhaps a cup of coffee might make you feel better, sir." He mimicked sipping from a cup with his pinky finger extended. Onion laughed even louder.

"Tea. Not coffee," I said through clenched teeth. I was beginning to wonder if Dave was further messing with me by selectively substituting words, knowing I would feel compelled to correct him.

"Won't you come in?" He gestured grandly toward the door.

"No. No, thank you." I spoke the line a littler edgier than in The Movie.

"Are you sure you're all right, sir?" He clasped his face.

"Yes, I'm quite all right." I glowered at him.

"Then goodbye, sir."

Dave curtsied again, turned stiffly and started back up the steps.

"Goodbye, Jamie."

Dave turned around with a totally shocked expression instead of the mildly puzzled look the scene called for.

I turned and strode away, glad it was over if Dave was going to spoil it with his maddening theatrics.

As soon as I stepped into the street, that was Onion's cue to step on the gas. She drove slowly towards me and beeped her horn. I raised my arms slightly and let them fall in kind of a daze, as if still contemplating my dear friend Filby's untimely demise just as the time traveler had. But instead of walking slowly so she could safely swerve in front of me, I went too fast, still fuming at Dave for ruining the scene with his silly faces.

Onion laid on the horn to get my attention, but it was too late. A horrible screech went up from the tires as she slammed on the brakes.

The grille of the Volvo bumped me just below the waist, hard enough to send me sprawling.

"Oh no oh no oh no," I heard Onion repeat, followed by the sound of a car door slamming and quick footsteps.

I pushed myself up off the pavement and stood up. My right hip hurt, but I was able to walk and knew right away it wasn't serious. All I was probably going to have was a good-sized bruise.

"Please tell me you're all right."

Onion's face was pale. I had never seen her look so frightened.

"Yeah, I'll be fine. That was my—"

"Hey!"

The voice boomed from down the sidewalk, where a man stood holding a set of keys. He hurried toward us.

"What are you doing by my shop?"

I hurried to the sidewalk to explain if I could, Onion by my side. Dave came down the steps and joined us. The man came up to me and looked us up and down.

"What's going on? Why are the three of you dressed like that? Say, you hit him with your car!" He stared at Onion. "I should call the police for that."

The very last thing I needed was to see the police again so I hastened to put him at ease, putting on my friendliest face despite my sore hip.

"No, I'm fine, just fine. This is all part of an act," I said lightly. "We're actors recreating a scene from a movie, that's all."

"A movie?" The man looked around. "I don't see any cameras. What are you talking about?"

"It's . . . street theater," I said. "We're an acting troupe. This location was ideal for the scene we reenacted today. We're done now and will be leaving soon."

Just as the man's face brightened as if he understood, Dave spoke up. Unfortunately.

"Look, we're really sorry. This whole thing is just retarded. We won't be back, I promise."

I stiffened at Dave's words and slowly turned around to face him. The anger I felt over him mocking the scene from The Movie was nothing compared to how I felt now.

Dave actually took a step back when he saw my face.

"Oh, David," Onion said.

"Well, no harm done, then," the man said, clearly unaware of how things had just changed. "I thought you were breaking into my shop or something." He laughed a little. "Well, you crazy kids take care now. I've got a business to run. And watch out for cars the next time you cross the street, will you? That looked painful, even if it was an act." He laughed again.

And with that, he went up the steps, unlocked the door, and went inside.

I took a step toward Dave. He backed still further away.

"Hey, I didn't really mean it. I was just trying to stop him from calling the police. After what you went through, I figured you'd never want to see another police car again."

He didn't sound like he believed it himself, and I was too angry to answer.

"Come on," Dave pleaded. "It meant nothing. I did you a favor!"

"A *favor*? Using the one word you know I hate is a favor?"

He seemed to kind of collapse in on himself then, no longer the least bit smug.

"I'm super sorry, man. It won't happen again, I swear."

I eyed him darkly. "That's what you said last time."

Dave looked shocked and indignant. "*What*? I haven't said that word in three years! I said I was sorry. What more do you want?"

I didn't answer, partly because I was still angry and partly because I didn't know what I wanted from Dave in order to forgive him.

Dave went on. "You're being unreasonable, dude. Yeah, it's a really bad word and I never should have said it, but it's not the end of the world."

"You don't get to decide that! I despise anyone who uses that word. You know that full well, no matter how long it's been."

Now Dave looked beside himself. "Oh, for . . ." He threw his hands up, turned around and walked a few paces away before turning around again to face me. "Tell you what. Let's ask Onion if you're being unreasonable. You trust her judgment, don't you?"

We both looked at her. She sighed a little.

"George, you know I love you like a brother, but what Dave said is true. You're kind of . . . overreacting about this." She put a hand up to her neck as if regretting having to tell me that. "What's wrong, George? What is it? What's this really all about?"

As hard as I tried, I couldn't stop this great big unexpected wave of sorrow from rising up from deep within me.

I covered my face with my hands and sobbed once—why, I didn't have a clue.

Onion squeezed my arm. "I know, George," she said quietly. "I know."

That calmed me down for some reason, and I took a deep breath to compose myself. At least, I thought with just a little solace, no actual tears flowed.

Dave stood head bowed, staring down at the sidewalk as if this was all his fault.

"Let's get out of here," Onion said, taking me by the arm. "Come on. I'll drive you home."

Dave quickly raised his head. "No," he said. "I will. That's my job."

Onion let me go.

I brushed past her without a word to Dave's car. Even though Onion had her own car and wasn't riding with us, I got in the back seat as if she were.

Dave and Onion glanced at each other and then parted.

We didn't speak most of the way home. Finally Dave cleared his throat.

"I don't know what to say, George, but this silence is killing me."

"You don't have to say anything."

"Yes, I do. I really upset you back there."

"That wasn't it."

"Then why did you—"

"I'm not sure." I paused. "Onion said she knew. I wonder what she meant."

Dave shrugged. "Ask her."

"No, I'm not going to put her on the spot, even if she is wiser than the two of us put together."

Dave said nothing in response, which told me he already knew that. We didn't speak again until we entered my neighborhood.

"What's going to happen to us, Dave?" I asked, staring out the window at nothing in particular.

"What do you mean?"

"I mean, the three of us are going to go our separate ways after we graduate, aren't we? Are we really going to keep in touch, or will that turn out to be just an empty promise?"

The three of us had picked colleges in different states and knew it would be tough to remain such close friends if we hardly ever saw each other.

"Don't say that!" There was more than a touch of desperation in his voice. "Of course we'll stay in touch! Absolutely."

Once again he didn't sound all that convinced. Why we were having such a deep conversation all of a sudden I wasn't sure, especially about such a touchy subject we usually went out of our way to avoid. The only thing I could figure was that the scene I had caused kind of opened the floodgates.

"Feeling better now?" Dave asked, as if anxious to change the subject. He glanced back at me.

"Yeah. Except for the hip. Sorry for making a scene."

"So am I."

I shook my head. "You're sorry I made a scene or you?"

"Me. I spoiled the reenactment by making fun of The Movie."

"You're always making fun of The Movie."

"Yeah, but I could tell you were ticked off about it but kept going."

I shrugged. "It doesn't matter now."

He looked back at me with a little satisfied grin. "Hey, I sure had my lines memorized this time though, didn't I?"

"Yeah, you did. Except for a few words." I glared at him, still suspicious about that. "And your delivery was perfect. I would have been really impressed if it wasn't for all the goofy faces."

He hesitated. "I practiced them in front of a mirror last night."

"You did? Why?"

"Because I thought they would be funny."

"Of course," I said drily.

"Well, Onion thought they were funny."

"So I heard."

He hesitated again. "Why *do* you love that old movie so much?"

Dave had never asked me so directly before. I guess it was his turn to be straightforward.

I took a deep breath to contemplate the question but couldn't formulate an answer. "I don't know. It just . . . means a lot to me, that's all. Something really important."

"Maybe it's got something to do with your mom. You know, like a way to cope for feeling abandoned all of a sudden, especially since you never found out why she died."

For some reason, that thought made me real uncomfortable in almost a pins-and-needles sort of way.

I shrugged; the creepy-crawly feeling went away. "No, that's not it," I said, but wondered if what Dave said wasn't at least a little bit true, if he wasn't on to something.

"Well, I won't ever make fun of The Movie again. Not if this is what happens."

Somehow, the thought of Dave not acting like Dave just for my sake bothered me nearly as much.

"Don't do that. If you think it's stupid then you think it's stupid."

"I don't think it's stupid. It's just that there are a lot better movies out there. Why you're so obsessed with that one I'll never know."

I shook my head. "Never mind. Just forget it, okay?"

"You want me to forget The Movie?"

"No, what happened back there."

Dave shifted in his seat, as if the pins and needles had jumped to him. "Man, that's going to be hard."

We pulled up in front of my house. I rubbed my increasingly sore hip, anxious now to get an ice pack on it.

"Try," I said.

# CHAPTER SEVENTEEN

# THE SAD SAGA OF SAM

My bruised hip ached for a few days, and then the pain faded away along with the ugly black and blue mark that kind of had the shape of the Volvo's front grille, which would have been amusing if it hadn't hurt as much as it did. I took kind of a small break from hanging out all day with Dave and Onion after that—probably more out of embarrassment than anything else—and hung out a bit more with Sam, our Geek Supreme.

I'm not sure what's up exactly with the nerds and geeks. What they lack in social skills they more than make up for in intelligence. You would think that the two would cancel out, but they don't. The problem is, their very nerdiness and geekiness make it difficult to relate to them. Sometimes it's like they're speaking in secret code when they try to explain some new technology or discovery that has them all excited; all you can do is smile and nod.

Another thing about geeks and nerds is that they're deadly serious about the most trivial elements regarding their beloved science fiction movies and TV shows, as if everyone should care deeply, too. I've seen them nearly come to blows in the science labs and classrooms about the smallest little details in *Star Wars* and *Star Trek*, as if the whole purpose of life is to get those things exactly right or die. Dave jokes that when I talk about The Movie, that's my inner nerd or geek trying to break out. That might be, but the full-time nerds and geeks take things to the extreme of the extreme.

As much as I can't relate to them, I can still empathize with their lower social status plight. Maybe that has something to do with the way some people treat Kenny; I don't know. My own status at The Big Brown Box is pretty much run of the mill—not revered, not ridiculed, just another face in the crowd—so I can't say that's the reason. The cruelest thing I've seen are the girls who feign interest in the guy nerds and geeks just to get help with some new tech toy they got for Christmas they just can't figure out. Despite the risk to their carefully cultivated reputations, some girls are actually brazen enough to be seen in public with them, smiling and standing oh so close, sending the boys to new levels of sweaty awkwardness and false hope regarding the opposite sex. Of course, it all comes crashing down once the tech lessons are over and the girls knows how to make whatever device they've got do what it is they want it to do. And yet the same nerds and geeks guys fall for that heartless trick over and over again, as if for all their intelligence, that's one lesson they just can't learn.

On the other hand, maybe they do know that the attention will be fleeting, but they're willing to play along for as long as it lasts because, well, that's still better than no attention from girls at all.

Either way, watching it happen was both painful and kind of sad.

Sam was still my favorite geek despite the bonfire fiasco at Homecoming. After that scare, I figured he would swear off fireworks altogether, but he actually seemed emboldened by the whole experience, as if he had decided he must be invincible.

"Aren't you pushing your luck?" I asked him once after he set off a long string of firecrackers right outside the gym doors, using the doors as shields to watch the display. Exploding firecrackers danced all about, with a few finding their way right between Sam's feet. He laughed his high-pitched staccato laugh.

"No really, Sam. Your luck's gonna run out someday."

"Nonsense. You make your own luck, my good man," he replied, preparing to set off another firecracker pack.

When Sam bought fireworks, that was one thing. It was much more worrisome when he started making his own.

At first I didn't think much of it. He seemed to know exactly what he was doing, until I realized that his homemade stuff often didn't work as advertised. And when I say "didn't work," I don't mean they were duds, although he had a few of those. It was the things that blew up in spectacular fashion rather than doing what they were supposed to do that really concerned me.

Once, Sam wanted to hold a fat homemade roman candle in his hand after lighting it. Given his dismal track record, I had my doubts about the wisdom of that.

"You know," I told him as he lit the long fuse, "maybe you should play it safe and stick it in the ground."

"Oh, ye of little faith," Sam said, watching the fuse burn.

"No, really, Sam. Please, do it for me, will you?"

I wasn't above groveling. Not this time.

"Okay. If you insist."

"I do. Quick!"

Sam stuck it in the ground just as the burning wick disappeared inside the long tube. We both took a couple of steps back.

It blew up in a loud shower of sparks and flames that sent us staggering backwards.

Sam was speechless. I wasn't.

"Wow. That might have cost you a few fingers," I said drily.

"Ouch," was all he could say as we stared at the smoldering bits and pieces scattered in a wide circle.

I tried to talk to Sam about The Movie once—thinking he might be as fascinated by the thought of time travel as I was since science was his thing—but to my dismay, he dismissed The Movie as pure fantasy, unworthy of serious discussion.

"Of course you know time travel is impossible, don't you?" he said, cutting me off as I speculated as to how the time machine might work. "It goes against causality. You know, the whole 'if I go back in time and shoot my grandfather I never would have been born so I wouldn't have been able to go back and shoot him' type of thing."

Dave had raised that very conundrum years ago, but somehow I still wanted to believe there was a logical way around it, only I didn't know what it could be.

I offered a lame counterargument instead. "And yet you talk about interstellar spaceships, which seem just as impossible."

Sam's face took on a bright "you're mistaken" look.

"Oh, but you're mistaken," he said brightly. "There's a warp drive theory that just might be possible, one that doesn't violate any of the laws of physics. We might be warping our way through space sooner than you think if we can solve the energy requirements. Faster-than-light travel has a *much* better chance of coming true than *time travel.*"

He made the last two words sound absolutely absurd.

Disappointed, I didn't mention The Movie to Sam again. I wondered if I should have befriended a *Doctor Who* fan instead, someone who wanted time travel to at least be a possibility like I did.

One day, before my chemistry class, Sam met me in the hall with some "great" news. We walked into the lab together.

"I've got it."

"Really? Well, I hope your doctor can help you get rid of it."

I was proud of that quick response. It was like something Dave would have come up with on the spur of the moment. I guess Dave was a bigger influence on me than I realized.

He frowned. "Very funny, wise guy. I'm talking about the new powder I told you about."

Sam was always experimenting with new explosive formulas. To his credit, rather than raid the school's chemistry supplies he had found some fly-by-night mail order outfits on the internet willing to sell him the chemicals he needed. Why he didn't get busted by the Feds or Postal Inspectors or someone like that was a mystery to me.

I sat down wearily in my chair at the back of the room. Chemistry wasn't my favorite subject, and Sam's quest for the perfect explosive was starting to get old.

I sighed. "Okay, so what's so special about this new powder?"

Sam was nearly beside himself with joy. He leaned closer to nearly whisper in secret even though the few other people in the room couldn't have cared less about his dangerous little hobby.

"It's one-point-five-micron military grade dark aluminum powder. That's really wicked small, man. This will create my most powerful explosive yet."

He held out a large, dark brown bottle he had been hiding behind his back.

I didn't especially like the sound of that, or the looks of the bottle with its multiple bright red warning labels. "*Military* grade? And they sold it to you? Sounds dangerous, dude."

When I tipped the bottle from one side to the other, the ultra-fine powder inside slide around almost like a liquid. It was actually kind of mesmerizing.

He nodded excitedly. "I know. Isn't that grand?"

More students drifted into the room, followed by Higgins.

Sam straightened up and grabbed the bottle from me. He didn't always see eye to eye with Higgins, even though Higgins gave him free reign to do pretty much whatever he wanted ever since Sam volunteered to keep the lab in tip-top shape and did. Somehow, I doubt Higgins had any idea that Sam was making his own ordinance.

Sam hid the bottle behind his back again and waved weakly to Higgins, who barely responded.

"Well, time to mix up my first batch." He motioned to the small chemistry prep lab next to us, more a supply room than an actual workspace. "Enjoy your boring class."

"Whatever."

Cradling the bottle in front of him, Sam crept quietly into the lab and shut the door. Through the thick glass-and-wire window, he held a finger up to his lips.

As if I would even bother to tell someone, and as if they would actually care if I did.

The class began and soon Higgins has us lulled into a trance. A few studious students up front took notes furiously as Higgins droned on in his monotone voice, but most of us slumped in our chairs, reading other things or just plain falling asleep, not even trying to disguise it.

Twenty-two minutes into class, it happened.

There was a muffled boom that shook the walls and rattled the ceiling tiles, a deep, penetrating sound that made everyone jump in their chairs. Even Higgins lurched backward, dropping his chalk. In unison, we all turned to look at the door to the small chemistry lab. Where there was normally white fluorescent light shining through, now there was a dense gray cloud of smoke that roiled behind the window.

The fire alarm went off, the shrill buzz pulsing in unison to the flashing light for the hearing impaired above the lab door.

"Something blew up," someone cried out, stating the incredibly obvious.

And then out of the dark cloud came a hand that pressed its palm firmly against the glass. The hand didn't move, as if signaling for help but unable to do anything more.

Sam's hand.

I leapt from my seat and raced to the door, two classmates right behind me.

"No!" Higgins' voice roared over the alarm. "Don't open it! The fumes could be toxic!"

I stood paralyzed, my hand on the doorknob, unable to do anything other than stare. It was a helpless, hollow feeling, one I've never felt before and never want to feel again.

"Come on! We have to get out! *Now*, people!" Higgins' voice was louder still.

The two classmates behind me slowly turned to leave with the rest of the class. I found myself powerless to respond, my shoulders hunched and my heart thumping in my throat. The whole scene seemed impossible, unbelievable. I stared at Sam's motionless hand as the fire alarm continued to blare, saw my own hand leave the doorknob and reach out towards his as if with a mind of its own, perhaps to make amends for recoiling from his shaky hands at homecoming. My hand perfectly covered his with only the cool glass between them, as if that were my other hand in there, as if that could have been me in that deadly, smoke-filled room.

And then Sam's hand withdrew back into the darkness. It didn't slide down like a drowning sailor as you might expect, it just pulled away and disappeared, and I found myself staring at the impenetrable gray cloud on the other side, the brief connection we had now gone.

I gasped several times in a row—how many, I don't know—as if I had forgotten how to breathe.

"No, Sam." I said quietly. "No."

That was all I could say, the most I could offer.

"*Wells!*" Higgins yelled. "There's nothing you can do for him. Let's *go!*"

I finally tore my gaze away from the door and turned to follow Higgins, who seemed exasperated by my delay.

He glowered at me as we walked quickly to the nearest exit, the last two people in the building as far as I could see.

"You want to die, too?" he asked.

With those words, I felt my heart jump up to my throat again. The thought of Sam dying or already dead in the lab gave me that queasy, surreal feeling again, as if somehow this was happening to someone else far away, not us here and now.

Most everyone outside milled about with bored expressions, unaware that this wasn't just another false alarm or someone's idea of a stupid prank.

As the door clicked shut behind me the fire alarm suddenly stopped as if it knew everyone was out of The Big Brown Box—or at least, everyone who was still alive. I immediately thought of the scene in The Movie where the Eloi who were lucky enough not to have been harvested by the Morlocks stood expressionless before those solid Morlock doors that had just closed, the wailing siren fading to silence, the Eloi who had marched hypnotically to the cruel death that awaited them already forgotten.

These people outside with me were the lucky ones all right, I thought with a sudden flash of anger, standing there like fatted cattle (as the time traveler called the Eloi then) unable to comprehend the seriousness of the situation. They had no idea how lucky they were. No idea at all.

I resisted the urge to lash out and berate them like how the time traveler berated the Eloi for their cold indifference to the horrible fate of their own. Then I realized I was afraid to tell them it was Sam who might be dead or dying and hear them laugh about it because, gosh, Sam was just a geek, wasn't he? Just some marginal nobody who nobody really knew or even cared about.

I felt isolated from the crowd and withdrew to a corner of the yard to sulk.

Onion spotted me and came forward. She stopped a few feet away and then approached warily.

"George? What is it?"

I struggled to put into words what happened and how I felt. "This isn't a joke, that's what. It's Sam."

"Sam? Sam the lab rat?"

"Don't call him that! He might be dead."

Onion's hands flew to cover her mouth.

"What happened?" she asked again, quieter this time.

"There was an explosion. Sam was trapped in a supply room full of smoke."

"Poor Sam."

My anger subsided a bit once I realized that Onion truly sympathized, as I should have expected.

The sound of several fire engines grew louder as they came around to our side of the building. I saw Higgins nearly yank a fireman off of one of the trucks before it even came to a stop, gesturing wildly at the door we came out of as if to make it perfectly clear that time was of the essence.

Then to my relief I saw an ambulance pull right up on to the main sidewalk, as if they already had the urgent message. Students scattered out of the way, and the happy, mindless chatter immediately ceased.

I was glad to see their astonishment and the slow realization on their faces that this wasn't a prank or a drill.

A murmur went through the crowd as the firefighters raced into the building wearing their breathing gear and carrying coils of hoses.

The paramedics were next, gurney in tow and wearing their own breathing gear. Higgins bounded in right behind them, red-faced and with his tie flapping over his shoulder.

After what seemed like an eternity, the paramedics reappeared just inside the doors with someone strapped to the gurney, an oxygen mask on the person's mouth and nose.

"Ouch, George. My shoulder."

I realized I was squeezing Onion's shoulder much too hard and relaxed my grip. All I could picture was my mom on a gurney, years ago.

"If they hurry, that's a good sign. But if they move slowly . . ."

She let the rest go unsaid.

The doors burst open and the paramedics flew with the gurney to the ambulance, shouting instructions to one another and into walkie-talkies. One of them held up an IV bag with a tube attached to Sam's right arm. They loaded the gurney into the ambulance in a matter of seconds, the driver jumped into the driver's seat, and the ambulance roared backward, lights flashing and siren wailing. It made a sharp U-turn to exit the way it came in, tires squealing in its haste to leave.

I felt myself able to breathe again.

"You okay now?"

"Not really. I'm exhausted."

Higgins came out, bent over and put his hands on his knees as if to catch his breath. Then he stood up and looked at me, his face pale and expression oddly blank.

I nodded at him and he nodded in return.

A crowd of other teachers and administrators soon surrounded him and took him to meet with the fire chief, who had exited the school with the other firefighters in no particular hurry at all.

Sam survived, although I never saw him again. I heard he had reduced lung capacity from smoke inhalation, permanent hearing loss, and dozens of scars where shrapnel was removed from his face, chest, and arms, but at least he was alive. He transferred to a private school for the physically disabled, where he continued his science studies—minus the pyrotechnics, safe to say. We stayed in touch by texts for a while, but the texts faded away in time as we ran out of things to say.

As for the chemistry store room, it came through in better shape than I thought it would have. All the ceiling tiles had come down, and there was shattered glassware on every shelf, but the only permanent damage was a black, moon-like crater in the middle of the countertop where Sam's mortar and pestle had blown up, with long burn marks extending like rays in every direction from the center of the explosion. It took months for the school to replace the countertop, but in the meantime it became kind of a geek shrine met with silence for all those who saw it for the first time.

"He's very lucky to be alive," Higgins reminded me on more than one occasion. "There was absolutely nothing you could have done to help him, you know," as if he sensed my pensive mood whenever we talked about it.

That was true enough, but what I won't forget is how sometimes, things happen in life way beyond your control, and how you react speaks volumes about who you really are.

# CHAPTER EIGHTEEN

# THE GROCERY STORE INCIDENT

Grocery shopping with my dad and Kenny was quite an adventure. My dad was an avid coupon clipper—"Just trying to save a few bucks," he would always say to justify his obsession—even though he bought things we didn't need or want only because he had a coupon for buy one, get one free or some other offer he couldn't refuse. As a result, our kitchen cabinets were full of unopened boxes of cereal and crackers and other weird things nobody asked for but my dad bought anyway solely because the offer was just too good for him to pass up.

While Dad searched for the items on his grocery list with all the seriousness of some hunter/gatherer caveman type, I tried to keep excitable Kenny under control as much as possible. That wasn't easy because he had a bad habit of bolting away to examine whatever he spotted on the other side of the store, usually something on display that was highlighted with bright signs and arrows. He would bring whatever it was back to us and put it in our cart without us noticing, and my job was to make sure it got put back so we didn't end up paying for it. Once we accidentally bought a tube of lipstick thanks to Kenny, which made us laugh when we got home and found it at the bottom of a grocery bag. My dad meant to return it but kept forgetting, until too much time had passed to get a refund. I gave it to

Onion and she tried it out, but only once because it was really dark and made her look "way too Goth," as she put it, so that was that.

One day my dad asked me to run to the store to pick up a few things without him because he had a meeting at the site of the old Post now that the insurance money to rebuild it had come through. Even though I had to take Kenny with me, that was a pleasure because it meant we wouldn't have to listen to Dad argue with the cashier about the validity of some obscure coupon while the shoppers in line behind us seethed and I had to turn away to avoid their wrathful gazes.

After dropping Dad off, I took Kenny to the new grocery store closer to our house rather than my dad's favorite one clear across town. My dad preferred the far away store only because they took expired coupons while the new one didn't. Never mind that we probably spent as much on gas getting to the distant store as what Dad saved in coupons; as far as my dad was concerned, I'm sure it was strictly the principle of the thing.

"George is driving the car," Kenny said, not looking up from his video game. "Why?"

"Because Dad wants us to buy a few things at the grocery store."

"Why?"

"Because he's too busy to shop with us."

"Why?"

"Because they needed his help with something for the new Post."

"Why?"

I sighed, knowing this could go on forever if I let it. Once Kenny started questioning why one of our usual routines had changed, he wouldn't stop until we either relented and went back to our normal routine or whatever it was we were doing different finally came to an end.

"Kenny, I'm not listening to you ask me 'why' the whole trip."

"Why?"

I didn't fall into his trap and respond, and mercifully he didn't ask me "why" again.

The new store was larger than the old one, which meant I had a longer way to go to chase down Kenny. And finding what was on my dad's short list wasn't as easy since I didn't know where things were. After a few minutes of looking in vain for the last item on the list—instant rice—and not seeing anyone on staff who could help me, I was beginning to think the old store wasn't so bad after all despite its distance.

As I searched down the row of boxed stuffing—feeling I had to be really, really close to the rice—I looked up and saw that Kenny was gone. Again.

I went to the end of the aisle and saw him by a display of beach towels. He was easy to spot because he was wearing one like a cape, darting back and forth.

Weary of having to go retrieve him once more, I took a few steps forward and called to him.

"Kenny! Put that down and get over here!"

At first Kenny shook his head no, then relented and came running toward me, still wearing the beach towel cape.

"And put the towel back, Kenny. I'm not buying it for you."

As he ran towards me, Kenny removed the towel and flung it in the air. It sailed high behind him. To my horror, I saw it land over the head of an elderly woman with silver hair pushing a cart of groceries. She let out a scream and fought to get the towel off her.

"You little monster!"

Kenny kept running, ignoring her, and didn't stop until he was by my side, still happy as always.

The woman marched towards us, her face twisted in anger, her cart chattering madly from the speed at which it was being propelled.

"What's the matter with you?" she yelled at Kenny. "Wipe that smile off your face! You think that's funny?"

A few people passing by glanced at us, but that was all. Standing there with a scowl that seemed to suit her much too well, she reminded me of one of those old people you meet now and then who are either perpetually distressed that society had dared to change without their permission or upset with the way their own lives had turned out, as if they had expected much more but were left wanting. One of those old people.

I knew I had to explain fast, and thought the best thing to do was just be honest and straightforward.

"I'm sorry about the towel, ma'am, but my brother is autistic. He doesn't understand why you're angry."

While most people who Kenny inadvertently annoyed would have backed off and even shown some sympathy after hearing that, the woman's expression didn't change.

"What kind of excuse is that? If you can't keep him under control, then he shouldn't be out in public, should he? He might hurt someone."

I cringed, but was willing to let it go if she was finished venting. The absolute last thing I wanted was some big confrontation when all I needed was instant rice.

Kenny finally looked at her and let out a little laugh. "Funny lady," he said.

And with that, he fell into her arms and gave her a hug.

She screamed even louder and flailed her arms.

Everyone around us stopped and stared. The woman shoved Kenny away, sending him flying at me. I caught him and helped him back on his feet. While his smile remained, I could tell from his eyes he was bewildered at what was happening.

"He attacked me!" she yelled, pointing an accusing finger at Kenny for everyone to see. "That's assault!"

No one reacted or did anything.

"He was just trying to hug you, ma'am. I think he didn't want you to be mad at him."

Someone tapped me on the shoulder, making me flinch away.

It was the store manager.

"What's going on here?" he said. He was a portly guy with wire-rim glasses who stood, arms folded, waiting for an explanation.

"I was attacked," the woman persisted, her accusing finger pointing again. "By this creature. He should be locked up."

I stiffened but didn't respond. Once more I found myself wishing I had a time machine that could take me back about five minutes—just five minutes, that's all I asked—so I could stop Kenny from tossing the towel and prevent all this.

The store manager eyed Kenny up and down with suspicion. "Is that true?"

"Sir, like I told her—or tried to—my brother is autistic. He just wanted a hug."

The store manager dropped his arms to his sides, his suspicion gone, replaced by a faraway look.

"Oh. Well, that's different then. No harm done, I guess."

The woman turned her anger on the manager.

"How dare you! I was assaulted and all you can say is 'no harm done'?"

"Lady, didn't you hear? The boy is autistic. What do you want me to do?"

"I want you to call the police! He needs to be put away for everyone's safety." She glowered at Kenny as if he were beneath contempt.

The store manager slowly shook his head. "I'm not calling the police. You can call them if you want, but I'm not."

The woman tossed her head back in indignation. "Then I'm leaving, and I won't be back. You just lost a valuable customer, I'll have you know."

The manager's face sort of glazed over at the threat. "Well, sorry to see you go," was all he said.

The woman huffed, turned her cart and marched to the front of the store.

The manger looked at the shoppers still gathered around.

"That's all, folks."

They went about their business.

"Thanks," was all I could say when they were gone.

"Glad to help," the manager said. He patted my shoulder, and then his expression turned serious. "My cousin has an autistic daughter about your brother's age." he said quietly. "You shouldn't have to put up with that."

"I know," I replied. "But sometimes we do."

He nodded sadly, patted my shoulder again and went on his way.

Kenny had wandered a short distance to look at bags of candy on an end shelf, as if nothing unusual just happened.

"Come on, Kenny," I said, taking him by the arm. "Let's get out of here."

I guided him down the aisle where our cart waited. Nearby, I spotted the instant rice section, grabbed a box and dropped it in the cart, scanning my selections to make sure Kenny hadn't added a surprise. He hadn't.

"This way," I said, and still holding Kenny's arm, steered both him and the cart to the front checkout.

Only three lines were open, and the one in the middle had the elderly woman who was never going to return. I figured it would be better to be in line behind her than next to her where she could stare at us with dagger eyes. That, and she would be gone before Kenny and I finished checking out, which meant we wouldn't meet again in the parking lot.

The line was slow-moving, and Kenny began to make little noises to show his impatience.

I was sure the woman knew we were right behind her, but so far she was ignoring us as I had hoped.

"Why did George drive?" Kenny started up again, at the worst possible time.

"Quiet," I said, quietly. "We'll talk when we get outside."

Kenny squirmed, laughed, and then bumped into the cart. I grabbed the handle just in time to stop it from banging into the woman, who was now putting her groceries on the conveyer belt.

"Kenny!" I whispered sharply. "Look what you almost did."

The elderly woman glanced back at us, her eyes indeed daggers, but she said nothing.

Kenny laughed again. "Funny lady," he said. "Funny—"

I put a hand over Kenny's mouth, something I had never done, and held him tight to stop his squirming. People waiting in line of either side of us—the same ones who witnessed the altercation in the aisle—stared at us inquisitively again.

"Please, Kenny," I begged. "Stop. Stop."

For just a few terrible seconds, I wished Kenny wasn't who he was, lamented he would never change, thought how much nicer it would be to have a brother I didn't have to beg, too often in vain.

The traitorous thoughts made my eyes well up. "Kenny . . ."

The elderly woman finished paying for her groceries, eying us again with derision.

"That's right," she said under her breath, just loud enough for me to hear without drawing the attention of the cashier. "You better keep him under control, or someday somebody will call the police."

She took the two plastic bags of groceries the grocery boy handed her and turned away.

I let Kenny go once she was gone, exhaled, and put the few items from our cart on the belt. The cashier rang them up and they were bagged in practically no time.

"Twelve dollars and twenty-three cents," she said, holding out her hand, even though I could see the amount on the screen right in front of me.

I slowly counted out the money my dad had given me, trying to delay the transaction to give the elderly woman plenty of time to leave. But it didn't take long to hand over two five-dollar bills and three singles, and soon I had stuffed a fistful of change in my pocket and we were on our way.

Kenny picked up an empty plastic bag he found on the floor, squealing a bit at his good fortune.

"Fine, Kenny. Keep it. It's time to go home."

I wiped the stubborn tears out of the corners of my eyes with the back of my hand and walked with our single bag of groceries to the exit, Kenny by my side.

Kenny broke free from my weak grip on his arm and raced out the door. I think I had held on to him too lightly to make up for the hard squeeze I had given him in line, as well as for my treacherous thoughts he didn't deserve.

"No!" I yelled, and ran after him.

Kenny made a beeline for our car, waving the plastic bag over his head like a victory flag. To my dismay, I saw that the elderly woman was walking down the same row. The sound of rapid footsteps behind her undoubtedly made her look to see who it was. When she saw it was Kenny, she gave a little cry and quickened her pace.

"Kenny, stop!" I commanded.

To my relief, he obeyed.

The woman kept hurrying, her two grocery bags swinging by her side. Then I saw one of them begin to tear at the bottom. The tear spread until all the contents spilled out, cans and plastic bottles rolling every which way.

I heard her curse, then turn and stoop to pick up a bottle. When she saw Kenny standing there staring at the scene and me not too far away, she gave another little cry.

"Keep him away from me!" She backed off a few steps.

Kenny lowered his head, and I wondered if he understood now what the woman thought of him. But then I realized he was just opening the plastic bag he held. Once he did, he went down on his hands and knees and began to collect all the scattered cans and bottles, reaching under cars and moving shopping carts out of his way so as not to miss anything.

When he was done and all her items were safely bagged again, Kenny crawled towards the woman and rose up on his bony knees.

"Groceries," he said. He held the bag out for her to take. "For lady!"

She stared down at him, stone-faced. For a few seconds she did nothing, and then she reached out slowly to take the bag as if this might be a trick and Kenny was going to yank it away at the last second. But Kenny didn't yank it away, and she took the bag and held it up to her heart—or whatever was in its place—her expression unchanged.

"Good," was all she said. Not "sorry I yelled at you," or "you're a fine boy after all," or even a simple "thank you." Just "good," as if that was an adequate thing to say after calling him a monster and a creature and demanding the police.

Kenny popped up to his feet and came running back to me with his usual happy face.

He stood by my side as we stared at the woman, who stared back for only a few seconds more. Then she turned and went to her car, walking slowly as if she knew that "good" wasn't nearly good enough, only she was too stubborn to admit it.

Kenny and I went to our car and got in. I set our bag of groceries on the seat where Mom used to sit and Kenny immediately returned to his video game in the back seat.

I started the car. The little four-cylinder engine sputtered to life.

"Kenny," I said before backing out, glancing at him in the rear-view mirror, "I'm very proud of you. I'll always be proud of you."

"Why?" he asked, not looking up from his game.

"Because," I said, feeling the tears well up in corners of my eyes again as I shifted into reverse. I figured that had to be from the glare of the sun through the windshield, nothing more. "Just because."

## CHAPTER NINETEEN
# THE SOCIETY GIRLS

Of all the cliques in the school, the most talked about and yet annoying has to be the Society Girls. They don't actually call themselves that, of course, but everybody else does. Besides their good looks, fancy clothes, and expensive cars, they're known for their grand entrances to school events, usually just oh-so-fashionably late to draw maximum attention, chatty yet poised in an over-rehearsed sort of way. Their goal was to turn heads—which they always did—and to always be the main topic of conversation wherever they went.

For the most part, Dave and I ignored them, while Onion just rolled her eyes when they went by. We didn't have any particular ill will toward them—we just didn't particularly care about social status in general. I did notice that the more someone berated the Society Girls, the more jealous they seemed, as if they were so incensed by their mere existence they just couldn't let it go. That always made me a little uncomfortable because you have to worry about the one who might decide to finally "do something about it" someday. That was the only time I was glad for the metal detectors at the front doors and the occasional surprise locker inspections.

The oddest thing was, the jealous ones were always the girls, never the guys. Maybe the guys thought the Society Girls were nice to look at even if unapproachable, while some girls were absolutely outraged whenever they were mentioned. Go figure.

The most noticeable among the Society Girls were Julia, Jennifer, and Jeanette, The J's as they were known. The three of them went and did absolutely everything together, which always led to some crass comments about their mutual trips to the washroom.

"They're not The J's. They're the jerks," Dave called them once, not really meaning it.

"You're right. They are," said Onion, who did.

Like I said, go figure, although Onion might have had an extra reason to dislike them since it was one of the Society Girls she had been unfavorably compared to by Freddie the Nerd back when she didn't want me to see her cry.

One afternoon I was in the school library with Onion, where we sometimes met to work on our assignments. Even though the library was as new as the rest of the school, it seemed much older with its dark woodwork and hemmed-in feeling. It even smelled old, but I was sure that was from all the dusty books that hardly came off their shelves. Most students make a beeline for the rows of computers when they came in; few ever bothered with the books.

Onion and I were sitting next to each other at one of the center tables. She was finishing an essay for her English class on one computer and I was researching my Geography paper on another. We were whispering and joking—in low voices, or so I thought—when one of the library ladies came over and shushed us.

"Please keep your voices down. You're disturbing the other students," she said in a not-so-low voice that made several students look up, thereby disturbing them. With her high buttoned-up blouse, granny glasses and hair in a bun, she seemed to identify with her role so much that if you saw her and had to guess her occupation, your first answer would be "librarian" in a living stereotype sort of way.

"Sorry," both Onion and I said simultaneously.

She nodded, apparently satisfied with our immediate apology, and then returned to her desk.

Onion and I worked in silence awhile longer when there was this sudden commotion by the entrance. The J's came grandly through the doors, chatty as always, in voices that sure seemed louder than the ones Onion and I were reprimanded for.

Nearly everyone in the place stared up at them as they strode in, as if we should be honored by their arrival. Most of us looked annoyed except for a couple of freshman guys who seemed enthralled instead.

Onion did her eye roll thing and then looked over at the librarian. "Observe. Any second now," she whispered to me.

The librarian kept her head down, as if she couldn't hear them.

"You've got to be kidding me," Onion whispered as the girls continued to chat quite loud not far from us. "We get chewed out but they don't? Why not?"

I shrugged. "Because they're special?"

I could tell from Onion's immediate dark expression that that wasn't a good answer. Not even close.

Onion waved her hand to get the librarian's attention. It might have been my imagination, but it sure seemed like she was trying hard to ignore Onion, too.

After a few seconds of waving so frantically I thought she was going to fall out of her chair, Onion finally stood up.

"Excuse me," she said in a perfectly clear voice.

The librarian winced, as if she had no choice but to acknowledge her.

"Yes, young lady?" the librarian said, still seated.

Onion pointed at the J's.

"I believe they're much louder than we were. Aren't you going to tell them to keep their voices down, too?" Onion smiled, but it was a snarling kind of smile, not unlike one of Dave's fake, sarcastic ones.

The librarian didn't look where Onion was pointing. Instead, she winced again and clasped her hands in front of her.

"They don't seem so loud," she said, unconvincingly.

"Oh, but you're mistaken," Onion replied over the J's chatter. "They're quite loud. You mean it's all right for them to talk in the library but not us? Seems like a double standard to me."

The librarian slowly stood up, and still not looking where Onion was pointing, wavered a moment as if uncertain and then turned and walked away.

Onion dropped her pointing arm to her side. "You've *got* to be kidding me."

She ever so slowly turned to face the girls, who were standing a scant six feet away from us, lost in their own little chatty world.

"Onion," I said, afraid of what she was going to say and the fallout that would follow.

She reached behind her to give me a stop hand signal.

"Excuse me, ladies! Excuse me!"

The J's paused mid-sentence to look Onion's way with blank faces. Nearly everyone else in the place looked at Onion, too.

"Would you mind keeping your voices down? You're in the library, you know." Onion laughed lightly, as if their chattiness was just a simple oversight.

With that, even the enthralled freshmen looked away, apparently wanting no part of the confrontation about to come.

All three girls frowned. One of them—I couldn't tell you which since I could never keep their names straight—took half a step forward.

"It's none of your beeswax if we talk in the library. You're not the librarian. You don't tell us what to do." She turned back to her friends.

Now it was my turn to wince. I actually felt a little sorry now for them.

Onion took a full step toward them. "Oh, but I think it is my beeswax. Here's the thing. George and I and everyone else here are trying to study. Perhaps that's a foreign concept to you, but that's mainly what people do in the library. They study. They don't stand in the middle of the aisle annoying everyone with their loud gossip. Understand now?"

The girl who spoke gasped. "How dare you! Don't you know who we are?"

I winced again. Of all the things she could have said to Onion that was clearly the worst, as she was about to find out.

"Yes, I do know who you are. You're students here, like me."

One of the girls scoffed. "Hardly."

I saw Onion draw in in a big breath, as if arming herself for the barrage she was about to unleash.

"You know what? You're right. I doubt your grades even come close to measuring up to mine. Believe it or not, that's what we're here for, to get an education. But I guess that's news to you. I've seen you and your exclusive little clique prancing about in your too-tight dresses, designer shoes, and perfect hair and matching manicures, full of your own self-importance, turning your noses up at everyone not part of your shallow, vain little group like we should all bow down before you. Do you have any idea how many people either hate you or make fun of you behind your backs? Why, it's practically the whole school, except maybe for a few fawning freshman boys who don't know any better."

The two freshman boys across from us blushed a little and stared down at their open books.

"What's the purpose of your clique, anyway? To celebrate that your daddies are rich and willing to buy you whatever you want? Is that it? Because as far as I can tell, that's all that really separates you from everyone else, despite how superior you pretend to be. But that's pretty sad, isn't it? It's sad and it's pathetic, and no matter how much money your daddies throw your way, you can't buy dignity or respect no matter where you shop. But I'm afraid that's a lesson you'll never learn because you're still trying, aren't you, still looking for that one thing to buy that will finally give you a sense of genuine self-worth without you having to lift a finger to earn it. Well, here's a news flash for you—it ain't gonna happen. You're wasting your time. Self-respect doesn't come in a bag or a box at any price from any fancy store or boutique. Buy yourselves all the expensive little trinkets you want with your daddy's money, but your exclusive little clique is worthless."

The first girl who spoke came up to Onion, stared hard at her a moment, then threw her arm back to slap Onion's face. Onion easily caught her by the wrist to block the slap. The girl tried with her other arm; Onion caught that one, too. Then the girl struggled to claw at her, but Onion calmly held her in place as the girl squirmed and struggled. Finally, Onion casually tossed her away as if she were inconsequential, the way you might brush off a pesky fly. The girl staggered back, breathing hard through her nose.

"Don't ever talk back to me again. And if I hear any gossip about me—anything at all—I'm blaming the three of you, understand? There will be serious and immediate and unfortunate consequences if there is." Onion stepped forward; the girl stepped back. "You can count on it. Now get out."

The girl spun to face her friends.

"Let's go," she said. "She's obviously crazy."

They marched out single file, faster than they came in, and without any chatter at all.

Onion sat down.

"Now," she said. "Where were we?"

I sighed, wondering what the repercussions of that little speech were going to be despite Onion's warning when a strange thing happened. Someone behind us began to clap, then someone else, then someone else, until everyone but the two freshmen were applauding.

Onion stood up, took two quick little bows to either side of the room—which drew some laughter—then sat down again. The applause died out.

The two freshmen grabbed their books and headed toward the door. They slowed as they passed our table, eyes wide and fixed on Onion and their mouths sagging open.

"*What?*" Onion said, barely looking up at them.

They shook their hands to indicate they didn't want any trouble and hastily departed.

I sat back in my chair and eyed Onion with apprehension.

"*What?*" she said again. She kept her eyes on her computer screen, typing again.

"You're going to pay for that somehow, you know."

She shook her head. "No, I'm not." She still didn't look at me.

"Why not?"

She finally looked my way. "Because they're the Society Girls, that's why. Do you think they're going to admit defeat, that someone finally put them in their place, that they're afraid of me now like they should be? They're going to deny it ever happened no matter who says what, mark my words. But we'll know the truth, won't we? And that's all that really matters."

She paused. "Besides," she added with a satisfied grin, "payback sure is sweet."

I had a sudden thought. "So how long have you been waiting to give that little speech? Ever since that incident in the cafe?"

Onion grinned coyly as if proud of me for figuring that out.

"Maybe," she replied. "All I know for sure is that we won't be hearing from them again."

And as the days and weeks went by and nothing untoward happened, it turned out Onion was right once more.

# CHAPTER TWENTY

# DEATH YET AGAIN

Onion got a strange look on her face and held up an index finger. We had just sat down at our table in the crowded cafe for lunch.

"Wait a minute. Listen! Hear that?"

"Hear what?" asked Dave.

I instantly knew what Onion was talking about. "I hear it. Something's up."

It was one of those unusual times when you could hear and feel and see it all around, that slight electric buzz that says something big has happened or is about to happen. Maybe it was the way people were hunched together at the tables, or standing in small groups rather than sitting, or the "floaters" who were moving methodically from one table to another as if on a mission to spread the news, whatever it was.

One of those floater-messengers appeared at our table. I knew that whatever the news was, it must be pretty big because our messenger was a tall metal-head wearing all black and sporting an ugly neck tattoo, someone I don't think the three of us had ever spoken to. He stood there grimly, like an angel of death or something, staring darkly down at us as if what he was about to say would forever change our world. His black shirt even had an ominous flaming skull above the name of some heavy metal rock band

I never heard of, as if our messenger knew this morning when he got dressed that he would be delivering awful news.

"Yes?" Onion finally asked, sounding more annoyed than curious.

"Did you guys know Maggie Sutherland?"

I shook my head. Dave shrugged. We glanced at each other, drawing a blank.

"Yeah, I know her. Well, sort of," Onion backtracked. "I went to grade school with her. We haven't talked in years."

I guess Dave and I still looked clueless, so Onion helped us out. "She's the short little cheerleader with the long curly hair who only smiles when she's cheerleading."

"Oh, yeah," I said, remembering her now. In four years, I had walked by her maybe a dozen times. Onion was right—she never smiled.

"So what about her?" Onion asked.

Our messenger's eyes flashed.

"She's dead."

Onion took a short, sharp breath. "What happened?"

Our black-clad messenger hesitated, almost as if savoring the suspense. "Her dad found her body in her room last night. They think she had a heart attack from being anorexic. They said she only weighed seventy-five pounds, all skin and bones."

He said that last part with a kind of creepy satisfaction.

"Wow," said Onion, looking away from all of us.

I didn't know what to say. Dave didn't say anything either.

Our heavy metal death messenger nodded once, his terrible message delivered, then turned to continue spreading the news.

"Another dead one," Dave said flatly. He stared down at his empty coffee cup.

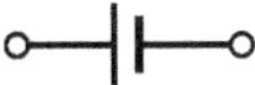

Unlike the private funeral for Paul, the line at the funeral home where Maggie was being waked went out the door and around the block. Most of the mourners were students, with just a sprinkling of teachers and other adults. Since Onion knew Maggie's parents, she thought it would be disrespectful not to go but didn't want to go alone. Dave couldn't or wouldn't attend, so it was just me and Onion. I think Dave had had enough of death for one year. Onion had borrowed her mother's car to get us there.

As we waited in the slow-moving line, we heard all the cliché remarks about "another death in the family," that we've "lost two in a row now," and "much too soon," and so on and so on. When we finally arrived at the front of the room, I could see there were flowers absolutely everywhere, with more still arriving.

As we crept our way forward to the front, we could see that Maggie was dressed in her cheerleader outfit, with two pompons on either side of her.

"Oh, no," Onion whispered to me in surprising indignation. "Our cheerleaders don't use pompons! That's the pompon squad! Don't they know the difference?"

"Do you want to tell her parents that, or would you prefer to yank the pompons out yourself?" I replied softly. "Let her parents bury her the way they want to. It's none of our business."

As we grew still closer to the open casket, I saw that like with most dead people, her face had been painted a living hue that wasn't quite accurate, as if they had tried to make her look natural in death but hadn't quite succeeded.

Then it was finally our turn to kneel in front of her if we wanted to say a silent prayer or goodbye or whatever.

"Go ahead," Onion said quietly. "I'll wait here."

Since I thought it would be rude if neither of us went, I kind of lumbered forward and knelt.

Up close, her tightly closed mouth was just as I remembered her from our few hallway encounters since I don't think she ever said a word to me. What was most unsettling though was how sunken her cheeks looked, probably the reason for the heavy-handed makeup. I guess not eating would do that to you.

I bowed my head, figuring that people were watching me. At least, it felt like all eyes were staring at the back of my head, true or not.

*So long, Maggie. Sorry you didn't eat enough.*

I stood up. Then, as if it were irresistible, I slowly reached out and touched her peaceful, folded hands with my fingertips—why, I didn't know.

Her hands were shockingly cold, like she had been in a freezer or something. I instinctively snapped my arm away, realizing almost immediately that if anything looked rude, that sure did. I swallowed hard to keep from make a sound as I backed away, wondering now if my mom would have been as cold had I responded to her beckoning hand and given her a hug the day she died.

When I returned to Onion's side, I half expected to see at least a few scornful faces for that bizarre action. Instead, no one seemed to be paying any attention at all.

Except Onion.

"What was that all about?" she asked quietly.

Two people brushed wordlessly past us to take my place by the casket.

"Nothing," I whispered back, still a bit rattled. "Her hands were ice cold, that's all. I was surprised."

"Well of course they're cold!" she whispered, louder than she had to. "What did you expect? She's a stiff! With no heartbeat or circulation, metabolism is no longer possible and hence no body heat is produced. As a result, the body cools down to the ambient air temperature. Sometimes that process is accelerated by the embalming fluids the mortician uses to replace the blood, depending how soon the body is prepared for viewing. Didn't you listen to *anything* they tried to teach you in anatomy?"

I cringed throughout her explanation as I frantically signaled her to not to whisper so loud.

"Will you keep it down?" I tried not to raise my voice, too, as I glanced around, desperately hoping no one was eavesdropping on our conversation. To my relief, no one was.

I took one last look at Maggie before we moved on to express our condolences to her family. It suddenly seemed strange that I would never see her walk by me again. Even though we were never friends, the hallways were going to be yet another person empty now, just a little less crowded in a sad sort of way.

I never know what to say to family members at a funeral. Sometimes I'll listen to what the people in front of me say so I don't repeat it and sound like a lame copycat, but no matter what I finally blurt out, I always manage to sound lame anyway.

It was finally our turn to greet the family, her mother and father first. Since I had never met either of them before, I wasn't going to throw my arms around them like I had seen a few of the cheerleaders do. The only reason I knew who all the cheerleaders were was because they had shown up wearing their uniforms in an obvious show of camaraderie. That was a nice touch, although an expected one.

Onion nudged me to go first.

I politely shook Mrs. Sutherland's hand. "So sorry for your loss," I said, not having heard that from anyone ahead of me.

Fortunately, that didn't sound too terribly lame.

She shook my hand rather mechanically, having already shaken what must have been hundreds of hands before me with hundreds more to come. I know wakes are meant to give survivors a chance to find some closure in addition to honoring the dead, but a long, crowded one like this had to be really grueling. So I wasn't upset at all when she just gave a faint sigh in response, her expression totally blank as if she had not only run out of words but emotions, too.

Mr. Sutherland was another story. He still had his emotions, all right—he looked angry and on edge, as if somehow this was all our fault, and here we were back at the scene of the crime. He fixed me with smoldering, bloodshot eyes, ones that nearly made me admit guilt by looking away rather than continue to return his gaze.

I was hesitant to shake his hand, afraid of being caught in a relentless bone-crushing grip, but I didn't want to seem impolite at a time like this, and so I took a chance and stuck out my hand.

His grip was surprisingly soft, and I realized he had no idea of the anger he was projecting.

I relaxed a bit. "Sorry about your daughter. I wish . . . I wish it could have been me instead."

If I could have done a face-palm without anyone noticing, I would have. Where on Earth did that come from? I didn't dare look at Onion to see her reaction.

Mr. Sutherland looked startled and his entire appearance softened. "Thank you. But I don't even know who you are."

"I'm George," I said.

"Oh," he said brightly, as if his daughter had spoken about me all the time, when in reality I don't think his daughter even knew my name.

Mr. Sutherland's expression turned profoundly sad and his shoulders dipped low. "I'm glad it wasn't you, George. This shouldn't happen to anyone. She lost weight so gradually, so slowly, and you think, 'look, she's still just your little girl . . .'"

For a few seconds nothing happened, and then he threw his arms around me and squeezed a bit too hard.

I stepped aside so Onion could face him. Her eyes were wide open as if she were stunned.

"So sorry," she said simply, then briefly touched his arm.

And she turned to look at me as if I had sprouted wings or something.

A few steps away was a young boy who sat on the floor playing with some toy cars. He looked to be no more than four or five. So close to Maggie's parents, the boy could only be Maggie's little brother. He was wearing black dress pants and a white shirt with a red bowtie. The mourners streaming by ignored him.

I squatted down to say hello.

"Say, that's a spiffy bowtie. Wish I had one like that."

He shrugged and kept pushing two of the cars across the carpet.

"Are they having a race?"

"Yep." He kept his focus on his cars.

"Who's winning?"

"This one." He paused and pointed to a blue car.

"Oh. Does he have a name?"

"Bluey."

"That makes sense."

He smiled a little, but still wouldn't look up.

"Is that your favorite car?"

"Yep."

I decided this conversation was much better than talking about what happened to his sister.

"Do you have lots of cars?"

"Yep. I only brought four of them. Daddy said that was enough."

"Is that how old you are?"

He nodded.

"Well, then, that's one for every birthday you've ever had, isn't it?"

His face brightened as he realized that was true.

"Say, I'll bet you brought your fastest cars, didn't you?"

He nodded again, more vigorously.

"Well, good luck and keep racing, okay? I hope Bluey wins."

He finally looked up at me.

"Okay. My name is Tommy. What's your name?"

"I'm George."

He stuck out his little hand.

"Well, thanks for coming to see my dead sister, George."

As we shook, I had to catch myself with my other hand to keep from falling backwards.

"Of course, Tommy. I'm so very sorry."

He went back to pushing his cars and then paused.

"George, do you think Maggie is in heaven now like everybody says?"

"Sure. What do you think?"

He looked up at me with a worried expression.

"I don't know where heaven is so I won't see her anymore."

I had no answer for that.

Tommy went back to his cars.

"Goodbye, Tommy. Take good care of yourself, and your family. I'm sure that's what your sister would have wanted. Okay?

"Okay."

I briefly patted his head, hoping to offer a bit more comfort than I could in words.

When I stood up and turned around, I was startled to see tears running freely down Onion's cheeks.

"Come on," she said. She practically pushed me out of building.

When we got outside, she glanced around then kissed me hard on the lips, bending me backwards.

Then she grabbed me by the lapels and shook me.

"I never kissed you, got it?"

"Well, I . . ." I didn't dare make a move to wipe the slobber running down my chin, a combination of spit and tears.

"You're a sweet, sensitive guy, but if you ever tell anyone I said that you'll really be sorry. Understand?"

"Sure, uh—"

"Good."

And she let me go.

I followed her to her mother's car, hastily wiping my face with my handkerchief only when I certain she wasn't looking.

We got in the car and she drove me wordlessly home, sniffing from time to time. When I got out, she raced away before I barely had the chance to close the door.

That was the first and only time Onion kissed me, or even paid me a nice compliment. And since it was always wise to take Onion's threats seriously, we never spoke about it again, just as she demanded. But it was something I'll never forget.

That night I wrote a short poem about what happed to Maggie. Like my poem about the anxious soldier at The Post, I'm not sure why I wrote it, but here it is:

> THIN IS IN
> "Pity the starving"
> He sighs at his party,
> While an unknown diet
> Rages in his daughter's room.

CHAPTER TWENTY-ONE
# GOODBYE, CRYSTAL

Dave finally showed up at our table in the cafe before the first bell, a strange little smirk on his face.

"Where have you been?" I asked. "You didn't have any breakfast."

He plopped his backpack down but remained standing. "Lady and gentleman. Some scuttlebutt for you. The police are here."

Both Onion and I hardly reacted to the news. The police had shown up at The Big Brown Box almost too many times to count for all kinds of reasons, either to conduct some random search or in response to an altercation of some kind.

"So what?" Onion said. "That's not scuttlebutt."

The little smirk remained on Dave's face.

"Ah, but it involves one of our most prominent students, none other than Crystal Lee. You know, Miss Wholesome Popularity, whose thorough wholesomeness actually makes my spine tingle." Dave wiggled a bit as if his spine was tingling right then.

Onion and I looked at each other.

"Wow," Onion said. "I take it back. That *is* scuttlebutt."

If anyone was "Miss Wholesome Popularity" at The Big Brown Box, it was Crystal Lee. Besides movie-star attractiveness, she had an uncanny knack for always being at the right place at the right time to garner all the attention. She was elected Homecoming

Queen by a landslide both times she ran for the honor, and nearly every issue of the school paper had at least one picture of her in it somewhere. That was probably because she was on the editorial staff, not to mention editor of the yearbook, co-captain of the girls' volleyball team, co-founder of the recycling committee, drama club treasurer, assistant to the after-school coordinator, student activities vice president and the secretary of the student government association.

She was such an endless flurry of activity, she made the rest of us look lethargic by comparison. How she found time to go to class and do homework I had no idea.

The one time I ever spoke to her, I realized what everybody meant when they said that conversations with her were mainly one-sided. I had just won a surprise award for "Best School Library Patron," one of those annual "feel good" awards that really didn't mean anything but was appreciated nonetheless. There had been an announcement over the intercom asking me to report to the library, no reason given. Naturally, I assumed I had done something wrong and went immediately, only to be pleasantly surprised (and relieved) when the library staff surrounded me and broke the good news.

No sooner did they hand me the award than Crystal appeared by my side out of nowhere as my picture was being taken for the school paper. She wore a smile so wide I thought her face had to hurt. I didn't think facial muscles could stretch that far.

"Congratulations!" she said, shaking my hand as the photo was snapped of the two of us together, as if she had either given me the award or was receiving it herself. "I won this award two years ago!"

"Oh! So, we have something in common," I said.

While her bright, eager expression didn't falter, I could see from her non-comprehending eyes in the brief moment she looked at me that we actually had nothing in common.

She turned away to face the small but appreciative crowd. "I think our library staff is the just the best ever, don't you agree? Woo-hoo!" She made a little fist and waved it around in a circle. The library staff and the few others in attendance tittered in approval and applauded.

I noticed that she kept her eyes on the audience as if to make sure everyone understood what she had to say was all that really mattered, as if I were no longer there.

"Just as a reminder, I'm trying to collect enough recycling materials to buy more library books soon, so keep on recycling, people! Woo!"

Everyone applauded again. Now that she had their full attention, Crystal had wandered off a bit, distancing herself even further from me. I wondered if I should take my award and slink away since I had apparently been dismissed.

"I would also like to take this opportunity to invite everyone to tomorrow's night home volleyball game. If we win, we're in the playoffs, so let's have a real good turnout, okay? Woo!"

More applause.

"Thank you, everyone! See you tomorrow night in the gym! Thank you!"

As she left, a small crowd of admirers formed around her and she took them with her out the door.

Nearly alone with my award, I did slink away, wondering what just happened yet knowing the answer.

Crystal happened.

"You know, I'm not convinced she's actually a student," Onion said. "I think she's here just to be popular."

"So what did she do that the police had to show up?" I asked Dave. "Kill somebody more popular than her?"

Dave laughed. "Nope. Some other sort of scandal. Besides, there's nobody more popular than her. She'll tell you that herself."

Onion's eyes widened. "Ooh, give us all the juicy details. Don't stop now."

Dave shrugged. "Unfortunately, that's all I know."

Onion slumped back in her chair. "Well, you're no use. You can't announce something like that and not have more information."

Dave sat down heavily as if dejected. "Sorry. Guess I'm not a very good sleuth." His face suddenly brightened. "Hey! We could always start a few nasty rumors about her and all that, see how far they'll spread. That's lots of fun."

Onion tossed a sugar pack at him. "You're not only useless, you're despicable."

Dave feigned a bright smile. "Why, thank you. That's my middle name." He yawned and stretched, but it sure didn't look authentic. "Never mind, then. I'm sure there's a perfectly good reason why the FBI showed up, too."

Onion and I looked at each other and then at him in shock.

"The FBI?" Onion finally said. "You didn't say anything about the FBI. What did they want?"

Dave shrugged. "Haven't the foggiest. I saw a bunch of them in Morgan's office with the police. They just left."

"How do you know they were the FBI?" I asked.

He gave me a scornful look. "Gosh, I'm not sure. Was it because they were wearing jackets with tall yellow 'FBI' letters written on the back? Yeah, that must be it."

Onion's gaze grew distant, as if she were contemplating that. "Weird," she said. "Maybe somebody is harassing or stalking her," I suggested.

"Could be," Dave replied. "Maybe her life is in danger."

Onion's eyes widened. "Whoa. Intriguing."

And with that, the first bell rang and our speculation ended. It wasn't until later that morning that news about the FBI visit spread, along with all kinds of expected and not-so-expected rumors about what they wanted with Crystal.

Dave laughed at one he overheard in a hallway. "Somehow, I just can't picture her robbing a bank," he said. "Besides, her parents are super rich. They give her everything her little heart desires. She's their precious little spine-tingling princess, you know." He wiggled a bit again.

Usually rumors like that would run out of steam and die the death they deserved. But for some reason, they grew in intensity, with people going out of their way to ask each other what was happening, if there was any fresh news. Freshmen, seniors, it didn't matter—the buzz was constant and heavy.

"It's like everyone's holding their breath, waiting for some big, official announcement," Dave observed at our next break in the cafe. "You can cut the suspense with a knife."

"Yeah," Onion agreed. "Somebody knows something, but they're barely talking."

When a police car pulled up to the front door at lunch hour and a cop in uniform and an FBI agent wearing a jacket just as Dave described hurried to Morgan's office, a small crowd drifted by from the cafe to catch a glimpse through his office window to see what was happening. Sad to say, that crowd included Dave, Onion, and me. Most of the girls stood with sour expressions like there was a bad smell in the air, as if expecting to hear the worst.

Morgan came out to put a stop to our gawking.

"Move along, everyone. Nothing to see here."

And he returned to talk to his visitors.

I followed Dave and Onion back to the cafe. To our surprise, coming down the hallway straight towards us was Crystal, head bowed with her hands shading her face, being escorted by two teachers as if they had been assigned as her bodyguards. I couldn't tell if she had been crying, but she sure seemed upset as she went by.

The teachers escorted her directly to Morgan's office then turned around and left once she was safely inside. Morgan sure didn't look too happy to see her. Neither did the cop or the FBI agent. Crystal stood there subdued, head still bowed, not at all her usual extroverted self. We could tell she was getting a few harsh words from Morgan even though we couldn't hear a word behind the closed door.

"Strange," Onion said. "I wonder what that's all about."

As if to explain, Morgan opened the door and let the cop and the agent escort Crystal back down the hall.

"Come on," Dave said. "Let's go the long way to see where they're taking her."

We hurried around the cafe like the three unabashed curiosity seekers we were. Since it was lunch, all the hall monitors were in the cafe, making our sleuthing easier.

As we peered around the corner, we saw Crystal standing in front of her locker, her escorts on either side as if expecting her to try to escape. Standing nearby was one of the school's maintenance men with an enormous pair of bolt cutters. Crystal defiantly crossed her arms. The FBI agent whispered something to her and she firmly shook her head, refusing to even look at him.

The agent then nodded to the maintenance worker. "Cut it open on my authority," he said.

The maintenance worker clipped the combination lock off the locker as if it the lock was made of wax. The cut lock fell to the floor and the maintenance man gave it a little kicked out of the way.

The agent opened the locker and began pulling everything out. He stuffed it all into a large plastic garbage bag the maintenance man handed him. The agent's expression was stony, as if the task were distasteful. I saw he was wearing clear vinyl gloves like the ones we wore in biology lab, like Crystal's stuff was dangerous or contaminated somehow.

"Really weird," Onion said. "This just gets stranger and stranger."

We saw a small group of girls walking slowly down the hall from the other direction, approaching cautiously. One of them I recognized as a friend of Crystal's. She was talking in a low tone, her lips pursed as if reluctant to say anything.

Onion marched over to join them. The group stopped in a circle a respectful distance away from the peculiar scene by the locker. When Crystal's friend finished whispering, there were a few faint cries and the girls quickly flew apart, almost as if something appalling had appeared right in the middle of them and they had to get away.

Onion walked back to us, her expression dark.

"Uh oh," Dave said. "This can't be good, whatever it is."

Onion didn't say a word. Instead, she stared with concern at the filled garbage bag as the FBI agent tied it shut.

"Well?" Dave finally asked. "Say something, will you? Don't leave us floundering like this."

Onion hesitated. Before she could answer, the FBI agent ushered Crystal toward the rear exit. I finally noticed the squad car with the lights flashing by the doors. As they approached us, I saw Crystal's hands shaking as she held them up in a kind of weak, scared surrender. For some reason I couldn't take my eyes off them.

This time I didn't shrink away like I had at Homecoming when I saw Sam's trembling hands. Instead, I boldly stepped forward and grabbed her right hand with both of mine. The FBI agent and policemen gave me cold gazes but didn't shoo me away.

"Whatever this is all about, you'll get through it just fine. I know you will, Crystal."

She stared at me with wide doe eyes, as if seeing me for the first time. To my surprise, her hands stopped shaking. I was glad about that.

"Thank you," she said. The words were soft, but it was the most sincere thank you I had ever heard.

I nodded and let her hand go, sensing that was what the FBI agent was about to order me to do. She stared back at me a few seconds as they continued on their way, her look of amazement still there.

I returned to where Dave and Onion stood with somber faces.

"Why did you do that?" Onion asked. "I thought you didn't even like her."

There was no way I could begin to explain it since I didn't quite understand it myself.

I shrugged. "I don't know. I guess I thought she could use some encouragement."

Onion nodded but still seemed puzzled.

Dave shook his head and gave a little huff in exasperation as if none of that mattered. "So what's going on already? Talk."

Once again Onion hesitated.

"It's about . . . sexting."

"*Sexting*?" David said. He staggered back in apparent disbelief. "Little Miss Wholesome was *sexting*?"

Onion looked at Dave with a humorless expression. "Yes. For years. And for a price."

Dave gasped.

"What does that mean?" I asked.

"She had clients. Older men, mostly. Some out of state. They paid her to pose. The cops took her stuff looking for evidence."

"Why? She didn't need the money," Dave said.

Onion took a deep breath. "I don't think it was about the money."

"For the thrill?" I suggested.

"That or maybe the sugar daddy money was really good," Dave replied. "I mean, *really* good."

"No," Onion said. "You're both wrong. It was to be popular."

There was a moment of silence. Unfortunately, I realized Onion was right. This was all about being popular.

"So why was the FBI involved?" I asked.

"George, Crystal just turned eighteen."

"So?"

She gave me an incredulous look. So did Dave.

"She was a minor. Underage. Don't you get it?"

It finally dawned on me. "So this was all about . . ." I couldn't say the words.

"Right," Dave said. "Child porn. Manufacturing and distributing across state lines for a price. She's in big, big trouble."

"Yes, indeed," Onion said. "But like you said, her parents are rich. I'm sure they'll pay for a top-notch lawyer to defend her."

"Yeah, but even if she goes scot-free, her reputation is totally shot," Dave said. "We'll never see her around here again."

"Are you sure?" I said. "People forgive and move on."

I wasn't exactly rooting for her since I hardly knew her—it was just that it would be strange not having her around to hog all the limelight.

Onion looked at me. "Dave's right. She won't be back. With someone like her, popularity isn't everything, it's the only thing. She'll never enjoy the same level of popularity she once did, not after this."

Dave went over and picked up the discarded, now useless lock. He looked at the cleanly cut shank, shook his head and tossed the lock into a trashcan. Then he went and gently closed the still-open locker.

"Goodbye, Crystal. Turns out we hardly knew ya. Hope you really can recover from this someday," he said.

"Oh, how the mighty have fallen," Onion said.

I said nothing as we stared at the locker door. The only thing I could think was that their words were my own thoughts exactly.

# CHAPTER TWENTY-TWO

# DAVE'S PETULANCE CATCHES UP WITH HIM

Dave either revered or reviled the teachers in our Big Brown Box. There was no middle ground.

Among the teachers he revered was Goodman, our English teacher. He was about as anti-establishment as you can get without actually going to jail. Dave and Goodman were two of a kind, and it was the only class where Dave paid rapt, wide-eyed attention to every word our teacher said, like a first-time altar boy or something. It probably helped that they both had impressive beards and were "big-boned" guys. Maybe Dave saw himself in Goodman thirty years from now, although Dave once said he would rather drill his own teeth than be a teacher. Still, plans and people can change, and if Dave ever did find himself in front of a class of high school kids, I'm sure he would carry on Goodman's take-no-prisoners attitude.

The other reason Dave liked Goodman was because Dave discovered early on that he could steer the classroom discussion to political issues pretty easily—in fact, Goodman not only seemed to encourage it, he looked positively delighted when Dave "reminded" us how corrupt politicians were, or bankers, or billionaires, or some other bourgeois group. Just a few words from Dave along those lines usually meant that whatever else we were discussing went out the window for the rest of the class. Dave usually tried to find a link between whatever author we were reading and some current issue—whether there was a connection or not—and Goodman was more than willing to go along until the bell rang. While their lively discussion often had nothing to do with Hemingway, Steinbeck, or Faulkner, the main advantage was that not only did Goodman forget to collect the homework assignments, he often forgot to give one as well.

Needless to say, not only was Dave getting a triple A-plus from Goodman, he was really popular with everyone in the class for making the class such a breeze. I think quite a few of us actually stopped reading the books we were supposed to, knowing that Dave would save the day by getting Goodman to launch into some anti-government tirade for half an hour or more.

The exact opposite of Goodman was Jorgenson, our Geography teacher.

To describe Dave's relationship with Jorgenson as sort of antagonist was like saying Captain Ahab didn't much care for that particular white whale. Not only did Dave hate Geography, but Jorgenson's style of teaching went back to medieval times, when students were flogged (I think) for giving wrong answers or not showing up on time. What really got Dave in trouble with Jorgenson and the other strict teachers was the usual problem with Dave—he was a pusher. No, not drugs. What Dave pushed were boundaries. And rules, regulations, and everyone's patience. Dave seemed to find it highly amusing to be not a totally destructive force, but a vaguely disruptive one, just enough to be hauled in for general misbehavior every now and then but not enough to be suspended or expelled.

"Do you ever stop with the sarcasm?" I asked him once, after a particularly annoying needling from him just because I had blanked out for a few minutes over what my locker combination was.

He smiled his devious smile. "Of course not. It's an art, a specialty. A calling, if you will."

"Well, whatever it is, someday it's really going to bite you in the butt."

He merely shrugged, as I might have expected.

One day Dave, Onion, and I were tooling around town in Dave's car, doing nothing in particular. Onion in front, me in the back behind her, our usual traveling configuration.

It was one of those nights without a breeze, the trees standing perfectly still as if holding their breaths, and flags head down, bat-like, as if asleep on their poles. If time could be frozen, it might look like this. The only thing moving was Dave's car as we rolled through the neighborhood, making our own brief breeze and commotion as we went by, like a time machine just passing through.

It would have been a shame to stay at home on a night like this and study for a history test, even if it was tomorrow.

Dave was in one of his usual moods, talkative and sardonic.

"Onion. What do you know about Jorgy?"

I had to think a few seconds before I realized Dave was asking about Jorgenson. Dave was the only one who called him that.

"I had his class. He's okay, I guess." Onion said. "He can be full of himself and pretty boring, but I've had worse."

"He's a jerk," Dave said. "A real jerk."

"Why?" Onion and I asked together.

"Because I'm getting a D-minus and deserve at least a B, that's why."

I was taking Jorgenson's class with Dave and didn't know until right then that Dave was on the verge of flunking, although I couldn't say I was surprised.

Onion half laughed and half gasped. "That's your fault. Do the homework. And turn it in on time." She gave Dave a scornful look. "Jorgenson hates late homework. You should know that by now."

Dave shrugged as if that shouldn't matter. He was notorious for turning in assignments late, with every excuse imaginable and a few that were hard to imagine.

Some teachers didn't care; others, like Jorgenson, apparently did.

"Why do we have to learn about those obscure Pacific land masses, anyway? It's not like we're ever going to vacation in the Marquesas Islands or some weird foreign place like that." He made the whole idea sound preposterous.

Half the time I couldn't tell if Dave was jesting or if he was semi-serious. This was one of those times.

Onion laughed. "So all you want to know about is the United States? Or maybe just our state? That's pretty narrow-minded, Dave."

He grinned, and I realized Onion had fallen for his ruse.

"Yeah, that's it! The good old U S of A. We don't need no stinkin' foreign islands. Away with foreign islands, that's what I say! America for Americans! Don't tread on me! Love it or leave it! We're number one, we're number one! USA! USA! USA!"

Onion sighed and looked away, aware now that she had been had.

Dave continued, like a bobblehead in a particularly good mood. "It's amazing how seemingly intelligent people can be so naive, isn't it, George? You know, those overly studious types who, despite their tremendous book knowledge, deep insights, and outstanding grades, can still be so gullible in such a cute and charming—"

Onions arms went up in the air. "*That's it!* Stop the car."

"What?" Dave seemed genuinely surprised.

"You heard me. *Stop.* Right here!"

Dave obeyed, a little faster than he had to. I grabbed the door handle to stay in place as the tires screeched. All Dave's books and junk slid off the seat next to me onto the floor.

Onion got out, slamming the door behind her.

Both Dave and I stared at her in astonishment as she marched to the sidewalk and walked away.

Dave pulled closer to the side of the road and kept pace with her.

"Hey! What's wrong with the USA?" he asked. "Are you a godless commie or something?"

She kept marching along, silent, head down.

I watched her walk, her knee-length skirt swaying, her calf muscles flexing with every step. A faint breeze had stirred up, and wisps of hair swirled behind her neck.

I thought she looked beautiful under the streetlights as she entered and exited them one by one, like spotlights on a runway for models, although I wouldn't have dared tell her so. That would have changed too much between us, and I didn't want anything to change.

Dave stuck his head out the window and spoke in an aged, creepy voice. "Say, little girl. Would you like a ride? How about some candy? How about both?"

She slowed, then stopped and turned to face him.

"You know, that's your whole problem right there, isn't it? Anything for a cheap laugh, even if it's disgusting." She put her hands on her hips.

He looked nonplussed and his creepy voice continued. "Hey, I'm not cheap. I'll have you know I have very expensive tastes. Like you." Then his normal voice returned and he sounded serious. "Look. We're in the middle of nowhere, Onion. You can't just walk home. It's way too far. You'll never make it."

She hesitated, then relented and got back in the car.

Dave beamed, as if proud of himself. "I really ticked you off, didn't I?"

"Yes. You can be rude and crude. And mean, too."

We sped up away from the curb, back to our mindless meandering.

"I'm not mean. I'm just charmingly pointless and witty." He grinned a big fake grin.

"More like witless," Onion countered. "Or a halfwit."

"Better a halfwit than a nitwit."

She laughed a little, and after that, things returned to normal. Or at least what passed for normal among the three of us.

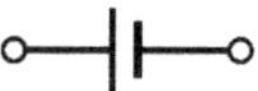

We were in Jorgenson's class the next day, waiting for him to show up. Dave sat next to me in his usual chair in the back row, randomly tapping his pen on his desktop. "Five more minutes and I'm out of here," he said.

There was supposedly some unwritten rule that if a teacher was fifteen minutes late to class, you could bail without any repercussions. I had never known anyone actually take advantage of that rule—if it even really existed—although it wouldn't have surprised me in the least if Dave was soon to be the first.

A minute later, Dave sighed exceptionally loud. No one paid any attention.

He cleared his throat as if to make a serious pronouncement. "You know, Jorgenson keeps telling us he's an original thinker. I wonder how original he really is."

That was true. Jorgenson often said he could have done a better job writing our textbook than its author since he had "better insights" into the material. It did seem rather boastful in an unabashed sort of way.

Dave went on. "You know what? I think that Jorgenson is so original, if he ever owns a male and female dog, he'll probably name them named Adam and Eve!" Dave beamed a fake look of adoration.

A few in the classroom tittered softly.

"Better yet, if he ever gets married and has three daughters, I'll bet he names them April, May, and June!" Dave banged a fist on his desktop. "Now *that's* original!"

The class tittered a little louder.

Dave slumped a bit, still bored despite his effort to amuse himself, and then slipped off his new class ring to take a look at it. We had gotten our rings last week and most of us were wearing them, at least until the novelty wore off.

Dave gave me a sly grin the way he always did when something mischievous occurred to him.

"Watch this, George."

He set his ring face down on the desktop and gave it a twirl. It spun and wobbled in a small circle.

"My name is of no consequence," he said, mimicking the line in The Movie.

I laughed in spite of myself. Dave had nailed the voice. "Very funny."

Then Jorgenson burst in the room, his face flushed and contorted in anger.

A few people jumped in their chairs. Dave jammed his ring back on his finger.

"Sorry," Jorgenson said. "Everything that could go wrong did on my way here this morning."

"Everything?" Dave asked, eyes mockingly wide. "You mean you hit somebody with your car and kept on going? A hit and run?"

Two or three people in the class covered their mouths.

I winced. Dave seemed totally oblivious to people's moods whenever he spoke up. As flustered as Jorgenson was, this was a particularly bad time for Dave to be pushing his luck.

Fortunately, Jorgenson ignored him as if he hadn't heard. I was hoping for Dave's sake that Jorgenson realized by now that Dave seldom said anything serious in class unless he was the one leading the conversation.

Jorgenson pulled a handkerchief of his pocket and dabbed at his shiny forehead. "All right. Let's make up for lost time. Pull out your homework. I want to hear what you wrote last night."

There was a flurry of activity all around as backpacks unzipped, books opened, and papers rustled into view.

I winced again. Jorgenson had given us this ridiculously pointless assignment to compare and contrast South Pacific islands, even though they seemed pretty much all the same to me. I had only managed to write a few sentences before giving up. Then I glanced around and realized that I wasn't the only one to have less than half a page of answers. Normally that would have been reassuring, but under the circumstances it didn't seem like such a good thing.

Then I noticed that Dave had nothing in front of him at all.

When I questioned him with a puzzled look, he gave me a little shrug and grin.

"Mr. Wells!" Jorgenson stared straight at me. "Name one of the most significant differences between the Pacific islands we studied."

Surprised to be singled out so quickly, I looked down at my scant handwriting.

"Um, some are volcanic landscapes while others have more vegetation?"

I had actually written that answer, but wish I hadn't said it in the form of a question.

Jorgenson seemed satisfied. "Good. That's one answer. Kathy?" He looked across the room at one of the few girls in the class.

"Uh, some are more mountainous than others?"

She answered in the form of a question, too. I was beginning to hope I hadn't started an unfortunate trend.

"Correct," Jorgenson said curtly. "Let's hear some other answers. Raise your hands, people."

No hands went up. Jorgenson waited, scanning the room. His frustration quickly returned, not that it seemed to have ever really left.

"Oh, come on, people! You've had all week to work on this. There are at least a dozen more."

Still no hands went up.

Jorgenson took a deep breath. "Fine. I'll call on someone." He looked about for his next victim.

*Please don't call on Dave*, I thought. Dave sat perfectly still, still nothing in front of him.

Jorgenson stepped forward, focused now on Dave's empty desk. "Mr. Baker. That's odd. You don't seem to have the assignment in front of you. Where is it?"

"Oh. The assignment," Dave said, as if he just understood what it was the rest of us had on our desks. He raised an index finger. "Just a sec."

To my surprise, Dave reached down and pulled a sheet of paper out of his geography book on the floor beside him.

It was all I could do not to react when I saw that the paper was blank; Dave was going to try to fake his way through it.

"Well!" Dave said brightly, staring at the empty sheet. "I believe some islands are much prettier than others, with double rainbows when it rains." He positively beamed.

There was a faint, collective inward rush of air throughout the class, a kind of mass gasp in reverse, then silence.

Jorgenson eyes narrowed, his lips pursed so tight it looked like he didn't have any.

"No?" Dave said, apparently too stupid to see that Jorgenson was on the verge of ballistic. "Well, then, maybe some of the islands are better tourist traps than others. They might sell carved coconuts, refrigerator magnets, key chains, bumper stickers . . . you know, just all kind of useless junk."

The silence was now deafening.

Dave blithely continued his suicidal commentary.

"How about Gilligan, then? You know, that three-hour tour. Gilligan, the Skipper, too. The millionaire and his wife. The movie star. The professor and Mary Ann. Maybe they're on one of those islands. But hey, they've all gotta be skeletons by now, right? That was way back in the sixties!"

Everyone looked like their heads were going to explode from trying not to laugh, their eyes bugging out.

Jorgenson came down the aisle towards Dave, walking slowly with a stiff gait like a mechanical man or something, like he was so angry his knees wouldn't bend.

"Let me see that paper." His voice was surprisingly soft and calm, even though I noticed with alarm that his hands were trembling.

For some reason I couldn't take my eyes off those hands. They were fascinating and terrifying at the same time.

Dave balled it up tight. "You can't. It's . . . incomplete. I'm sure I can do much better."

Jorgenson arrived at Dave's chair, breathing hard through his nostrils, and actually pried the balled paper away, although Dave didn't put up much of a fight.

Jorgenson carefully opened it and glanced at both sides.

"This paper is blank. It's a blank paper."

It was spoken more as a statement of fact than an accusation.

"Yes. Yes, it is. Guilty as charged, Your Honor. I throw myself on the mercy of the court. Or something like that."

Jorgenson didn't respond for what seemed like an eternity.

"You think this is all a joke? That this class is a *joke*?"

The last word was spoken so loud, everyone flinched. Except Dave.

"No, sir. Not at all. I'm sure we'll all find what you're teaching immensely useful someday. I'm just not sure when."

If I could have disappeared straight through a hole in the floor I would have.

There was another long pause.

"Get out. Pick up all of your belongings and get out. I'm talking to Principal Morgan right after class about having you suspended if not expelled for your endless, mocking behavior."

Dave nonchalantly gathered up his stuff and looked at Jorgenson as if contemplating yet another snide remark.

"Dave," I said, my hands folded politely in front of me on my desk. "Shut. Up."

Jorgenson shot an angry glance my way. "*Quiet*, Wells."

Dave wisely took my advice, got up, and brushed by Jorgenson on his way out, seemingly hardly troubled. He didn't even look back to see the class's frozen-in-disbelief reaction.

Jorgenson lumbered back to the front of the room, his knees still not cooperating.

He turned to face us. Even in the back row, I could see veins in his scrawny neck throbbing. He swallowed hard, refusing to look directly at us.

"All right. That's fine. Since no one completed the assignment, take out your textbooks. I'm going to patiently explain the differences between those Pacific Islands since you can't seem to figure it out for yourselves."

There was an explosive flurry of activity as books appeared in record time on desktops.

A faint grin appeared at a corner of Jorgenson's mouth. Dave might have been a rebel, but the rest of us were clearly meek sheeple. Including me.

The remaining thirty minutes crawled by painfully, Jorgenson's droning voice like Chinese water torture, which I've heard is supposed to be really bad. As soon as the bell sounded, I resisted the urge to burst out of the room in search of Dave to ask what he possibly hoped to accomplish by belittling Jorgenson in front of his own class.

For a really smart guy, at times Dave could be really dense.

The class filed out of the room in subdued, orderly fashion. I picked up my pace when I was sure Jorgenson wasn't behind me, convinced that I knew exactly where to find Dave.

I turned the corner to the cafe and stopped. Sure enough, there was Dave at our table, calmly drinking some obscenely large drink with a straw as if the imminent possibility of being expelled didn't bother him in the slightest.

I approached him cautiously, as if the trouble he was in might jump and infect me somehow. Guilt by association, I figured.

He beamed his usual fake beam when he saw me.

"George! Good to see you! Have a seat. Just taking a nice long break here between classes. I usually don't get this opportunity."

I sat down heavily to emphasize my agitation. "What is wrong with you?" I said softly, even though no one was near enough to hear me.

Dave cupped an ear. "What? I can't hear you. Did you say something?"

I spoke up. "Are you *trying* to get expelled? Is that your goal in your senior year, just a few weeks away from graduation? You saw what happened to me when I tried to prank you by the football field, and I wasn't even looking to cause trouble. You were so concerned I was going to be expelled, yet you aren't the least bit concerned about your own future? What's going on?"

Dave took a loud slurp from his drink. "Okay. So maybe I got just a *little* carried away back there." He wagged his hand as if to emphasis the "little." "It took on a life of its own, that's all. Sometimes it's hard to stop when I'm on a roll." He slurped again. "Besides, the assignment was stupid. Admit it."

I sighed. "You just don't get it, do you?" I lowered my voice again, just in case. "We have to play *their* game, not ours. We're on *their* turf, remember? We're the pawns here, just passing through. Nothing more."

Dave set his drink down. For the first time that morning he looked serious.

"Maybe you, but not me. It would stink to go through life thinking you're a nobody."

"You know what I mean. We toe the line, get the grades so we can graduate, then say *adios* and *arrivederci*. You don't ever have to come back here again or even admit you were a student here if you don't want to. If people ask, 'Say, Dave, where did you go to high school?' you're free to say 'Gosh, I don't remember.'"

Dave looked away. "That still stinks."

"Maybe so. But you know what? You get a job and treat your boss the way you treat Jorgenson, you won't have a job."

Dave was quiet a moment. "Guess I'll have to be my own boss then."

"Whatever. Just don't throw everything away, okay?"

Dave eyed me with suspicion. "And all along I thought you embraced your individuality. Sorry to hear you're just one of the sheeple now."

I leaned forward across the table. "You know what? This close to graduation, you should be one of the sheeple, too. Or at least pretend to be. What you do after your graduate is your business."

"So basically you're telling me to sell out, like you have?"

"No. I'm telling you to be practical. There's nothing wrong with that. You're whole anarchy thing is not just wearing thin, it's getting you nowhere fast."

Onion appeared by my side. I hadn't even heard her approaching.

"Hey, Dave. Heard you got kicked out of Jorgenson's class," she said. "I'd say sorry to hear it, but you probably had it coming. You can be so stupid and stubborn at times, can't you?" She shook her head in dismay.

Dave looked her up and down.

"Wow. Way to gang up on me. And here I thought you were my friends."

The static-filled intercom system sputtered to life over our heads.

"David Baker, please report to Principal Morgan's office. David Baker."

Dave took one last, long slurp, belched, then stood up.

"Gotta go."

I stood, too. "I'm coming with."

"Me too," Onion said.

"What for?"

Onion and I glanced at each other.

"For moral support if nothing else," she said. "We *are* your friends, Dave. You know that."

He shrugged. "Fine. Suit yourselves."

Dave strolled down the hall as if still unconcerned about his fate, waving to the people he knew, stopping briefly to chat with someone in our English class. When we arrived at Morgan's office, both Morgan and Jorgenson were waiting.

To my surprise, I saw Goodman waiting, too, hanging back a bit from the others. Then I remembered that Goodman was on the dreaded Student Disciplinary Committee, as was Principle Morgan and—extremely unfortunate for Dave—Jorgenson.

Of all people.

"Hey, Dave. George." Goodman fist-bumped both of us. He nodded at Onion. "Nancy," he added.

Neither Morgan nor Jorgenson looked pleased.

"What are you doing here, Wells? This doesn't concern you." Jorgenson asked. Not surprisingly, he didn't question why Onion was there. Probably because not only was she a stellar student, she never caused any trouble.

I decided to try the "I'm on your side" route to weasel my way into the meeting.

"Well, Mr. Jorgenson, Principal Morgan, Mr. Goodman, I've been trying for some time now to talk some sense into Dave, here. It's important that he understand that school rules and regulations are made for a reason, a lesson I learned last semester the hard way, as you well know." I gave my best hat-in-hand appearance, even though I didn't have a hat. "I think I'm finally getting through to him and thought my presence could be beneficial."

Morgan's cold expression warmed just a bit, but Jorgenson's looked unchanged.

"That's very admirable, Mr. Wells, even if a bit contrived," Jorgenson said coldly, "but this matter still doesn't—"

"No, wait." Morgan cut Jorgenson off. "Maybe a couple of his more sensible peers could make a difference here. George did learn a valuable lesson last semester, didn't you, George?"

I nodded vigorously, like a good little schoolboy.

"And what about you, Nancy?" Morgan said, finally acknowledging her. "Why are you here?"

She smiled faintly. "I'm here to keep both of them in line. You know me."

"Fair enough," Morgan replied. "Do you mind if George and Onion—I mean, Nancy—join us in our discussion, Mr. Baker?"

Dave seemed to take a cue from me and straightened up, serious-looking now for a change.

"No, Principal Morgan. I know and trust both of them. If anybody can talk some sense into me, they can."

Morgan nodded, pleased. Jorgenson still looked skeptical.

"Wait a minute," Jorgenson said. "They can't join us. There are all kinds of confidentiality laws involved with student discipline."

His eyes glued on Dave, Morgan didn't even glance at him. "Oh, let me worry about the confidentiality laws, will you, Floyd?"

For some reason, the way Morgan said that gave me pause. I had to wonder if he was up to something, if we weren't making a big mistake.

Standing quietly in the background, Goodman had an amused look on his face as if in on our scheming ways, which didn't surprise me in the least.

We all entered the one room in the school everyone hoped never to go, Principal Morgan's inner sanctum, his private conference room. As we entered, I wondered how many students had been suspended or expelled here, their futures altered forever, how many tears had been shed, how much trauma and drama had played out over the years in between these four unadorned walls.

Again I wished I had a time machine so I could go back and see for myself.

We took our seats, Morgan at the head of the table. He put his hands together as if in prayer, which made me wonder who—and what—he was praying for.

"Mr. Baker. Everyone is well aware of your . . . propensity . . . to question authority on just about every occasion. While a healthy dose of skepticism can be a good thing in moderation, your habit of challenging convention at every turn is becoming highly disruptive and counterproductive to the primary mission of this institution, which is to educate our students in a safe and secure environment, free of unnecessary distractions. Today's inexcusable incident in your Geography class is yet another prime example of your perpetual insolence that is completely at odds with our stated goals. Would you agree with that basic assessment, Mr. Baker?"

Dave blinked, his glazed eyes focusing again as he roused himself.

"Uh, sure. Yes, sir."

"Good. What do you think we should do to solve this problem, Mr. Baker?" Morgan's hands remained folded, as if praying now for the right answer.

Dave hesitated. "I would imagine some kind of corrective measure is in order."

Morgan immediately pressed his palms on the tabletop as if his prayer had been answered. Jorgenson sat back in surprise, and Goodman raised an eyebrow.

"Excellent! I'm glad you can acknowledge the need for discipline in this matter. If we let it go unpunished, what kind of message would that send to the rest of the student body?"

"Not a good one," Dave replied, even though I was pretty sure Morgan was asking and answering his own question.

"Precisely."

For an awkward spell, no one said anything more.

"Well, then." Morgan said finally, breaking the awkwardness. "What do you think that punishment should be?"

Dave looked thoughtful in a rather forced way. "Detention," he said firmly, as if resigned to that fate.

Morgan didn't respond.

"For quite some time, of course" Dave added hastily.

Morgan glanced down. "Mr. Baker. If this were an isolated instance, I might agree. But given that this has been an ongoing problem that shows no signs of abating, I'm afraid detention would be an ineffective solution. My records show that you've served multiple detentions over the years for exactly the kind of infraction we're discussing her today, yet here we are still trying to resolve the problem, still trying to put a stop to your endless insurgency. Do you really think another detention—regardless of its length—will result in a different outcome?"

"Yes, sir."

"I disagree."

Morgan stared hard at Dave, who finally flinched.

Jorgenson's hand flew up to his mouth in a failed attempt to hide a sudden grin.

"What do you think, Nancy and George? Mr. Baker allowed you to participate in this discussion. What do you have to say?"

Onion and I glanced at each other. Neither of us said anything. I was immediately aware that our inability to answer only made it seem we had to agree that detention was pointless. That made me wonder what we had hoped to accomplish by being here; if we weren't going to jump to Dave's defense, then our presence was doing him more harm than good.

Maybe—it occurred to me too late—that this was Morgan's intention all along. He had allowed us in on the meeting to help him make his point. The trap had been set and sprung.

Morgan drew in a deep breath. For the first time since we sat down, he looked genuinely concerned, sympathetic even. "Mr. Baker, as much as it pains me to have to do this to a student so close to graduating, I'm afraid I have to—"

"Can I say something?" Goodman interrupted.

Morgan paused. "Yes. Of course," he said, still staring straight at Dave.

I hoped whatever Goodman had to say would prevent Morgan from saying what I was certain he was going to say.

"I think we have to consider the possibility that David is a very troubled young man."

Jorgenson gave out a single, high-pitched, derisive laugh as if that were the funniest thing he had ever heard. "No kidding! Tell us something we don't know!"

"I am. I think there could be psychological issues here that need to be addressed, ones we should have recognized long ago. That was our failure. The rules regarding how we administer to students with special needs are very specific, you know."

*Special needs?* I thought. *Dave?*

I glanced at Dave, who looked like the proverbial deer in the headlights at that remark.

Morgan's expression changed to one of growing apprehension, his mouth slightly agape. He sat back.

Jorgenson's smug grin vanished.

"So you're suggesting that before we do anything, Mr. Baker should have a psychological evaluation?" Morgan asked. You could almost hear the gears turning in his head as he tapped his chin, eyes narrowed.

"Yes, I am. The procedures for that are quite clear, as are the penalties for non-compliance. If he's suspended or expelled before an evaluation, we would be held liable if it's determined he fits the criteria for an Individualized Education Program as outlined by the Individuals with Disabilities Education Act."

Jorgenson practically exploded in his chair. "Oh, for...he's nothing more than an undisciplined troublemaker! Don't try to hide him behind all this *special needs* nonsense!"

Goodman turned to him, spoke in a measured tone. "Are you suggesting that special needs students don't exist? Are you a psychologist or a behavioral therapist or any kind of mental health professional qualified to determine David's particular needs?"

Jorgenson looked perplexed. "Well, of course not! It's just that . . . we can't . . . how can we . . ."

He wavered a bit and then slumped, glowering in defeat.

When Goodman turned back to face us, I swear I saw the same twinkle in his eye he had when I had bluffed our way into the meeting.

Morgan cleared his throat, spoke even slower than he normally did. "Unfortunately, now that the issue has been raised, we can't ignore the possibility that Mr. Goodman's assessment is correct. Discrimination against those with disabilities is not tolerated by the school district, nor should it be."

He looked at Dave now as if Dave had just morphed into someone brand new.

"Mr. Baker, I am going to send you home with a letter for your parents requesting that you make an appointment for a thorough psychological evaluation as soon as possible. They are to call me right away to discuss the matter. Depending on the results of that evaluation, we would need to move quickly to set up an IEP meeting." He pulled his phone out of his suit pocket and began to tap on the screen. "Let's see now. There's a lot to do and not much time to do it in."

Goodman winked at me, and I suddenly understood.

Jorgenson abruptly stood up. "Excuse me. I think I've heard enough. Am I still needed here?"

Morgan glanced up at him. "No, Floyd, you're not. You may go."

Jorgensen stared hard at Dave, then Goodman, then Dave again before he strode out of the room.

Morgan looked up at the three of us. "You may leave as well. Mr. Baker, wait outside my office. Nancy and Mr. Wells, if you have class starting soon, go there now."

Only too happy to oblige, the three of us were gone in a flash.

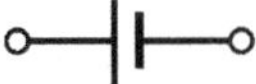

We stood in the hallway outside Morgan's office.

"What just went on in there?" Dave asked.

"I think Goodman saved your skin, that's what," Onion said.

"By calling me a *special needs* student?"

"Well, it worked, didn't it?" I said. "You weren't suspended or expelled."

Goodman came out into the hallway, as chipper and bright as could be.

"Gentlemen!" he said. "And lady. That went about as well as it could have, didn't it? Here. This is for you." He handed an envelope to Dave. "It's a letter saying that you require a psychological evaluation due to ongoing disruptive behavior, with the results to be made available to the school counselor ASAP."

Dave took the envelope gingerly, as if it might detonate any moment.

"Great. Now I have to see a psychiatrist or psychologist or somebody like that. Just my luck."

"A small price to pay, don't you think?" Goodman said.

Dave sighed. "I appreciate you helping me, but *special needs*? I hate to break it to you, but I think Jorgenson's right. I'm just a troublemaker. You were just gaming the system in there."

Goodman's chipper appearance faded fast. He got right into Dave's face, real up close and personal.

"Yeah, I'm gaming the system. We all game the system at some time in our lives. I've known you since you were a freshman, Dave. You can be a real pain some times, but in all my years of teaching, I've never had a student who's made me question my own assumptions about life and politics and literature like you do. If you were suspended or expelled, my class would suffer. I can't let that happen. I can always count on you taking me down a notch if I get too full of myself, but not everybody appreciates that like I do. The problem is, you still haven't learned how to play nice with people. I don't think it's because you don't care—it's because you're tone deaf when it comes to recognizing that not everyone likes your brand of sarcasm. You're like a bull in a china shop, only a very clever bull. Maybe you do need an evaluation to figure out why you can't notice that sometimes you take things too far. You understand?"

Dave nodded.

"Good. So get your evaluation, which will undoubtedly claim you do need help because there's lots of money to be made in that business and they're always looking for new customers to come walking through their doors. In the meantime, Morgan is in there trying to figure out how to place you in an IEP program before you graduate, which is impossible with only a few weeks left, only he doesn't realize yet or won't admit it. What I really did in there was buy you enough time to get your butt out of here with your diploma without having to repeat half your senior year or finish it somewhere else. Got it, my friend?"

Dave nodded again.

Goodman took a step back.

"Great! See you tomorrow in class."

His chipper face returned and he strode merrily down the hall

I started to laugh, keeping it as soft as I could. Onion joined in, undoubtedly thinking what I was thinking.

"What's so funny?" Dave asked.

"A clever bull," I replied, still laughing. "I've never heard a better description of you. Sorry."

Dave looked resigned, then looked away. "Glad you like it, George."

He stared down at the envelope again as if still not sure exactly how it ended up in his hands.

# CHAPTER TWENTY-THREE

# THE HILL OF PAIN LIVES UP TO ITS NAME

Our final exam in Physics started out mundane enough, but ended . . . well, bizarre.

Dave helped me prepare as usual. I didn't get the straight A's he got, but still, the tutoring made a big difference in my grades. Since Conway was Dave's second-favorite teacher, at first I wondered if that wasn't the reason for Dave's stellar performance, if Dave wasn't extra motivated to do well by him. But then I realized that Dave didn't have the kind of mutual admiration type relationship with Conway the way he did with Goodman, and that Dave simply "got it" when it came to physics like he said he did.

Conway's tests were tough but fair. He didn't have trick questions, "show all your work" demands, weird extra credit bonus stuff, or anything like that. He just gave you a reasonable number of questions that you could solve in fifty minutes, and you just gave him the answers. Every question he asked was one we had studied and discussed in class.

Other teachers could have learned how to give a test from Conway as far as I was concerned.

I worked my way through the test, pleased that only a few questions this time had me stumped and certain I was going to get a decent grade—or, at least, one good enough.

Then, just minutes before time was up, there was an outcry from the front of the room.

"*Cheater!* You *cheat!*"

Darryl Schmidt, mild-mannered, front-seat nerd who only spoke up to proudly answer questions in class, stood pointing at the student next to him, fellow nerd and compatriot Gordon Hicks.

"Now, now, Darryl, take it easy." Conway looked stunned by the accusation almost as much as Gordon did, who stared up at his accuser.

"What are you talking about?" Gordon demanded to know.

"I saw you looking at my answers, Gordon. You copied them. You *copied!*"

Gordon gave the loudest gasp of indignation I've ever heard, immediately making me doubt its sincerity.

"How *dare* you! I would never cheat!"

"I saw you!"

"Darryl . . ." Conway persisted, now halfway up out of his chair.

Still pointing at Gordon, Darryl turned to face Conway.

"We can't have a cheater like this in class! It's disgraceful!"

And that's when the real weirdness began.

Gordon shoved Darryl away.

It was a mild little shove, hardly anything really, but Darryl clearly wasn't expecting it and stumbled into his chair. He knocked the chair over and fell clumsily on top of it, his test papers spreading across the floor.

"Now look what you did, cheater!" he said as he angrily grabbed each sheet. Gordon stood up, his hands balled as if ready to rumble.

With surprising speed, Conway came around his desk and stood between them before things could get too crazy. The class bell sounded in the hallway.

"What's the matter with the two of you? You're the last ones I ever expected to cause any trouble. Give me your tests." He grabbed their tests from them and looked at the rest of us, still sitting and staring in disbelief despite the dismissal bell. "All of you, put your tests on my desk on your way out. *Move*, people! You two stay right where you are."

We slowly complied, giving wide berth to the two angry nerds now staring hard at each other, their faces flushed.

None of us wandered far from the classroom door, waiting to see what was going to happen next, if there was going to be another altercation as soon as Conway let Darryl and Gordon go.

Sure enough, the two of them immediately resumed their argument in the hallway.

"Thanks for the week detention, Darryl."

"You deserve it, you cheater!"

"I didn't cheat!"

"I know you did!"

"You take that back or after school I'll . . . see you at The Hill!"

"Fine! See you at The Hill."

"Fine!"

And they turned and went their separate ways.

"Oh, wow," Dave said. "They're meeting at The Hill. I wouldn't miss this for anything. This could be as big as *Homecoming*," he said.

Facetiously, I hoped. But with Dave, you never knew.

The Hill was on the south side of the school, in front of the main parking lot. It wasn't all that tall, but it was the highest point around, and the place where some people went to settle their differences with their fists after school when nothing else worked. Whoever won the fight was then obviously "King of The Hill," at least for the time being. It was also where the jocks gathered to have their pictures taken after winning some significant game, a more benign purpose. As a result, The Hill went by several names—Victory Hill, Pride Hill, and Dave's favorite, Hill of Pain. Of course, if the administration got wind of any planned fight, they waited around to prevent it from taking place, so the trick was to spread the news as surreptitiously as possible to draw a large crowd but leave the administration clueless—which honestly, wasn't all that hard to do.

Fights at The Hill—so I was told back when I was a freshman—were a school tradition, even though our Big Brown Box wasn't really all that old.

Onion giggled when she heard the news. "Too funny! I might watch it, too."

I couldn't say I was all that surprised. Usually Onion abhorred violence, but I guess the intrigue of a fight between two skinny, rather feeble-looking guys you would never suspect even knew how to throw a punch was clearly too much to resist. Even I planned to be there, and I didn't particularly like violence any more than Onion.

As the day wore on the buzz over the impending fight grew exponentially, like a chain reaction. In the cafeteria, you could tell who just heard about it when someone whispered in their ear and they burst into laughter, only to turn and whisper to someone else, who then reacted the same way. And instead of producing a sense of foreboding that pending fights usually did, this time there was almost a jovial mood in the air, kind of a party atmosphere. I guess its main attraction was its total incongruity; nobody could quite believe it.

The only problem was that it was becoming such a hot topic, I had to wonder if the administration would soon hear and put a stop to it before it could even begin. I was kind of torn about that—on one hand, that would undoubtedly be good for Darryl and Gordon, but on the other, the letdown after such a tremendous buildup would be immense.

I contemplated what Dave had said when Darryl and Gordon first agreed to fight—in some ways, this *was* going to be as big as Homecoming.

When the last bell rang for the day, I half expected people to make a beeline for The Hill, tipping off the administration that something was up and spoiling the party. Instead, almost as if rehearsed, people left quietly and without any fuss, as if it were just an ordinary end to an ordinary day. Once safely outside, though, people glanced back to make sure no teachers were watching, then grinned at each other and raced to the south side.

Dave patted my shoulder as we watched the brilliant deception unfold.

"I'm so proud of them," he said, pretending to wipe away a tear of joy.

By the time the three of us got to The Hill, the whole area was packed. Not ever having gone to a fight before, I wasn't sure if this was normal or unusual.

"Man, I've never seen so many people here," someone behind me said. "Look at the size of this crowd!"

That answered my question.

The other surprise to me was the number of girls present. I guess I thought the only ones interested in fistfights were those of us awash in testosterone, yet almost half the crowd was female.

I mentioned it to Dave.

"You know, you would think this would be more of a guy thing, wouldn't you?"

He gave me a disdainful look. "Yeah, right. Like girls never fight. Don't you ever watch YouTube?"

From our vantage point, we couldn't see what was going on at the top of The Hill. Dave, being the big, commanding guy he is, steamrolled his way closer, and Onion and I followed right behind until we could see Darryl and Gordon standing a couple of feet apart, fists up, ready to go at it. Both had taken off their glasses and looked a little blurry-eyed trying to focus on their targets.

"Good," Dave said. "We didn't miss a thing."

The circle of students surrounding the pair were all still grinning, as if the sight of two spindly guys on the verge of thrashing each other—or trying to—was the funniest thing imaginable.

Darryl took the first swing and missed. The crowd cheered the start of the action. Gordon tried next, connecting awkwardly with Darryl's shoulder, which made Darryl slide a bit sideways. It had rained the night before and the grass had just been cut, making the hill slick.

"That was nothing," I heard Darryl say. "You'll have to do better than that."

Gordon followed up with another swing, missing again. Darryl grabbed Gordon's arm as it went by his head and yanked it. Gordon lurched forward, his feet went out from under him, and he did a face plant on the hill.

The crowd laughed uproariously.

Gordon got up and charged Darryl, tackling him around the waist. Both went down and rolled over each other.

"Get off me!" Darryl said, and pushed Gordon away.

They staggered to their feet, wet and covered with grass clippings, which caused more laughter.

After sizing each other up a few seconds, fists raised again, Gordon threw a long punch that barely connected with Darryl's chest. Darryl didn't even flinch.

"Stand closer," someone in the crowd yelled.

"Yeah," some else agreed. "You're too far apart."

I guess if you've never fought before, some impromptu coaching from the sidelines was probably in order.

Gordon and Darryl circled each other warily, drawing nearer to each other until they were finally in decent striking range.

"That's better," someone said.

Darryl and Gordon threw a punch at exactly the same time. Their fists met in midair with a smack.

They both backed away, grimacing and shaking their affected hands.

The crowd half murmured and half chuckled.

"Didn't hurt," Darryl said.

"Nope. Didn't hurt," Gordon echoed.

You could sense growing restlessness in the crowd as the two wannabe boxers circled slowly again, feigning jabs.

"Come on! Somebody hit somebody!" someone finally said, more than a hint of impatience in their voice.

"Yeah, what are you waiting for?" someone else chimed in. "We don't have all day."

People nodded in agreement. At this rate, the two of them would still be circling at midnight.

Gordon finally threw a punch that looked at first like it might connect, until Darryl quickly held up a palm and caught Gordon's fist like a baseball pitch. They appeared to arm wrestle a while with both arms, slipping and sliding, their faces contorted as if the effort took all their strength, and then they went down again in a heap. They tried to get up but only made it to their knees, clutching each other and giving really short little jabs to each other's sides that seemed way too puny to do any harm. After about a minute of that, they fell over and started rolling again—this time, straight down The Hill.

The crowd hurriedly parted to let them through.

Down they went, over and over and over and over, all the way to where the ground leveled out. The parking lot curb finally brought them to a stop.

They separated and lay on their backs, their hands on their foreheads, panting mightily and streaked with grass and mud.

The crowd approached them cautiously.

"Are you kidding me? They're exhausted!" someone said, as if that wasn't possible after such a short fight.

"That's it?" someone else asked. "It's over?"

Several in the crowd groaned. A few people booed.

"Lame!" someone shouted.

"Worst. Fight. Ever," someone else chimed in, and with faces drawn, the crowd turned away and dispersed. After all the hype, it ended not with a bang but a whimper, as someone once said.

Dave, Onion, and I joined the exodus and headed toward Dave's car in the far parking lot.

"Well, at least no one got hurt. Much," Onion said

Dave shook his head. "Talk about anticlimactic."

Both Onion and I turned and walked backward to look at Gordon and Darryl. They were alone now, sitting up and talking to each other. Neither seemed particularly animated or upset. They were just talking, probably like they always had.

Nothing much to see there, Onion and I turned to walk forward again.

"I guess they just had to get it out of their systems," Onion said. "This was probably about a lot more than just cheating on a test."

Dave shook his head again. "You would think they could have done that without wasting everyone's time."

"Hey," Onion said. "That was their moment in the sun. Maybe it didn't turn out as planned, but now everybody's going to remember them. I mean, isn't that what everybody really wants, just to be remembered?"

Neither of us answered. I didn't know what Dave thought, but what Onion said was exactly true. I didn't know all that many people all that well at The Big Brown Box—or what they accomplished their four years here—but I would always remember Darryl and Gordon's Big Fake Fight as it came to be known, a permanent part of school lore now that would likely be told for years to come.

I took one last glance over my shoulder and saw the two of them standing now and shaking hands, as if to congratulate each other for achieving fame at last.

# CHAPTER TWENTY-FOUR
# A PROM LIKE NO OTHER

Senior prom was kind of our last formal hurrah before graduation. Years ago, the only ones permitted to attend were opposite-sex couples only, thank you very much, but now anyone who could afford a ticket was allowed in. Some parents still grumbled about that—not too many—but frankly it didn't matter to me or anybody I knew because, well, it wasn't a matter of life or death, it was just a fancy dinner and a dance.

Onion, Dave, and I have been going together to the prom since our sophomore year. It's amazing how well Dave washes up when he really wants to; he's almost unrecognizable with slicked-back hair, neatly trimmed beard, and a tux. Onion, too, can really dazzle in a dress, although it's odd to see her with just one layer of clothing. As for me, I don't take proms all that seriously, so I always try to add some outrageous element to what I'm wearing that nobody will forget. People think I'm trying to make some kind of statement about proms or society or something like that, but really, I'm just having fun. This year, I found a fluorescent green bowtie with matching handkerchief square and cummerbund to wear with my tuxedo.

When I put the whole outfit together, I just had to show Dad and Kenny before Dave picked me up to go the banquet hall where the prom was about to start.

"Too bright," said Kenny, briefly covering his eyes. "George should wear something else."

My dad just laughed when he saw me.

"You look like a leprechaun ambassador. Well, if the power goes out, people will know where you are."

I heard a horn beep in the driveway. Dave was right on time.

To my surprise, not only had Dave washed his car, he'd cleaned out the inside as well.

"Wow, Dave," I said as I got in. "Lots of room back here. How hard was it to wash?"

He snorted. "The dirt was caked on. I really had to scrub. It looked like some of it in the wheel wells was still there from your little football field excursion. Remember that?" he said, looking back at me, as if it were even possible I could forget.

"Sure, Dave. I remember," I said, as pleasantly as I could.

I didn't have the heart to tell him was that after all his scrubbing, every dent and scrape stood out now like the proverbial sore thumb. He had the only car I knew that actually looked better dirty than clean, all the damage camouflaged nicely by all the layers of crud.

Onion came out of her house looking like a fashion model, wearing a sparkling silver dress and her hair styled way up like I had never seen it before. When she got in next to Dave, she had to keep her head down so her hairdo didn't get crushed. I noticed she was clutching a little silver purse of some kind.

"You look great," Dave said.

"Thank you, David."

"What's in the purse?" I asked. "You've never carried one before."

"Nothing's in it. It's an *accessory*, okay?"

She did a double take glancing back at me.

"What are you supposed to be? The leprechaun president? It's not a costume party."

I was beginning to think I should have gone with some other fluorescent color if I was going to hear leprechaun comments all night.

When we arrived, the front entrance was lined with limousines of all shapes and sizes, including some that looked half a block long. Dave honked several times as he drove past them to park in the lot next to the building.

"Why did you do that?" I asked.

He shrugged. "Just to let the beautiful people in their fancy rides know that the truly important people were here."

The banquet hall was really an aristocratic kind of place, with wide, sweeping staircases, lots of intricate woodwork and the plushest, bounciest carpeting I had even walked on. The tables all had these tall brass cardholders with guest's names printed in fancy script on gold-bordered cards. We spread out to search for our names in the sea of tables, each one elaborately set with fine china, crisply folded linen napkins, and glimmering silverware. The room was about half full, with more people trickling in behind us.

"I don't believe it," Dave said by one of the few tables that didn't have someone already sitting at it.

We abandoned our search for our names to see what Dave had found.

"Oh, no," I said when I saw what Dave was pointing at. "It can't be."

Dave had found our name cards. The good news was, we were sitting together as we had requested. The bad news was, we were sitting at the head table with Principal Morgan. And his wife.

"Who made these table assignments?" Dave demanded to know.

"I don't know, but they sure have a twisted sense of humor." Onion said.

Dave looked around to see if anyone was watching, then snatched his card out of its holder.

"Come on. Grab yours. Let's switch with someone before Morgan gets here."

"Too late. Put it back." I whispered.

Principal Morgan walked through the entrance with a primly dressed woman who looked to be his age holding on to his arm.

Mr. and Mrs. Morgan had arrived.

With a faint sigh of resignation, Dave surreptitiously slipped his name card back in its holder as they approached.

"Good evening, gentlemen. Nancy. Are you our tablemates?"

Mrs. Morgan beamed at us even if Mr. Morgan didn't.

"Yes, sir," I replied, knowing David wouldn't.

"Splendid. This is my wife, Agatha."

"Pleased to meet you," I said, and gave a little bow.

"Agatha, this is George Wells, and this is David Baker."

Agatha's cheerful expression quickly faded, and she briefly touched her face. "Oh. I see. Nice to meet both of you."

"And this is Nancy Gordon."

Agatha cheerful expression returned just as fast as it had disappeared.

"So very good. You look wonderful, my dear." She took Onion's hand in hers.

"Why, thank you," Onion said. "So do you."

Principal Morgan gave Dave and me a brief look of disdain.

"Your reputations precede you, don't they, gentlemen? Shall we take our seats?"

"Right away," I said. After that introduction, I was all too happy to no longer be standing face to face with them.

The room was nearly full now, with most guests having found where they belonged. Soft piano music started up from somewhere as we took our seats. A few feet in front of us was a lectern with a microphone.

"Excuse me," Morgan said, getting back up. "Now that just about everybody is here, I have to make some opening remarks."

He strode purposefully to the lectern. Those who noticed immediately fell silently.

"Welcome to your senior prom, ladies and gentlemen. Dinner will be served shortly. Let's give a round of applause to the prom committee for making this event happen. As usual, they've done a wonderful job."

There was enthusiastic applause. Even though everyone looked around to see who it was exactly they were supposed to be applauding, no one waved or stood up to take credit.

"After dinner, there will be dancing in the adjacent room." He pulled a small card out of his coat pocket. "Music tonight will be provided by . . . DJ Outofmyway." He looked closer at the card. "Is that right? Well, it's music. I think." He shrugged and put the card away. "Oh, and joining me at the head table this evening are three of your classmates I'm sure you all know, Miss Nancy Gordon, Mr. David Baker, and Mr. George Wells." He glanced back at us with a stiff little grin. "Enjoy the evening, everyone."

Now the applause was so anemic it was almost nonexistent.

"Oh, great" Dave said quietly, hunched over as if trying to hide his bulky frame behind the water pitcher in front of him. "Now we look like three brown-noses, like this was our idea."

Morgan returned and took his seat.

As I looked out over the unsmiling, nearly hostile-looking crowd from our head table vantage point, something told me this was going to be long, long night.

We helped ourselves to the rolls in the breadbasket at our table. No one spoke. I hoped someone would start some kind of conversation to break the uneasiness that quickly settled in.

Dave spoke first. "You know, the three of us were surprised to have been selected to sit with you, Principal Morgan, especially after our recent history together. Isn't that right?" He looked at me and Onion.

Onion and I nodded meekly. I wondered where Dave was headed with this, if he wasn't leading us into some new kind of slaughter.

"I know," Morgan said, not looking at any of us. "I saw you pull your name card and hastily put it back as we approached. I can only imagine you were attempting to sit anywhere else but here."

Dave sputtered a bit in his water glass. "Oh. You saw that, did you?"

"Yes. But I haven't been completely forthright with you, either. The truth of the matter is I requested that the three of you be seated with me."

"Why?" I said, without really meaning to.

Dave hung his head, as if already regretting what he was about to say. "I hope that wasn't because you wanted to keep an eye on us this evening, like unruly children."

Morgan gave a dry little laugh. "Perhaps to some degree. No, mainly I wanted to follow up on our 'recent history', as you put it, and see if you truly learned the lessons you claim to have. In short, I wanted to see if you're sincere or if you believe you've pulled the wool over my eyes. I hope that's not the case because I would be very disappointed."

"I would never do that," Onion said.

Dave and I didn't respond in kind. By the time I thought to agree, it was much too late.

"I never thought you would, Nancy," Morgan said. "Unfortunately, I can't say the same about your two friends."

We were silent again.

Principal Morgan cleared his throat as he buttered his roll.

"Interesting color selection for parts of your tuxedo, Mr. Wells."

I wasn't quite sure how to respond. "Well, thanks," was all I could say. At least he hadn't mentioned anything about leprechauns.

He paused. "Weren't you the one who wore the spinning bowtie that lit up last year at the junior prom? That caused quite a sensation as I recall."

I was amazed he remembered. "Yes! That was me!"

His stern expression remained. "I thought so."

No one spoke again for an uncomfortable amount of time.

"So, Mr. Wells. Our groundskeeper Mr. Fields tells me you did a wonderful job helping him to restore the football field after you damaged it with Mr. Baker's car."

Dave nudged me hard in the ribs, and I knew why. Morgan made it sound like Dave was partly responsible.

"Yes, sir, but of course David didn't know I had taken his car, as I'm sure you remember."

I saw Dave nod as he chewed, satisfied with my response.

"I like Mr. Fields," I added. "He's a nice guy."

Principal Morgan looked at me as if surprised I would say such a thing.

"I like him, too. He does excellent work."

"He knows a lot about old movies, you know."

Morgan's eyebrows went up.

"No, I didn't know that. Do you like old movies?"

"Yes, sir. One in particular. My favorite. Mr. Fields knew some things about it I didn't."

"Oh? Which movie is that?"

"The 1960 version of *The Time Machine* with Rod Taylor and Yvette Mimieux." I beamed, certain that Morgan would be impressed.

Instead, he put his roll down, tossed back his head and laughed.

"That old thing? It's terrible! *That's* your favorite movie?"

I heard both Onion and Dave chortle. They didn't even try to hide it.

"Well, I think it's a fine movie," Agatha said. "Don't pay any attention to him."

Principal Morgan shrugged, picked up his roll, and took a bite. I was beginning to like Agatha a lot more than her husband.

"And how are you doing, Mr. Baker? Feeling better now?" Morgan asked, staring over the top of his glasses at Dave.

Dave's amused reaction to Morgan's comment about The Movie vanished.

"Yes, I am. The doctor I'm seeing is helping me with my . . . mood issues."

Agatha set her roll aside and looked at Dave with concern.

"You do whatever is necessary to get better, young man. I'm sure you'll be fine."

She gave her husband an icy stare. He coughed politely and looked away from her.

Now I was beginning to think that the wrong Morgan was our principal.

A gaggle of waiters appeared with trays at our table. Apparently, the head table was going to be served first, which so far was just about the only benefit of having to sit there.

Dave nudged me again. "Good. I'm starving," he whispered.

It was going to be family-style dining, I soon realized, as the waiters set heaping bowls of twice-baked potatoes, vegetables, roasted chicken, and salads on either side. It all smelled wonderful, and I waited to see who would serve themselves first, figuring it would be Agatha and Onion.

Before anyone could reach for the food, the sound of dishes crashing and a yell came from the entrance to the hall.

"No, you watch out!" someone said in a loud, slurred voice.

A senior who I vaguely recognized came charging in, wearing a disheveled tuxedo that looked slept in. He staggered toward us, arms raised.

Both Principal Morgan and Dave stood up when he stopped in front of our table.

"Morgan!" he said. The smell of alcohol from his breath overpowered the smell of the food. "What do you think you're doing, man?" He wavered unsteadily in front of us.

Morgan signaled for help from the waiters, who didn't seem to know how to respond. Dave ushered Onion and Agatha away from the confrontation. Agatha in particular looked distraught.

"What's the meaning of this?" Morgan demanded.

It was then I remembered that this was the glassy-eyed guy who insisted I have a beer at the house party months ago. I had to wonder if he had ever sobered up since then or if he was perpetually drunk, which was really a sad thought.

"Meaning?" he rasped. "There's no meaning in any of this. I'm supposed to be here with Maria, but I guess I'm not good enough."

He turned around and staggered to the lectern.

"Maria? Where are you?" The sound system screeched from his too close encounter with the microphone.

The crowd fell silent and finally looked our way.

"Did you disappear, Maria? Did you just vanish? How about that. Must be magic."

He turned and staggered back to our table.

His face brightened considerably. "Say, do you like magic, Principal Morgan? Well, do you? I'm gonna do a little magic trick for you. Watch this!"

And with that, he grabbed the front of our tablecloth and yanked, falling backwards in the process.

You know, if you really could have a time machine, you could watch time go by not only fast but slow as well, so you could see everything in the smallest detail that normally happens too fast to be observed. As if I had set the controls of a time machine to make the next second or two last much longer than normal, I watched as the tablecloth tried to escape from under all those place settings and bowls of food. Done properly, the trick of course is to yank the smooth tablecloth so quick, everything stays right where it is and drops the imperceptible thickness of the cloth straight down to the now-bare table, no harm done. But this tablecloth was bunched up and moving just a little too slow, I saw in my altered state of mind. The empty cups and silverware reacted first, lifting up and tumbling end over end. Then the plates took off, wobbling into the air. Finally, the food quaked and launched up out of their heavy serving bowls, chicken and potatoes and lettuce and tomatoes, each piece taking its own unique trajectory. Some came right towards me; others, toward Principal Morgan. Even Dave, shielding Agatha and Onion as best he could, was standing within range of the flying food projectiles. One by one they found their targets, striking with a distinctive splat—face, chest, outstretched arms and hands. As the tablecloth laboriously made its way off the table, there was that silent pause like after a flash of lightning, then the thunder as everything came raining back down, breaking and ringing and bouncing and spinning, until finally all was still.

After that, as I sat there covered in food, I looked up and saw everyone on their feet, mouths hanging open. Where there was steady chatter and the clinking of glasses, now there were only stares.

And then there was a single guffaw, an old-fashioned kind of snort, right behind me. I turned around.

Agatha was pointing at Principal Morgan, who was covered in more food than even I was, with half a potato upside down on his head like a tiny little hat.

"Charlie, you look ridiculous!" And she guffawed again.

That was all the permission we needed for everyone to laugh—even, to my faint surprise, Principal Morgan, whose laughter seemed restrained but laughter nonetheless.

The only one not laughing was Dave, who had taken the fewest hits but was still food stained.

He stood there looking indignant, as if shocked that anyone would find it funny.

"How come . . . why is everybody . . ." he stammered, apparently unable to comprehend the humor in the situation.

"Dave, our head table is a wreck and our Principal is covered in food. That's funny," Onion explained.

Agatha laughed along with her.

Dave kind of slumped then, as if defeated.

"But I was really hungry," he said.

Onion patted him on the shoulder.

"Now, now. I'm sure they'll give you plenty to eat."

Dave seemed consoled by that and finally smiled a bit.

Only then did I notice our wannabe magician, still lying on the floor in front of us, clutching the tablecloth up to his chin like a blanket. His eyes were shut.

Dave and I went over and stood on either side of him. A few others joined us.

"Is he dead?" someone asked.

"I don't think so," Dave replied.

"He looks peaceful," I said.

"Serene," Dave added.

A puzzled look came across Dave's face. He bent down and turned an ear toward the motionless figure.

"You know why?" Dave said, straightening back up. "He's sound asleep. I thought I heard snoring."

We let him slumber as we pitched in with the waiter staff to clean up the mess the failed magic trick left behind.

The mood the rest of the evening was upbeat after that, boisterous even. Dave finally got his meal, as did the rest of us at the head table. Despite my mottled, greasy appearance—or maybe because of it—I actually went out on the dance floor and danced the night away, figuring I had nothing left to lose—at least, not my dignity. In a way, it was totally liberating. Dave danced too, in his stiff, jerky fashion. Perhaps not surprisingly, we were both quite popular with the ladies, who not only wanted to dance with us but have their pictures taken with us, food stains and all. When Onion wasn't dancing, she was laughing hysterically on the sidelines at our awkward dance moves, which we exaggerated just for her.

It reminded me of the time I danced with Kenny at The Post, only sillier still.

Before Agatha and Charlie left, they took to the dance floor when a slow song started. The dance crowd stepped aside and applauded. And when Agatha put the half potato she was secretly carrying back on Charlie's head, the crowd roared its approval.

"You know, I never thought I'd say this, but tonight, Morgan's all right," Dave said as our principal danced proudly with his potato hat. "I had no idea he had it in him to act like a regular person."

"I think Agatha brings out the best in him," Onion said. "She's pretty cool."

"He should bring her to work, then," Dave replied. "Maybe that would improve his image."

"Think we convinced him we're sincere?" I asked

"Sure," Onion said. "Dave shielded his wife from a whole bowl of flying chicken."

The crowd thinned as the night wore down. Since Dave was our ride home and he wanted to leave, complaining that his feet hurt after all that dancing, we went to hunt for Onion's lost accessory purse, which had gone flying with our plates and food hours earlier.

To our great surprise, our failed magician hadn't budged from his spot, still reposed and covered by the tablecloth.

"He's still here? Really?" Onion said. "Nobody kicked him out or called the police or an ambulance or anything?" She picked up her purse from under our table.

"Nope. Still sleeping like a baby," Dave observed.

"What should we do?" I asked. "We can't just leave him here."

"Sure, we can. Not our problem. Let Morgan or the banquet hall people deal with him. We're outta here."

Onion stepped over him to head out, and we obediently followed.

When I got home and walked through the door in the wee hours of the morning, my dad was nearly ready for bed.

"Good heavens!" he said the second he saw me. "What happened to you?"

Like Homecoming, once again I didn't know where to begin.

"Dad," I said, going the simple explanation route again as I walked by, "it was prom night, remember?"

"Oh. Of course," he replied in a voice that said he understood, even though his expression clearly said he didn't.

On my way to my room, I looked in on Kenny, who was asleep in his usual curled position. I wondered what kind of proms he would attend in the future—and I was sure he would—and if he would have as much fun as I did that evening.

He stirred a bit and opened his eyes.

"George is home," he said, as if reassured to see me.

"Shhh," I hissed, finger to my lips. "Sorry. Don't let Dad hear I woke you up."

"Did George have fun?"

"You bet."

"Did George dance?"

"Yes, I did. You should have seen me." I sat down on the edge of his bed in the semi-dark, the only light coming down the hall from the kitchen. "I made a real fool of myself."

"Kenny dances, too."

"I know you do. You're a good dancer."

"Lots of pretty girls there?"

"Lots of pretty girls. You'll dance with some when you go to your proms someday. You'll see."

He reached out and touched one of food stains on my tuxedo where a stick of butter had stuck.

"Uh oh. George made a mess," he said.

"Yes, there was a big mess. But that's all right. We cleaned it up."

Kenny yawned. "Good night, George."

"Good night, Kenny. Sleep tight." And I got up and softly closed his bedroom door, glad to be home and glad the prom had turned out the way it did, magic trick fail and all.

# CHAPTER TWENTY-FIVE

# THE END OF THE BEGINNING

The day before graduation, there was a "Senior Appreciation Event" in the auditorium, a tradition at The Big Brown Box where the administration and staff get on stage and we all reminisce like one big happy family. At least, for the most part.

The event is a chance for the seniors to hear some "thank you and farewell" speeches from the people who do most of the actual work at the school—the cafeteria ladies and custodians (who got the usual standing ovations), Frank the groundskeeper (who also got a standing ovation thanks to my jumping right to my feet when he was introduced), and all the overworked, probably underpaid office secretaries. For that reason alone, the event is pretty well attended, with only a few no-shows.

That, plus they gave us unlimited snacks on long tables in the back of the room, which meant we weren't above being bribed to attend.

Before they started the tradition, the day before graduation was an unofficial Senior Ditch Day, which the administration fought hopelessly to squelch. Senior Appreciation Day was one of the administration's rare good ideas that everyone actually liked and serves a useful purpose. What's particularly amusing is that when all the usual high-level suspects get up and speak—Principal Morgan, the school district supervisor and the other bigwigs—the seniors have their own tradition of folding their arms and not applauding. Yeah, the silent treatment is rude, but it's our last chance to protest some of their insane policies that made our lives miserable and theirs easier. It's satisfying in a cringe-worthy sort of way to watch Morgan and the others finish their speeches and go sit back down in you-can-hear-a-pin-drop complete silence—especially after all the whistles and stomps we gave the school workers—but frankly, that's the way it goes. And yeah, they deserved it.

Needless to say, Dave was eagerly looking forward to the event. At least he *was*, until the administration showed a particular video I had forgotten all about for the entire graduating class to see.

"And finally, we've got a special treat for everyone," Morgan said innocently enough after everyone on stage had spoken. "It's someone you know, sending us all an important message. Watch." He went back to his chair.

And with that, the auditorium lights went down, the projector in the back of the room turned on, and all eyes focused on the big screen on the front wall.

At first all you could see was an empty classroom, with rows of motionless chairs. Some of us looked at each other and gave a little shrug, unsure what this was all about. And then, rising up as if from the depths was Dave's face, gigantic and scowling, just inches away from the camera.

My jaw literally dropped when it hit me all at once that it was Dave's security camera rant back at the start of the school year.

I don't think there was any way the administration could have extracted a bigger revenge on Dave than by showing what followed, although I doubt that was their intention. And even though there was no sound, it wasn't hard to read Dave's lips and follow along with every curse, foul word, threat, and innuendo for the next five long minutes.

The class not only roared with laughter, they were beside themselves.

Sitting right next to me, Dave looked like he had just been hit in the forehead with the proverbial two-by-four.

"Oh, no. Oh, no no no no no," he said, and then began to gradually slide lower and lower in his chair until I thought he might slide off and disappear completely.

I would have shown some concern for Dave's reaction—and probably should have—only I was laughing uncontrollably myself. I think what made it so incredibly amusing was that you could see the administration sitting there on stage beneath that silently ranting Dave just smiling at each other and at us, totally clueless as to what it was it was that ranting Dave was mouthing, as if they had no idea at all how to read lips and this was just some cute video they found of precious kittens playing the piano or something like that, not an endless stream of all too obvious four-letter words.

The whole thing was so incongruous, I had to wonder if they had even bothered to preview what they were showing.

I finally had to look away from the spectacle so I didn't pass out from lack of oxygen, that's how hard I was laughing. Through tear-filled eyes, I could see others had to do the same.

When ranting Dave on the big screen gave his pair of obscene gestures to wrap things up, the entire audience doubled over as if on cue.

Now I knew for certain that Morgan and the others hadn't really paid attention to the recording; they couldn't possibly have known *that* was coming.

But then, for just a few curious seconds, I stopped laughing and wondered if the administration *did* preview it and knew we would find it funny because even though we were graduating, in a lot of ways we were still kids. Maybe they were letting us have one last, immature laugh because they knew this was it, that from this day forward things were going to have to change, that we were going to have to grow up sooner rather than later and put all our childish behavior behind us. But with everyone around me still rocking with laughter, I decided this wasn't the time to be so serious and laughed along with them again.

And then, mercifully—for Dave, anyway—the film came to an end. Morgan got up and went back to the podium as the audience caught its breath and began to settle down.

"We thought you might like that," he said, starting a fresh round of laughter. "Now how about a nice round of applause for the star of the film, Mr. David Baker!"

By this time, Dave had slid so far down in his chair only his head was visible.

Not only did the class spring to their feet to cheer, they began chanting Dave's name. The chants started in one corner of the auditorium and quickly spread.

Sitting right in front of Dave, a nerd whose name I could never remember turned around and gave two enthusiastic thumbs up at Dave's low face. Dave stared up at the thumbs as if in disbelief.

And then there was a slow change in Dave's demeanor. His look of utter shock and horror gave way to a thoughtful, almost pensive expression, and he began to slide back up in his chair as if pulled by some mysterious force. As the chanting continued, Dave rose to his feet and a grin appeared that blossomed in a full-fledged smile, almost as though he had decided the best thing to do was just accept the accolades.

He stood up on the chair the way he did in that classroom months earlier when the video was recorded, raising his arms like a prizefighter victorious in the ring. As he shook his fists and gave a rebel yell, the crowd cheered all the louder.

Dave in all his glory, indeed.

"That ends our program, everyone," Morgan said, still at the podium. "See you tomorrow at graduation."

As the cheers died down and we filtered out of the auditorium—a happy, noisy, kind of bouncy bunch now—Dave was swarmed by well-wishers who patted his back and shook his hand, as if everyone wanted to be like Dave.

"I feel sorry for those who ditched and missed this," someone said, wiping his still-teary eyes. "That was even more epic than last week's fake fight."

And so, at the end, Dave joined the ranks of those immortalized at The Big Brown Box, his exploits likely to be exaggerated with each generation until he achieved near mythical status.

If anyone deserved that fate, it was larger-than-life Dave.

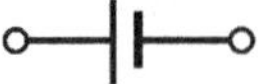

Graduation day started out hectic. Kenny, Dad, and I went out for breakfast, to a restaurant that was packed with cheerful near-graduates and their families. While the mood was festive, we had to wait quite a while for a table, which meant once we were done we had to rush home so we could start getting ready. I tried on my graduation robe and found out it was badly wrinkled. Fortunately, they told us during rehearsal to hang it in the bathroom when you took a shower to steam it a bit, and that would smoothed it out enough to make it look presentable. That little trick worked.

After putting on my dress pants and shirt, I slipped on the robe and put the mortar board on to see the finished product in the mirror behind the bathroom door. There was something a little unsettling about the way I looked, as if I was staring at someone other than myself, somebody far more advanced and mature than the more familiar guy under the robe. Today was one of those rare major life transitions as I knew full well, and just like a time traveler stopping for a spell in his machine to see what had changed, I tried to memorize every detail of the near-stranger in front of me so when time resumed and I raced into the future, I would always remember what I looked like just a few short hours before I was handed my diploma and became an ex-high school student, the transition now complete.

Next to the mirror on the door frame was a faint pencil line with a two-letter word written above it that I hadn't paid attention to in years. I wasn't sure if anyone else had ever noticed it—if they did, they probably didn't think it was important enough to even mention. Back when I was seven years old, I had stood with my back pressed up against the frame and best I could, drew a short line to record my height, then added the word "me" on top. I had only done that once—what compelled me, I have no idea—and now that, too, was a snapshot in time.

I touched the line as if to bridge the gap between who I was then and who I was now, thinking of all the time that had raced by in between. My mom before she died, Kenny still a baby, high school just a distant dream . . . the line was about two feet lower than my current height, which probably wasn't going to change much no matter how long I lived. It was difficult to remember how the world looked to me back then. It must have seemed a whole lot bigger, infinite at that age, the future filed with limitless possibilities.

There was a knock at the door that yanked me back to the present.

"Yes?" I asked, pulling the door open.

"Perfect! You're ready," my dad said, "Hold it right there."

And the camera he was holding went up fast to his face, followed by a bright flash as he took my picture.

Now I had an actual snapshot of the moment, I thought, although I was certain I would never need to look at it to remember.

So we piled into the car for the short ride to the school—my last official one—the day breezy but sunny, the sun brighter somehow than I ever remembered it being. We drove in blissful silence, the trip like a waking dream. After four eventful years, the last one in particular, it was all coming down to this. I savored the trip, studying the familiar landmarks as we went by, knowing I would never view them quite the same way again.

We had to park in the far lot near where Dave always parked. I saw his car in its usual spot and realized with a twinge of sadness it would likely never be there again.

I sighed, wondering if I was going to wallow in nostalgia all day. I hoped not.

We walked the too-familiar route to the school. What was different this time was having Kenny and Dad with me rather than Dave and Onion.

"This is the way I walked to school every day, Kenny, rain or shine," I announced, pointing forward to The Big Brown Box, still reminiscing and sick of it already.

People streamed into the school from all directions, those wearing a robe like mine appearing now and then. When people saw me, they smiled and offered me heartfelt congratulations—some of them with actual tears in their eyes—even though I had no idea who they were or why they were already so emotional when the ceremony hadn't even begun.

The stream turned into a boisterous crowd in the gymnasium. All the kid brothers and sisters were dressed in their finest, parents walked by with bouquets of flowers, searching for the best place to sit together, and balloons bobbed at the ends of their strings here and there above the loud sea of churning people. Add to that the sound of the school band tuning up, and the noise was incredible.

We reached the back of the audience chairs.

"Dad, I have to go join up with the other grads."

I practically had to shout to be heard.

"Okay," he replied just as loud. "When it's over, wait by the side doors. Kenny and I will go get the car and pick you up. It might take a while. You know how pokey Kenny can be."

"Okay."

And Dad and Kenny were swallowed up by the forward crush of the crowd.

Since my last name started with a W, I was in the second row from the front. While that meant I would have a great view of the commencement stage, it also meant my name would be among the last to be called.

In the hallway, it was impossible in the long, snaky line of grads standing two-by-two to catch a glimpse of either Dave or Onion, although I hadn't really expected to. Still, I looked.

"Lose somebody, George?" Carl Wentworth asked. He was the grad next to me.

"No, just looking for a couple of friends."

"Well, forget it. Wait 'til it's over. This is a madhouse."

Wentworth was right, of course. Dave and Onion and I had a plan to meet by the south doors after the ceremony, a former emergency exit that led nowhere. Since nobody ever went out that way, we figured that would be the best place to meet up and escape unscathed.

Shortly after one o'clock we heard the slightly off-key strains of some song the school band started playing in the gym, our cue to get going.

We all followed a scrawny-looking underclassman in a red robe who struggled mightily to carry a large American flag on a long pole. Next to him was a muscular underclassman in a blue robe carrying a brass bell. Why their roles weren't reversed I didn't have a clue.

Once our robed guides entered the gym, they came to an abrupt halt. There was a mild pileup of grads behind them, which soon straightened out.

The bell ringer rang the bell three times, and the band abandoned the song they were playing in favor of "Pomp and Circumstance," which they played much better.

We entered to a standing ovation, near deafening in its intensity.

I took my seat, listening to "Pomp and Circumstance" play over and over again as my fellow classmates made their way in. It seemed to take forever just to get everybody seated.

I had lost track of the flag bearer, then spotted the flag on the stage next to the wooden lectern. After Principal Morgan and the rest of the dignitaries climbed the stage steps and lined up in front of their chairs, from somewhere offstage the bell rang again and the crowd fell mostly silent.

Morgan step up to the microphone. "Please rise for the singing of the national anthem."

Everyone stood, the grads slipped off their mortar caps, we all sang as the band tried to accompany us, and then we put our caps back on and sat down for the long haul.

The ceremony itself was kind of a blur. The commencement speaker wasn't nearly as funny as he thought, whoever he was, his jokes not making a lot of sense or maybe just way over our heads. The only ones who actually laughed were the others on the stage and a smattering of adults in the audience.

And then they started reading the names. I was surprised at how fast they read them, the graduates streaming across the stage at almost a frantic pace. Even Dave and Onion were hardly up there for long. I tried to discreetly catch their attention, but they just motored on off the other side with hardly a glance the audience's way. That was a little disappointing, but at least Dave didn't make a scene in some final act of defiance, so that was a big relief.

The school had warned the audience multiple times not to shout out or otherwise disrupt the ceremony when the names were read under penalty of instant death or something, so there was hardly a peep throughout. Finally it was my row's turn to get up and go stand by the steps. As I grew closer and closer to the stage, things kind of took on a surreal feeling, like this wasn't really happening. I wouldn't call it an out-of-body experience or anything like that, but I had to consciously order my uncooperative, suddenly jello legs to move when my turn arrived.

"George Rodney Wells."

One leg forward. The other leg forward. Repeat. Shake Morgan's hand. Smile like you mean it. Now four more steps. Take diploma from some really serious, rather scary-looking guy. (*Diploma!*) Smile again. Keep those legs moving and walk down the steps on the other side without falling flat on your face or otherwise embarrassing yourself.

Mission accomplished, I relaxed on my way back to my seat, my legs operating normally again. Once there, I opened my diploma and read the first few lines:

DIPLOMA OF GRADUATION
*This Is To Certify That*
*George Rodney Wells*
*Has Hereby Satisfied All Requirements For Graduation*
*As Prescribed By The Board Of Education*

I closed it and set it carefully on my lap as if it were fragile, like a priceless Picasso or something.

After a few closing remarks—mainly to warn the audience not to block the recessional so we weren't all stuck in the gym—the band struck up another song and we were on our way. The audience noise returned with a vengeance after an hour and a half of nearly complete silence, and dozens of cameras and phones held high flashed at us from all directions. We had to kind of waddle our way out, hemmed in on either side by family and friends desperately looking for their special graduate.

In the crush, I didn't see either my dad or Kenny, not that I really expected to.

As soon as I saw a narrow gap in the crowd out in the lobby, I said goodbye to Wentworth and broke free to head to the south exit doors.

Dave and Onion were both there, comparing their diplomas and grinning like little kids with brand new toys. They were still wearing their caps. I had yanked my off and tucked it under my arm as soon the recessional ended.

Before they could even ask, I opened my diploma as if to prove that I had actually graduated, too.

"Awesome," Onion said.

"Finally," Dave said, looking down at his own diploma. "There's my name. *My name.* It's finished, and not a moment too soon."

He clutched his diploma to his chest and threw his head back with an overly dramatic, deep sigh of relief as only Dave could do.

We could hear the muffled sound of hundreds of voices grow fainter as the festivities moved outside.

"Are we ready for it?" Dave asked

"Ready," Onion and I replied.

"Great. Let's do this," Dave said

We marched around the corner into the deserted cafeteria, right up to our now former table to pay a final homage.

Dave saluted and clicked his heels. "Thank you for your fine service, Table One and Table Two. You shall always be remembered."

Onion laughed and shook her head. "Well, that's just ridiculous. Like you said, it's only a table, isn't it?" But then she stepped forward and gave it a few gentle pats. "Thanks," was all she said.

I glanced around the cafeteria for a final look, the serving area dark and still, the chairs empty and mute. It was hard to imagine that the place would no longer be a part of our daily routine.

From the hallway came three young guys wearing dress shirts with collars open and neckties loose. I thought I recognized them as freshmen, kind of poised but kind of not.

They came up to us with overly serious expressions.

"Just so you know, we're taking this table next year," one of them said.

Why they felt they had to tell us I had no idea. I guess they just wanted to make it official or something.

"Who are you?" Dave asked.

"We'll be sophomores next year," their spokesman continued. He had a straggly goatee that was no match for Dave's fuller facial hair, but at least it was a start. "My sister just graduated. Now that the three of you graduated, too, this table is ours." He tapped on it. All three of them wore a defiant look.

"Is that so?" Dave said. "What makes you think you're worthy?"

*Leave it to Dave to mess with them*, I thought. They didn't have to explain anything to us.

"Because we'll continue the fight against the system, that's why," their spokesman said. He shook a fist. "They're not going to keep us down, man."

Dave's tough guy stance immediately softened.

"Oh. Actually, that's a great answer."

He pulled his chair out from behind the table.

"Are you the ringleader? Here, take my chair."

"Wait a minute," Onion said, pulling her chair out, too. "If he's their leader, he wants *my* chair."

The three young guys looked surprised that we were so willing to acquiesce, not that we had any real choice.

All three of them sat down and smiled as they touched the tabletop, like they were claiming a throne or something.

Dave stepped back and nodded. "Looking good," he said. Then his voice dropped. "Good luck, guys. Just . . . take good care of it for us, will you?" He patted the tabletop the same way Onion had. "It helped us get through."

They nodded solemnly.

We turned and headed back to the south exit. I took a brief glance at the three of them sitting there as we rounded the corner. They were laughing and clowning around now like the three of us used to do, and I had the gratifying sense we were leaving our beloved table in excellent hands.

The seldom-used exit doors didn't want to open at first. Dave gave one of the stubborn panic bars a hard hip shove and the three of us spilled outside.

Onion shaded her eyes from the sun. "Wow, it's bright out here."

"Yeah," I said. "It's a beautiful day, isn't it?"

Dave shook his diploma at us. "I wouldn't care if there was lightning, hail, and tornadoes all at the same time, it would still be a beautiful day now that we've got these."

The stoop we were standing on was barely big enough for the three of us. Since it was an exit that led nowhere, there was no connecting sidewalk or really anywhere to go. There was a big step down to some loose gravel and then rows of overgrown thorn bushes that blocked us in. I seemed to remember that there was a path between them to the parking lot years ago, but clearly not anymore.

The only thing we could do was go back in.

I tugged on the door handles. "Uh oh."

"Uh oh, what?" Onion asked.

"It's locked. We're locked out." I tugged frantically again as if that would make any difference, and then peered through the thick glass at the long rows of now empty lockers. There was no one in sight who could let us back in.

"Dude," Dave said. "Don't."

"What do you mean?" I asked.

"We don't have any business in there anymore. It's all over, remember? We're alumni now."

The finality of it sank in right then, even though I always knew this day was coming. I stared a bit longer at the inside of our now former school. The once familiar hallway suddenly seemed foreboding, like the entrance to the Morlocks' underground workshop at the end of The Movie when that other George fought them single-handed to get his time machine back and escape their grasp.

I turned around to face our new problem. Our own escape wasn't going to be a walk in the park either.

"So what do we do now? There's no way out."

Dave looked resolute. "There will be. I'll make one. Follow me."

And with that, Dave jumped off the landing and went crashing through the bushes. Onion and I followed behind as Dave plowed through them like an icebreaker clearing a path. We could hear the frequent and alarming sound of fabric ripping and an occasional faint cry from Dave as the thorns on the bushes struck home.

"Are you okay, Dave?"

"Never better," he said, to the sound of another fabric rip. "Ouch."

We broke through to The Hill on the south side of the building where only a few other grads stood waiting for their rides home. No one seemed to notice our sudden appearance out of nowhere, as if a time machine had just deposited us there.

"Oh, man." Dave turned around to face us. "Look at this."

What we saw left us speechless. On the front and sides, Dave's robe was in tatters, with big chunks missing.

"You know what? If this is the price I have to pay to finally get out of here, it's worth it," he said, then pulled the robe off and wadded it up. A slender strip from it went fluttering to the ground.

In a show of solidarity, Onion and I took our robes off and wadded them up, too.

"Give them to me," Onion said. "Your caps, too. I see someone who can return them for us."

She waved at a girl walking down the sidewalk with her own robe and cap in neatly folded bundle.

"Suzie? Suzie! Are you returning your robe?"

"Oh, hi, Nancy! Yes, I am."

"Would you mind taking ours, too?" She smiled overly bright.

Suzie grimaced when she saw the big black ball of robes Onion was holding.

"Uh . . . okay," Suzie said, but her eyes said she wasn't too happy about it.

Onion handed over the robes and Suzie nearly staggered away, trying to see where she was going over the tall, bulky load. Another long sliver of Dave's robe blew away in the breeze.

A boxy yellow car sputtered up the drive and screeched to a halt at the bottom of the steps.

Onion hardly needed to shade her eyes and peer down the hill to know who it was. "Yep. That's my ride."

"Call us tonight if you're not busy," I said. "We'll figure out something to do."

"Sure," was all Onion replied, and promptly headed down the steps to the car. She gave us a brief "tootle-oo" wave of her fingers over her shoulders but didn't look back.

We watched Onion and her mom drive away, and that was that.

Another car soon arrived and picked up the few other new grads waiting for their ride. The only ones left now were me and Dave. We stood silently side by side, enjoying the pleasant day and lost in dreams of days gone by.

Or so I thought.

To my surprise, Dave suddenly grabbed my shoulder and turned me to face him, his gaze intense as if angry about something.

"All right," he said. "Before I leave, we have to have a little talk."

"We do? About what?" I asked, even more surprised.

"Filby."

I searched Dave's face for some clue as to what he meant. None was there.

"So? What about him?"

"I'll tell you what about him. For years I've had to listen to you moan and whine and complain about how you didn't have a Filby, nobody really loyal or worthy like that. Well, you know what? I've been way better to you than Filby ever was to George the time traveler and you know it. Who went out of his way to drive you to and from school nearly every day? Who helped you pass Physics with a pretty good grade? Prevent the cheerleaders from beating you up when you wrecked the football field? Saved you from being hit in the head by a flaming board when the bonfire blew up and then protected you from the angry bonfire builders? Helped bail you out of jail? Make you feel better when you thought you burned down The Post? Put up with all those silly movie reenactments? Take you to a drag race so you could win fifty bucks? I did, that's who. If you've been waiting for the perfect friend, you can just keep on waiting the rest of your life because nobody's perfect, not even your imaginary Filby. Maybe I do have some kind of mood disorder or something like that, but I've been there for you whenever you needed me, which is more than you can say about anyone else, not even Onion. Don't ever mention Filby's name to me again, you understand?"

To my further surprise, beneath Dave's ireful appearance I saw brief flashes of dismay and hurt in his eyes. Even his tone conveyed them.

"Sure, Dave. I'll never mention him again. Sorry. Just . . . sorry."

Dave nodded and stepped back, but I could see he was still upset.

"Fine. Good. I'm leaving. Maybe I'll see you tonight," he said, as if that was far from a sure thing. "And I'm angry that I even had to remind you what a good friend I've been."

He turned and started down The Hill.

"Wait!"

Dave stopped and turned around, his expression still dark.

I always thought it would be years before I would say what I was about to say, waiting for just the right person and just the right time to say it. But what Dave said about perfection was spot on and I knew it, that if I was waiting for the perfect friend then that moment was never going to come. With sudden clarity of mind I had never had before, I finally realized that right here, right now, with this very special friend in front of me, the time had arrived.

I took a deep breath, knowing what I was about to say was going to change everything forever.

"Thanks for being such a good friend, David. Always."

Dave gasped and his eyes grew wide—maybe even a little misty, I couldn't tell. He knew as well as I did that those were the time traveler's final words to Filby before climbing back on his time machine and heading into the future, never to return.

"I never thought. . . I will see you later. Thanks, man." He grinned.

Dave reached out and we shook hands. I don't know why, but we had never shaken hands before. His grip was firm and warm and full of life. And friendship.

And then he turned and flew down The Hill as if I had set him free.

My shoulders sagged as if finally speaking those final words affected me almost as much as they did Dave, as if I had brought the last few years to their ultimate conclusion. And suddenly—perhaps not unexpectedly—The Movie didn't seem indispensable anymore, as if it had served its purpose, outlived its usefulness.

In a way, I guess I had set myself free as well.

Alone now, I climbed to the top of The Hill and looked around. I had never stood at the peak before, but now seemed the right time. Other than a few birds chirping there was hardly any sound. The sun was starting to get low, casting a long shadow of The Big Brown Box across the nearly empty parking lot. Once I left this place, I knew it would be impossible to return with any real sense of belonging. With diploma in hand, I already felt disconnected, the four fast years I had spent here just a blur now, no more than memories of brief moments in time.

We were all time travelers of course, even if our travel is only one steady speed forward into the unknown. I knew then it really was the journey that mattered, not so much our destinations as the old saying goes, and what we said and did to each other along the way. I thought about all the others who just graduated, now streaming in all directions, most to never return here again. And I thought about those whose journeys were done forever, or drastically altered—Dave's friend Paul, Maggie Sutherland, Crystal, Sam.

And my mom, who would have been so proud of me today. Even if she did live only in our memories of her, that was comfort now enough. Comfort now enough.

My dad's car pulled around the drive. He beeped the horn to signal their arrival as Kenny waved at me from his usual place in the back seat.

I descended The Hill without looking back, faster and faster, forward through time to whatever the future held for me, to whatever new journeys lay ahead, leaving that old George far behind to forge a new beginning.

THE END

2006 EPPIE Award Winner - Best Science Fiction Novel
First Place - 2003 Authorlink International New Author Award"
Best Debut Novel - Fountainhead Press 2002/03 National Writing Contest
Finalist - WriteMovies.com International Writing Competition, Spring 2003
Finalist - Dream Realm Awards, best science fiction novel 2005
Finalist - 2019 ScreenCraft Cinematic Book Competition
Semi-Finalist - WriteMovies.com 2020 Screenwriting Contest